TH

DOCTOR WHO
THE POWER OF THE DALEKS

Based on the BBC television series by David Whitaker by
arrangement with BBC Books, a division of BBC Enterprises
Ltd

JOHN PEEL

Number 154 in the
Target Doctor Who Library

First published in Great Britain in 1993 by
Doctor Who Books
an imprint of Virgin Publishing Ltd
332 Ladbroke Grove
London W10 5AH

The BBC producer of *The Power of the Daleks*
was Innes Lloyd
The director was Christopher Barry
The part of the Doctor was played by Patrick Troughton

ISBN 0 426 20390 9

Printed and bound in Great Britain by
Cox & Wyman Ltd, Reading, Berks

Phototypeset by Intype, London

Dedicated to the memories of David Whitaker
Patrick Troughton
and William Hartnell

and with special thanks to June Barry

Prologue

The Antarctic winds howled mournfully about the battlefield. Driven snow was already covering the bodies of the casualties. At first glance, the fallen figures might have been mistaken for human, but they had surrendered their humanity centuries earlier. Now their electronically enhanced lives had also been surrendered.

The Cyberman invasion was over.

Within the nearby *Snowcap* space tracking station things were beginning to return to normal. The technicians were tracking the *Zeus Five* spacecraft that they had to guide in. Troops were cleaning out the debris and securing their base once again. Everyone was much too busy to pay attention to the three strangers who had helped the human race to defeat the Cybermen. By the time that anyone would get around to checking the immobile Cyberman saucer, there would be no trace of Able Seaman Ben Jackson, nor of his young friend Polly. And that mysterious old man known only as the Doctor had vanished as abruptly as the life from the Cybermen.

All around the world, the human race shook itself free of the shackles that the Cybermen had imposed in their attempt to drain the energy of Earth to feed to their own world, Mondas. Mondas was now no more than planetary dust, blowing on the cosmic winds to the far reaches of space. The Earth had survived the experience, but it could hardly be said to be unchanged.

A fleet of heavy transport aircraft and dark helicopters bearing the logo of UNIT – the United Nations Intelligence Taskforce – settled down later that day by the Cyberman saucer. A select team of men led by Lieutenant Benton of the English division of UNIT secured the saucer, but found no signs of life. As soon as it was considered safe, the scientific team under Professor Allison Williams headed inside. It was, as UNIT's official chronicler Sarah Jane Smith later phrased it, 'The Aladdin's lamp of applied technology'. No matter where Williams and her team probed, fresh discoveries awaited them.

Nowhere was this more true than in the heart of the ship, where the awed scientists discovered the key that would eventually unlock the stars for the human race.

'At one and the same time,' wrote Sarah Jane Smith, 'the Cyberman invasion was both the greatest disaster and most astonishing blessing ever to have happened to the human race.'

In the general euphoria, only a cursory search was made for the three missing people. When no trace was found, they were promptly forgotten. The human race concentrated on more important issues.

1

We Must Get Back to the TARDIS

Ben staggered against the wall of the Cybership as it shook again. He barely managed to keep his grip on the Cyberweapon he clutched. He felt pretty certain that all of the invaders were dead, but there was no sense in taking chances. As the ship setted again, he pushed himself away from the wall and peered down the dimly lit corridors. Only the emergency lights were in operation. Which way?

Choosing to go left, he slipped silently along the starkly efficient walkway. The Cybermen had long ago surrendered their emotions and any passions they might once have possessed. This included any aesthetic senses, so the ship – like their weapons and the Cybermen themselves – was completely utilitarian.

One of the fallen creatures lay in a puddle of gunge in the corridor. Ben stepped over it, holding his breath. The Cybermen had replaced almost all of their living tissue with metal and plastics. The energy drain they had faced when Mondas had been destroyed had fused their circuits, melted their plastics and short-circuited their cybernetic brains. The few remaining pieces of organic tissue in each Cyberman, without the life-sustaining energies of the Cybersuits, had immediately collapsed and begun to decay. It had left an awful mess and an even worse stench.

Somewhere in this tomb were Polly and the Doctor. They had been taken captive by the Cybermen, and Ben hoped that they were still alive. The Cybermen killed only when they thought it necessary – never for human reasons like gain or revenge. There was no reason Ben could think of that the dying Cybermen should have killed their captives.

Which didn't mean that they hadn't, of course.

Ben was a practical kind of man. He had to be, given his background. He'd spent his formative years on the streets on East London, barely keeping on the right side of the law. As soon as he was old enough to be accepted, he'd joined the Navy, to see the world. The idea of travel had appealed to him.

Then he'd met Polly and the Doctor . . . Since then, he'd seen plenty of travel, most of it in the fourth dimension. Time travel . . . Sometimes after a lonely watch out at sea, Ben had stared up at the brilliant stars, spinning in the heavens. He'd sometimes wondered what it would be like to sail right out and join them. And he'd read a couple of books, to try and improve his mind. Talk about lost causes! One book had been *The Time Machine* by H G Wells. The idea of bunking in a time ship – talk about tall tales! Until he'd discovered that it was true by stepping out into seventeenth-century Cornwall. And if that wasn't bad enough, here he was right now – thirty years in his own future. Maybe somewhere in this world there was a Ben Jackson looking forward to his own retirement . . . It was just too much for him to get used to.

Ben liked things simple. Pol – well, she was a looker, all right. Long blonde hair, a pretty face and a charm that went right down to her soul. True, she was far from his own working-class background, but that didn't really bother either of them. She was no snob, and he didn't hold her upbringing against her. Polly was really easy to get along with.

But the Doctor!

Ben turned a corner in the corridor, the Cyberweapon ready for use. Still nothing. One of the side doors had jammed, half-open. It led into some kind of a recharging booth. Maybe where the Cybermen plugged themselves in for breakfast. No cornflakes for them. But there was no sign of any humans, though. Ben moved on, thinking about the Doctor. Anything to keep himself believing his friends were still alive.

The Doctor had the appearance of an elderly man. Tall, thin, with a pinched face and expression to match. His eyes held a depth of almost cosmic proportions. His silvery hair hung neatly down to the nape of his neck. If he had been human, Ben would have guessed his age at around the sixty mark.

One of the few things that Ben was sure about concerning the Doctor, though, was that he was not at all human.

The old man had never told either of his human travelling companions anything about his background. 'I'm a wanderer,' he had said at one point. 'An old man out for a stroll in the cosmic wastes. No more.' Ben had been utterly certain that the Doctor had, well, not exactly lied – but he'd only told a part of the truth. A very small part.

Take that Heath Robinson craft he travelled about in – the TARDIS. It was a lot like the Doctor himself, very deceptive. On the outside, it looked like a battered London Police Telephone Box. On the inside, it was an incredibly sophisticated and complex time machine, many times larger than its exterior dimensions would have suggested. Just like the Doctor – far more inside than there should have been, and just as unreadable, unpredictable and uncontrollable.

The Doctor could be irritating, condescending, brusque, callous and unthinking. On his *good* days. Yet, underneath all of his annoying habits, there was a flame of more than human decency about him. Ben felt drawn to the strange traveller. Like a good officer, the Doctor had an aura of command and self-assurance about him. He needed help, though, and as long as was practical Ben knew he'd stick with the old man.

If he could find him again.

In the gloom, he could make out another half-shut door. Probably nothing to worry about, but he slid softly into the room, his stolen gun before him.

'Ben!'

His face cracked into a wide grin as he saw movement inside the room. Polly was strapped into some kind of silvery chair. Beside her, apparently asleep, was the Doctor. He hurried over to them.

'Hello, Duchess,' he said, slinging the Cyberweapon over his shoulder.

'Did you have to give us such a fright?' Polly asked, trying to sound angry with him. Ben could hear her relief under the words. As he bent to examine the bonds that held her, she nodded her head towards one of the panels in the wall. 'The controls to free us are over there.'

'Okay,' he replied. 'Sit tight.' Crossing to the panel, he followed her instructions to the right switches. Praying that there was enough power left in the system, he reversed their settings.

With a faint whine, the straps receded into the arms of the chairs. Polly rubbed her wrists to gt the circulation going again. The Doctor merely slumped forward. Ben rushed over to catch him.

'What's wrong?' he asked over his shoulder at Polly. 'Did the Cybermen . . .?' His words trailed off, not wanting to give voice to his fears.

'No. They just left us here, waiting till they won the battle.' Polly knelt beside Ben, her face drawn in concern. 'He just fainted a moment ago.'

Ben was getting really worried. Despite his apparent age, the Doctor had always been lively and possessed more vitality than any six normal people. But for the past couple of weeks, he seemed to have been slowing down. Sometimes he'd almost collapsed on little walks. Ben had even caught him napping over the TARDIS controls. And he seemed to have become older and frailer.

Gently raising the Doctor's face, Ben was shocked at what he saw. The old man's features were almost grey. The skin was cold to his touch. There was only the faint fluttering of the Doctor's nostrils to show that he was even breathing.

'Come on, Doctor,' he said gently. 'Wakey-wakey! It's all over now.'

A faint groan escaped the old man's lips. Then his eyelids fluttered. It seemed to take him forever to focus on the face of his young companion. 'Ben.'

'That's right.' Ben felt like dancing with relief. It worried him to see the Doctor like this. 'It's okay. Time to get moving.'

The Doctor closed his eyes as if drawing on the last meagre reserves of his strength. 'Over?' he repeated, his voice thin and reedy – nothing like his usual sergeant-major pay-attention-to-me-you-'orrible-little-man voice. 'No, it's not over. Not by a long way.' He sighed.

'What are you going on about?' Ben asked, puzzled. 'The

12

Cybermen are all dead. It's just a matter of mopping up now.'

'No.' Taking a deep breath, the Doctor managed to find the strength from somewhere to push himself to his feet. He stood there swaying for a moment, but shook off both of their offers of help. Drawing his long cloak protectively about his frail form, he said with a spark of his old authority: 'We must get back to the TARDIS! Immediately!'

Polly stared at him in shock. She could see the changes in him as well as Ben could. 'You need to rest first,' she said, gently.

'No,' he snapped back. 'There's no time. We *must* get back to the TARDIS.' He started for the door.

'What's the rush?' Ben asked. He caught Polly's worried look and tried to give her a reassuring smile. It didn't feel very convincing.

'Don't dawdle,' the Doctor said. He led the way unsteadily back down the corridor towards the airlock. Ben and Polly fell in close behind him in case he needed their help. They both knew better than to argue with him when his mind was made up. They always lost in such situations.

The cold blast of air from outside almost sent the Doctor sprawling. Once again, though, he summoned up the energy he needed from somewhere. Gripping the edges of his cloak, he plunged out into the frozen wasteland. Ben and Polly sealed the parkas they'd borrowed from the *Snowcap* base and stumbled out after him.

Wind sliced through them both, trying to strip the flesh from their frozen bones. Heads down, they staggered after the Doctor. How the old man was bearing up in these conditions was a mystery to Ben. He'd looked so worn and frail, but somehow he forced his feet to plod on through the snow.

As they plodded through the swirls of snow, Ben looked around. The still bodies of the Cybermen lay where they had fallen. There was no pity in his heart for them – they wouldn't even begin to understand such an emotion – but it just seemed like a horrible waste. To die like this, for no real reason. Polly hugged closer to him, chilled by more than the wind.

Ben looked up. The Doctor had vanished ahead of them.

He and Polly had slowed to look at the bodies of the fallen warriors. The Doctor must have rushed on ahead of them. Ben could see the line of the Doctor's unsteady footprints in the snow. Half supporting Polly, he stumbled on through the numbing wind.

Finally, the TARDIS came into view. Snow had been driven around it, but the dark blue of the police box seemed to repel the flakes. There was a gap of an inch or so all around the doors. They were closed, and there was no sign of the Doctor.

'Ben,' Polly said, fear in her voice, 'where's the Doctor?'

'He must have beaten us to it, Duchess,' Ben said. He pointed to the line of tracks leading up to the doors. 'See?'

Polly tried the handle of the door. It was locked. She gave Ben a quick, frightened look. Ben understood her perfectly. If they were out here in the freezing wind much longer, they would be as dead as the Cybermen.

Ben started to hammer on the doors. 'Doctor!' he yelled, hoping that his voice was carrying inside the craft. 'Doctor! It's us! Ben and Polly! Let us in!'

It seemed like he was banging his fists on the doors for an eternity. Finally, the doors gave way. He and Polly stumbled through them and into the timeship beyond.

'Warmth at last!' Polly laughed, rubbing her hands together. Ben shook himself like a dog, his eyes focusing on the frail form of the Doctor. He had been standing just inside the doors, operating the manual controls to open them for his companions.

The old man stumbled across the large room from the doors to the mushroom-shaped control panel. His cloak was still wrapped around him, only the tips of his fingers protruding. He grabbed the edge of the control console, obviously fighting to stay on his feet.

'Must close the doors . . .' His voice was thin, almost ghostly. He lurched like a drunkard, hitting the switch more by accident than design. With a faint whine the double doors to the outside world closed behind him.

'You okay, Doctor?' Ben asked, worried. He didn't look it,

but the Doctor could get very touchy about personal questions.

Ignoring Ben completely, the Doctor started to throw switches and set controls. It seemed to be draining him of all his remaining energy. Ben could see beads of sweat trickling down the Doctor's face. He seemed to be fighting not simply to stay conscious but to stay alive.

There was a sudden gasp from Polly, and she clutched Ben's arm in panic. Ben put his hand over hers and felt the tremors in her fingers.

'Ben,' she whispered, 'he looks like he's dying!'

He didn't want to admit how close her guess was to his. 'It'll be okay, Duchess,' he said. 'Just a bit tired, I reckon.'

The Doctor must have caught some of their exchange. He glanced up. His eyes appeared to be filled with pain. 'This old body of mine is wearing a bit thin,' he said weakly. 'I *must* get the TARDIS's help!' He returned to his tasks, frowning in concentration and pain. He had to hold on to the rim of the panels to drag himself around.

With an ear-splitting roar, the central cylinder set into the console lurched into life. Rising and falling steadily as it wheezed and groaned, the time rotor inside the glass column began to spin. The Doctor had once explained that this was some esoteric form of monitoring system for the thrust provided by the TARDIS's engines. It meant that the ship had taken off.

They had left the South Pole and the 1990s behind them.

Journeys in the TARDIS were highly unpredictable. The Doctor had admitted that sometimes they could be travelling inside the ship for days on end; at others barely fifteen minutes. The Doctor hated explanations and had never bothered to enlighten them on why this should be. This journey, however, seemed destined to be very different.

The column stopped dead in mid-thrust. Only the rotor within it continued to spin. The Doctor hunched forward, almost collapsing. His eyes were fixed on the rotor. In the spinning lights, his face went from shadow to ghostly light and back to shadow. His eyes burned brightly, but the rest of him seemed to be collapsing inwards.

The soft roar of some mechanism made Ben and Polly look up. From the ceiling, a large octagonal device was slowly descending. In its centre was a huge light that began pulsing on and off. In exact time, there seemed to be a gigantic heartbeat deep within the ship.

Polly almost clawed her way inside Ben's skin. He hugged her protectively, though he had no idea what he was supposed to be guarding her from. They had only been travelling with the Doctor for a short time and this was completely outside their experiences.

The Doctor stiffened. The light pulsed over him, ebb and flow. Shadows writhed across his features, snaking in and out across his almost transparent skin. Ben could see the blue veins inside the Doctor's skin pulsing in time with the beat from the huge light.

With a loud cry, the Doctor fell backwards on to the floor.

2

It's Begining to Work Again

Ben and Polly dashed over to the prone body. The lights were pulsing like crazy now, and the heartbeat in the ship was almost deafening. It was hard for Ben to concentrate. At the back of his mind he could feel *something* plucking at his mind, trying to twist it, to change it.

'Stop it!' he yelled, falling to his knees beside the Doctor. 'Stop it!' He wasn't sure if he was addressing the Doctor or the TARDIS itself.

The Doctor was beyond hearing anything. His chest was rising and falling in short, sharp breaths. His features were contorted. His thin, silvery hair looked lifeless and ready to fall out.

'Is he . . . dead?' asked Polly.

Ben shook his head. He couldn't find any words, so he simply pointed.

As they watched, the Doctor's face began to change. The skin seemed to be in motion, like some sentient carpet creeping over the Doctor's bones. Then the face began to shift and fall. Ben wondered in sudden terror if the Doctor was going to crumble and fall apart, like Christopher Lee did in those *Dracula* films. Or like the Cybermen had done. He forced himself to watch, to be strong for Polly's sake. She gave a short, sharp sound of disgust and fear and buried her face in Ben's arm.

The silver hair started to curl up and vanish. The cloak that covered the Doctor shifted, though the Doctor was obviously neither conscious nor moving.

Was this the end?

Then, incredibly, the changes began to show. First the skin settled down. It was no longer pale and transparent, but almost tanned and thicker. The silver hair was gone completely. In its place was a shock of jet-black hair. The familiar lines in the Doctor's face were gone, and fewer lines now marked the visage Ben stared into.

It was no longer the Doctor who lay on the floor before them but a very different man.

'Ben . . .' Polly said in a very small, frightened voice. 'His face . . . his hair . . . Look at him!'

Ben couldn't take his eyes off the man who lay there in the Doctor's cloak. The pulsing lights overhead seemed to be slowing down and the pounding sound in the TARDIS walls was getting softer. It was now merely incredibly irritating. 'He's still breathing,' Ben told her, then caught himself. Who was *he*?

'What are we going to do?' Polly asked helplessly. 'We can't just leave the Doctor there.'

'Him?' Ben pointed at the stranger in front of them. 'The Doctor?'

'Well, who else could it be?' Polly sounded as if she were on the very edge of panic, about to plunge into a maelstrom of madness from which there was no return. Ben could understand and sympathize with that – he was tottering on the brink himself. 'He came in through the doors just ahead of us. We saw him standing there and there was nobody with him but us. And we saw him collapse. Don't you remember what he said? *This old body of mine is growing a bit thin . . .* '

Ben shook his head. 'So he just got himself a new one? No . . . no, that's impossible! Do me a favour!' He stared at the man on the floor. 'Somebody must have come in with us, while we were watching the Doctor.'

'We didn't take our eyes off him for a second, Ben.' Polly dug her long nails into the back of his hand, making him want to scream. At least it meant he wasn't dreaming all of this. 'The Doctor fell down, and this man is here, in his cloak.'

Ben reached forward and with a swift motion he jerked the cloak from atop the unconscious man. Not only the Doctor's face had vanished – so had his clothing.

The battered black coat and trousers were different. They were now a loose, stain-covered black jacket several sizes too large for the small man who wore it. The trousers were yellow, with a large chequered pattern on them. He wore a faded shirt with a very large bow tie that seemed to have been tied by a blind man in a rush to be somewhere else.

'And I suppose he not only changed his body but his tailor as well?' Ben snapped. 'It's impossible, I tell you.'

Polly seemed to be getting a grip on herself again. 'Not long ago, we'd have called many of the things we've seen *impossible* too.'

'Yeah. But . . . this!' Ben waved his hand over the stranger. 'I don't think this is the Doctor. I think it's somebody else, who's taken the Doctor's place.'

Polly gave him a funny look. 'What are you talking about?'

'Well, like you said, Duchess, we've seen lots of funny things. I reckon that one of his enemies must have found some way to swap places with him.' He rubbed his chin thoughtfully. 'You know, snatched him out of the TARDIS and taken his place.'

Polly's eyes flickered from the man on the floor to Ben and back. 'And done all that *inside* the Doctor's cloak?' She didn't sound convinced.

'Yeah, well, is it any dafter than thinking the Doctor's gone and grown himself a new body then?' Ben knew he sounded angrier than he felt. Fear was not that far away.

'If you're right,' she said cautiously, 'then that man must be one of the Doctor's mortal enemies.' She bit her lip, uncertain. 'And if I'm right, that's the Doctor.' She shook her head. 'Ben, we need some way to tell.' Then she grabbed his arm again. 'Ben – look!'

The stranger's eyes had flickered open, then closed, and now open again.

There was a world of pain in the dilated pupils.

Agony. That was the first thing that he felt. A burning sensation inside all of his bones as they settled into their new forms, then in the muscles and the softer tissues. No point in cataloguing them all, he knew: they were all filled with pain.

It was hard to concentrate. If he could work out how to get his mouth and larynx working he might manage a scream or two. Well, that could come later. Right now, it was important to get his bearings. What could he feel apart from the pain?

There was some flat surface under him. Right – he was on his back. A bed? A floor? The ground? No way to be sure. When this happened to one, there was no way of being certain of anything for a while. It took the body time to adjust to its new parameters. And the new synapses. Not to mention a new way of thinking.

Well, that was a start. He was on his back somewhere and very much in pain. There was a horrible ringing sound in his ears, as if he'd stuck his head into all of the bells of Notre Dame de Paris at once. Or perhaps the Cloister Bells of . . . Of where? His mind refused to provide the answer to that one. Well, it would come in time – or it wouldn't. There was no helping it along. And sooner or later the maniacs who were ringing those bells in his head would pack in and go home for supper. Then he'd be able to hear the external world again.

External world. Oh yes, that was what he was doing. Working out what was happening. Concentrate, concentrate . . . He'd already checked on touch and hearing. Didn't this stupid body of his have any more senses than those two? Taste! No, that wasn't much use right now, unless this had happened while he was eating, and that didn't seem at all likely. Smell? Nothing there. But wasn't there some other sense?

Sight, that was it! And a very important form of information gathering it was, too. How could he have forgotten about that? Come to think of it, how did this *sight* business work? Wasn't it associated with some organs? Not the liver, he was pretty certain. Something closer to the surface. It was so infernally hard to concentrate amidst all of that pain and din!

Eyes! That was it – eyes. Two of them, if he remembered correctly, on the front of his head. Now, how did they operate?

The covers to his eyes slid open. A terrible light flooded in. He snapped the eyelids shut again, then tried a second time. Better. Not much, maybe, but better.

He couldn't see anything at all clearly. There was some powerful light shining down on him. The sun? Could be – but which sun? He'd been to so many of them. No, perhaps it wasn't a sun. He didn't feel any heat, just light.

Light! That was it. He was on his back, staring up at a light. His eyes refused to focus. Apart from the glow, he could make out nothing clearly.

'Slower,' he told himself. He couldn't hear his voice but he knew he'd said it aloud. 'Slower!' There was just too much information for his mind to process. He had to try and organize it. That meant taking samples of bits of information, not trying to process it all at once. 'Slower.' It did seem to be working. The noise in his head was falling off, and the room didn't seem to be spinning quite as fast.

'Think of one thing,' he told himself. He could just hear the sound of his voice. It seemed a little odd, but he'd worry about that later, when his head was in a state where it could begin to worry. 'Concentrate on one thing . . .' He managed to sit up. The blurry images shifted into different blurry images. He wasn't sure that it was an improvement. 'One thing.'

The vague shape he was staring at gradually became more and more real. The edges sharpened; the contours became cleaner. He could start to make out some details of what he was seeing. It was a hexagonal console and it looked vaguely familiar. If he thought about it, he could probably identify – no! One thing. Just get the shape into focus.

The bells had faded away, and now all he heard was a low humming sound. He felt pretty certain it was not inside his head. Finally, his sight became crystal-clear again. He could see the dials flickering on the panel he was facing.

'That's over,' he announced happily. He realized that he had been pressing the palms of his hands against his temples. He moved them away and looked at them. They didn't seem familiar, but that was hardly surprising, considering everything.

Two people moved into his line of sight, staring at him in shock and with no hint of recognition in their eyes.

Ben gazed down at the improbable figure on the floor of the TARDIS. The stranger smiled back. He thrust down with his left hand and sprang to his feet.

The Doctor's cloak seemed to hang very oddly on the small man and threatened to trip him up if he moved. Clicking his tongue in annoyance, the stranger reached up to unfasten the cloak. The heavy woollen garb seemed to come apart in his hands. The threads evaporated; the fabric tore silently, and settled to the floor as a very thin smattering of dust. As Ben watched in astonishment and worry, there was a metallic tinkle. A ring had fallen from the stranger's hand and rolled under the console.

Twitching his face as if he were unused to the muscles, the little man then began to do a quick series of callisthenics. Bend at the knee, arms straight out to the sides. Bend at the elbow, touch the nose with the left middle finger and out. Bend at the elbow, touch the nose with the right middle finger and out. Straighten, bend at the knee, straighten.

'The muscles are still very tight,' he announced, and gave them each a cheery smile. Then, sucking on one finger, he spun about on the balls of his feet until he was facing the door that led from the control room to the other quarters. 'Right.' He charged across the room and plunged through the door.

Ben finally found the power to speak. 'Here!' he yelled angrily. 'Half a mo!' The strange little man didn't seem to have heard, or else he simply ignored Ben. The sailor turned a puzzled look on Polly. 'What are we going to do?' he asked.

Polly stared at the open door uncertainly. 'It's the Doctor,' she said. 'I know it is.' She bit her lower lip nervously. 'I think . . .'

Ben could hardly believe his ears. 'It isn't only his face that's changed,' he pointed out. 'This geezer doesn't even act like the Doctor.' Convinced that his theory of an intruder was correct, Ben decided that it was time to take action. 'Come on, it's time to sort him out!' Ben marched resolutely through the inner doors.

On his left, the door to the TARDIS's wardrobe was open. Ben could hear the racks of clothing being pushed aside, and then the sound of the old sea chests the Doctor stored his souvenirs in being shifted. Gritting his teeth, Ben stormed into the room closely followed by Polly.

'Here, hold this.'

Taken aback, Ben clutched at the object that was thrust into his hands by the maniacal stranger. It was a large mirror with an elaborate brass frame. The little man peered into it, then wrinkled his nose.

'Tilt it back a bit further,' he commanded. Ben did as he was told. The stranger stared into the mirror as if he were seeing a ghost, then shook his head slightly. Satisfied, he pulled the mirror back out of Ben's hands and seemed about to drop it into one of his baggy jacket pockets. Even they weren't big enough for the mirror, though. He glanced around and tossed it casually on to a pile of feather cloaks. He was about to dive off into the trunks again when Ben clapped a firm hand on his arm.

'Now just a minute,' Ben began.

'Don't worry, I'm quite fine,' the little man said, giving what he obviously felt was a winning smile. 'Everything's settled down now and working properly.' He stuck his tongue out and almost went cross-eyed trying to peer at it. Then he grabbed his left wrist in his right hand and began counting pulses. They seemed to be quite far apart.

'That's not what I meant,' Ben told him, his temper starting to rise. Was this idiot really as daft as he seemed, or was it a put-on for their benefit? 'Where did you come from?'

Letting go of his wrist, the stranger peered curiously back at Ben. There didn't seem to be any worry in his eyes, just a kind of puzzlement. If this bloke was an imposter, he was a good one. He didn't seem to be acting oddly – more like this was his natural state.

'That's rather a strange question to ask me, isn't it?' He smiled innocently at Ben. 'Do you really want me to tell you my life story here and now?'

'No. I just want to know who you are.'

Polly held up her hand. Her fist was clenched around something. 'And who are we?'

'Why?' the odd figure asked her. 'Don't you know?'

Ben glared at him angrily. 'Look, enough of this mucking about. I want some straight answers.'

The little man stared at them as if realizing for the first time

23

that they were worried and scared. Then he nodded. 'Yes, yes, of course you do. I'm sorry, Bob – '

'My name's *Ben*!'

'Ben! Yes, of course!' The stranger banged the side of his head quite hard. 'Still, I got the first letter right, didn't I?' He smiled happily at Ben. 'Yes, this must be a bit confusing for you.'

'A bit?' Ben was taken aback by the remark. 'Blimey, you don't exaggerate, do you?'

The little man turned to look up at Polly. His eyes sparkled and a grin tugged at the corner of his mouth. He suddenly jabbed a finger towards her and she jumped back.

'Keep away!' she cried.

Frowning, the stranger folded his finger swiftly back into his palm. 'I don't look as bad as all that, do I . . .' He concentrated. 'Polly? Yes, Polly!' He clapped his hands and laughed in childish glee. 'It's beginning to work again!'

'What is?' Polly asked, obviously interested despite her fears.

He didn't answer her directly. Instead he gripped the bridge of his nose between a finger and thumb and shook his head slightly. Then he tapped his temple. 'Just like a whirling roundabout in here, you know.' He gave her a knowing look. 'Very painful.'

Ben had had quite enough of this clown. He glared down at him. 'What have you done to the Doctor?' he demanded.

The stranger drew himself up to his full height, staring Ben right in the chin. 'I *am* the Doctor,' he announced.

3

I Think We'll Make Some Changes

'No, you're not!' Ben snapped back.

The infuriating little man just cocked his head to one side and raised his right eyebrow slight. 'Because I look different?'

'You're completely different,' Polly told him.

'I assure you – ' he began, but Ben cut him off.

'You can make all the assurances you like, mate, but you're not the Doctor.'

Biting his lower lip, the stranger turned his brown eyes from one to the other. He seemed to have suddenly realized that they didn't trust him. 'I see,' he said quietly. 'Two against one, is it?'

Polly opened her clenched fist. In her palm lay the ring she had picked up from under the console. 'The Doctor always wore this,' she said, challenging him.

Ben grabbed the other man's hand and held it up. Hesitantly, Polly slipped the ring on to the man's finger. It was far too large for him. Ben gave a triumphant grin. 'That settles it, doesn't it?'

Pulling his hand free of Ben's grip, the little man sniffed loudly. 'I'd like to see a butterfly fit back into a chrysalis case after it spreads its wings.'

'What's that supposed to mean?' Ben demanded belligerently.

'It means that life depends on change and renewal.' He stretched up high, then bent to touch his toes before straightening up and smiling again. 'I have just been renewed.'

Polly slipped the Doctor's ring into her pocket, staring at the man with wonder. 'Then you did change!' she exclaimed.

Darting a filthy look at Polly for going over to the enemy side, Ben refused to surrender his suspicions so easily. 'Must be very useful,' he said sarcastically, 'this renewal business.'

Refusing to back down, Polly jumped to defend the person she was now almost certain was the Doctor. 'It sounds like fun.'

That was the wrong thing to say. The maybe-Doctor turned on her angrily. 'It can be agonizing!' he snapped. 'No one would ever submit to a process like that voluntarily!'

Even Ben was taken aback by the ferocity in his voice. 'But you said . . .' he started to break in weakly.

'I fought it!' The little man came down from his angry pinnacle almost to sorrow. 'I couldn't stop myself.' He shook his head. 'But I couldn't resist. It is a part of the TARDIS. Without it I could not survive. It is over seven hundred and fifty years since I left my home planet.'

Polly touched his arm gently, as if trying to soothe his pain. 'Then it hasn't happened to you before?' she asked.

The maybe-Doctor looked up at her. 'May I have my ring back?' he asked abruptly, holding out his hand.

Polly flushed, as if she'd been accused of stealing it. Pulling it from her pocket, she handed it over. The little man took it from her and crossed to another of the many trunks in the room. He threw the lid open to reveal a glittering array of jewellery. Polly let out an astonished gasp, and Ben couldn't blame her. Neither of them had had any idea that the Doctor possessed such a stock.

The stranger smiled knowingly at them, and Ben was a little shaken. If this man wasn't the Doctor, how had he gone straight to this trunk? His doubts were not helped by what the little man said next.

Holding up an ornamental dagger inlaid with precious stones, he commented: 'A gift from Saladin, during the Crusades. The Doctor was a great collector, wasn't he?'

'But *you're* the Doctor,' Polly protested. 'Aren't you?'

'Am I?' He stared at both of them.

Ben didn't like the way that the odd man had referred to the Doctor using the past tense. As if he were dead. An awful suspicion slipped into his mind: he'd been assuming that the

Doctor had been kidnapped and replaced by this foe. But what if this man had killed the Doctor and taken his place? Then what? Would he try and eliminate them next?

Turning back to the chest, the newcomer held up a large earring. 'I used to wear this at one time. Very fashionable once . . .' He replaced it and then held up a thick bracelet that looked as if it were solid gold. There were odd pictures on it that Ben couldn't quite make out. Putting it back, he gave them a cheery smile. 'I really must dip into my collection more often.' He was like a child playing with new toys. With an excited gasp, he pulled out a jade brooch. 'A memory of a visit to the Aztecs,' he told them. 'It was given to me by Cameca, a most extraordinary woman.' He sighed. The next item he picked up was a dull triangle of metal. It looked worthless to Ben, but it clearly meant a lot to this odd figure. 'My granddaughter Susan gave me this,' he told them. 'We were on Skaro, fighting the Daleks. She picked this up on one visit to their control room.' He dropped the piece back and slammed the lid.

Peering at them, he shook his head sadly. 'Still not convinced? Well, it'll take time, I suppose.'

'It'll take a lot more than that, mate,' Ben told him angrily. Were they supposed to have been convinced by his so-called 'memories'? There was no way they could have checked what he was claiming. 'Like common sense. The Doctor falls down in agony and then you get up – dolled up in new togs and everything. Do me a favour!'

The little man gnawed at his lower lip. 'I don't understand your brand of common sense, Ben,' he said. 'Does it grasp the principles of time travel?' He raised an eyebrow inquisitively.

'Well,' Ben blustered, 'I don't know all of the ins and outs, of course, but – '

'But you do know it's possible?'

'Well, yes,' Ben had to concede.

Turning to Polly, the stranger said: 'And you, Polly. You can, of course, explain how the TARDIS has the shape of a small police box outside and yet is far, far bigger once you step through the doors?'

'No,' Polly admitted. 'No, I can't explain it.'

'Yet both of you accept the two things.' The man spread his hands and looked at them expectantly.

Ben was confused and angry. 'Well, we know that they happen!' was the best he could manage.

'Exactly,' the maybe-Doctor replied. 'Then accept what has happened to me – even if you don't understand it.' He began gnawing on his thumb-nail. 'The Doctor kept a diary, didn't he?' he asked rhetorically. Ben realized he was speaking as if the Doctor were someone else again. These abrupt shifts in pronoun were making Ben's head whirl. 'Now, where would it be?' He started to ransack the chests again. After a moment, he gave a happy cry and straightened up.

It wasn't a diary that he held but some sort of flute. No, Ben realized, remembering his days at school, it was a recorder. Putting it to his lips, the stranger blew a single note. It was ear-piercingly high and sharp, and Ben winced. Then, as if he were trying to remember how to work the recorder, the little man ran through the first couple of bars of a tune that Ben actually recognized – The Fisher's Hornpipe – and shuffled his feet in time with the music. Abruptly losing interest, the man stuffed the recorder into one of his huge pockets and dived back into the trunk again. A moment later he emerged clutching a large black book. It was one of those leather-bound volumes with a strap on the side and a lock. Ben caught a glimpse of the words 500 YEAR DIARY on the cover before the volume joined the recorder in the odd man's pocket.

What was he up to? Ben couldn't recall the Doctor ever writing anything in the book, but there was an awful lot he didn't know about the Doctor. Was that book filled with some of the Doctor's secrets, and was this fake trying to steal them? Ben was wondering if he should try and get the book back when the other man leapt to his feet again.

'We must have landed some time ago,' he announced. 'I think I'll just pop out for a stroll.' He scuttled back towards the control room. Polly and Ben gave each a quick, puzzled glance, then shot after him. They couldn't risk him mucking about with the controls unsupervised until they were sure of him.

If that time ever came.

Ben skidded to a halt as he reached the control room. The odd figure now had a ridiculous-looking stovepipe hat crammed off-centre on to his head. It made him look even more like a tramp than before, but he seemed to be very happy with this latest addition to his wardrobe. Ignoring the console, he was heading for the doors, which already stood ajar.

'Oy!' Ben called out, alarmed. The little man frowned and then paused.

'We don't know where we are,' Polly said, shocked.

'You should have checked the oxygen, the temperature . . .' Ben gestured towards the dials. 'The *Doctor* always did.'

'Yes,' the other man agreed. 'Bit of a stickler for such things, wasn't he?' He sniffed, clearly not in approval. Raising his eyes to look at the ceiling, he recited: 'Oxygen density one-seven-two, radiation nil, temperature eighty-six degrees Fahrenheit, faint suggestion of mercury.' With another of his cheery smiles, he looked back. 'Now are you satisfied? Are you two coming or not?' He walked towards the doors. Then he paused and looked over his shoulder. His eyes flickered about the room, settling briefly on Ben and Polly. 'Yes, I think I'll make some changes.' Then he ducked out through the doors.

Ben felt a hill that wasn't from the cold. *Changes?* he wondered. What did this man mean? Was he talking about redecorating the TARDIS? Or . . . was the man referring to him and Polly? Was he even now setting a trap, or simply planning to lure them outside and leave them there?

'Ben,' Polly said quietly. He looked at her and saw mirrored in her own eyes the aching indecision he felt. 'What do you think? He must be the Doctor! He knew the readings on the panels!'

Ben felt a need to be more cautious than that. 'Come off it,' he said, a little more roughly than he'd intended. 'He could be making those figures up, for all we know. Can *you* read these things?' He gestured at the panel. 'It's all double Dutch to me!'

'He did make a sort of sense about time travel and the TARDIS dimensions,' Polly said, changing the subject.

'Yeah, well,' countered Ben, 'I don't think we should believe him blindly, Duchess.' He tapped the side of his nose. 'We'd do as well to watch him every second.'

Polly gave an exasperated sigh. 'And what are we going to call him?' she demanded. 'The only name he's given us is "Doctor".'

Shrugging, Ben replied: 'Then we may as well call him that – for now. But let's not forget he's got to provide us with some sort of proof that that's who he really is.'

Polly nodded. 'Then let's be careful, Ben.' She gave a faint smile. 'If we're supposed to watch him every second, shouldn't we be out there now?'

'Strewth!' Ben bolted outside and then halted in wonder.

4

So You've Come At Last

The Doctor had his nose planted firmly in his diary. He hated having to read the chicken-like scrawl of ancient High Gallifreyan that his old self had inscribed on the pages in tiny, precise and infuriatingly neat letters. It had kept the contents of the diary safe from prying eyes, but it was such an infernal strain on the eyes to read and the brain to translate. Of course, such things used to be a matter of pride to him at one time – not so long ago – but now they were of utter indifference to him.

Or, at least, they would be if he could read this nonsense. Squinting at the page, he tried to concentrate on the work of translation. He had to discover what he once knew. The problem with this entire regenerative process was that it scrambled the neurons up a bit. It might be a while before his thought-processes settled down into their new lines. Until then, he needed all the help that he could get.

Another section of his mind was ticking over quietly on his other problem: Ben and Polly. The Doctor knew that they hadn't believed his story. They hadn't entirely disbelieved it, of course, but they would be demanding proof for quite some time yet. And, of course, it would be almost impossible for him to give what they wanted. He wasn't entirely certain, but he was pretty sure they hadn't been with him for very long yet. Was it long enough for them to accept his rebirth? Or would they continue to fight belief?

There was just so much to think about. It was a good job he could take a walk outside like this in such . . .

He paused, pulled a large handkerchief from his pocket and coughed. 'Not a very healthy place,' he muttered. For the first time, he lowered the diary and peered around at the landscape.

It was an incredibly desolate-looking place. Not the worst he'd ever seen, of course – virtually nothing was worse than the radioactive slag and ash that the Daleks called home on Skaro – but it was pretty wretched. Volcanic rocks jutted up all about, or lay in tumbled ruins. The aftermath of one too many earthquakes, he supposed. There wasn't an ounce of colour in the whole place, except for the depressing grey of the rocks. Vents of steam whispered awy in the background. The place must still be volcanically active. Maybe a youngish world, then? But without the slightest sign of even the most primitive plant life. The Doctor bent to examine the soil. Good volcanic residue, perfect place for plants. He could get a good vegetable garden going here, if he had the time.

A slight bubbling noise caught his ears. Nice to know they were working well. He trailed the sound through the rocks to a pool of seething liquid. The vapours gathered in the air left him in no doubt as to what the pool contained – pure mercury. Maybe he should take a cup of it back to the TARDIS. You never could tell when the fluids links would need topping up. He began to rummage through his pockets, hoping he'd remembered to bring along a tin mug or something.

After a moment, he realized that he hadn't. Well, when he returned to the ship he could get one and make a quick trip back. After all, he needed to test out the state of this new body. His eye fixed on a large, flat rock, about six-feet long. His fingers fastened around a tape measure. Pulling it from his pocket, he measured the rock. Twenty-nine kroliks. Kroliks? Oh yes ... He'd picked this up on ... Now what was the name of that planet? Oh well. He dropped it back in another of his pockets and slapped his legs.

'Time I put you through a few tests, I think!'

He peered through his shaggy fringe at the rock. Really, he had to get that hair cut! He chuckled. Freshly regenerated, and already in need of a short back and sides. Anyway, first things first. Rubbing his hands together happily, he took several strides backwards. He had almost backed into the mercury pool when he decided he had enough of a runway. Giving a quick mental countdown, he dashed towards the rock, then leapt into the air.

He cleared the far edge quite handsomely and landed with a bit of a clatter in the loose volcanic sand. A glint of metal caught his eye, and he instantly concentrated on the rocks close by. Traces of mercury on the edges. Hmmm ... He glanced back over his shoulder at the mercury pool. Maybe not so much of a pool as a geyser, he thought. It might not be all that safe here after all. The nagging thought that had been troubling the back of his mind finally stepped out into the light: *mercury is quite poisonous to human beings*. And Ben and Polly were human beings.

Time to find them and tell them that nothing could live here for very long. A desolate wilderness of rocks, volcanoes and geysers. No signs of life having –

A man stepped from a clump of boulders ahead of him. The Doctor stopped dead, astonished. The stranger was a little taller than him, and quite clearly human. Hints of grey at the corner of his temples suggested an age in the late forties. Craggy features, but shrewd eyes. He was dressed in a casual tunic, boots and thick trousers.

As he caught sight of the Doctor, his eyes widened. Not in shock or surprise, but relief. Odd.

'Ah!' he said briskly. 'So you've come at last. I'm from Earth. I'm the Exami – '

His eyes suddenly bulged. From somewhere off in the jumble of rocks, the Doctor heard the *crack* of a gun of some kind. The man in front of him started to speak again, then raised his hand towards his head before collapsing in a crumpled heap.

The Doctor's first instinct was to run for cover. He almost followed the impulse, until he realized three things almost at the same time. Firstly, the man in front of him might not be dead, but could need immediate medical help. Secondly, there wasn't any cover close enough anyway if there came a second shot. And thirdly, Ben and Polly were probably utterly oblivi- ous to whatever was going on here.

What *was* going on here? He had to find out.

Overriding the impulse to duck and hide, the Doctor edged

over to the fallen man. Nervously scanning the rocks, he turned the man over quickly. There was neither sight nor sound of the gunman – or gunwoman – so he chanced a quick look at the victim.

It was instantly clear that he was dead. He'd been struck by some sort of energy beam that had fried the left side of his head. Nobody could live after such a wound, but the Doctor checked for a pulse anyway. As he'd expected, there was none.

He did see something clutched in the man's left hand, though. It was a small wallet of some kind. Prying it from the dead man's grip, the Doctor saw that it opened up to show two pockets. On one side was a metal badge. It looked terribly official, like some sort of police badge. The other pocket in the wallet held a small laminated card. The Doctor reached from habit into his pocket for his spectacles. He pulled the wire rims over his ears and then bent back to study the card.

It was a white blur. Puzzled, the Doctor waved his hand in front of his eyes. It looked like a package of sausages, waving around like that. Then he realized what was wrong and chuckled at his own stupidity. Of course! He'd been renewed, hadn't he? That included his eyes. He didn't need his glasses any more. He pulled them off and stuck them in his pocket. To his relief, he could make out everything on the card perfectly.

EARTH EXAMINER, it read in solid, official-looking lettering. *ACCORD EVERY ACCESS*. Under this and an illegible signature had been typed the single word *VULCAN*.

Curious. What could this all mean? The Doctor pondered the meaning, oblivious to what was happening around him.

The assassin slipped through the tumbled rocks carefully. He was watching where he placed his suited feet. It wouldn't do to alert this stranger by kicking a rock at the wrong moment. Whoever it was, he wasn't one of the colonists. Was it possible that the Examiner had brought an assistant? Sometimes they did work in teams.

There was no chance he'd be recognized. Not only was this interloper a stranger to the planet, but also the assassin wore an atmospheric suit. Typical of these Earth bureaucrats to

34

ignore the warnings of danger in this area and forget their suits. The killer chuckled to himself – they could get a fatal case of mercury poisoning.

The pistol he'd used to kill the Examiner rose slowly to target the silly-looking figure who was stooped over the dead body. Well, two corpses were as good as one.

His finger tightened on the trigger.

Polly joined Ben outside the TARDIS doors, pulling them closed behind her. She stared around the bleak landscape and shuddered. 'What a dump,' she muttered.

Ben seemed to be fascinated, though. He moved away from the safety of the ship, staring around as if he had been suddenly transported to paradise. 'Pol,' he breathed, 'just look at it!'

She sniffed in contempt. 'What a hole,' she said.

'Don't you realize where we are?' Ben asked her, the light of wonder still in his eyes. 'Look at the sky! Look at these rocks!'

'Margate on a rainy bank holiday Monday?' she suggested sarcastically. Honestly, sometimes Ben found the most absurd things interesting.

'Pol,' he said happily, 'we're on an alien planet!' He gestured at the grey-tinged sky and the washed-out colour of the rocks. 'There's nowhere on Earth like this. Believe me, I know.' He shook his head in wonder. 'An alien planet! The Doctor always said his old ship could make these journeys, but I never really believed him. I mean, all we ever seem to have seen was the Earth. But this . . . it's . . .' He seemed at a loss for words.

'A real dump,' Polly finished for him. She did feel a sort of sense of wonder though, knowing that Ben was right. For the first time in her life, she no longer walked on the surface of the Earth. This was a whole alien planet, most likely one that no other people from the Earth had ever even imagined, let alone seen. She and Ben – and the maybe-Doctor – were most likely the first people ever to step out on to its surface.

But . . . Well, she'd have been a lot more impressed if the place had been more interesting. No signs of life, no faerie castles or beautiful grottoes or anything. Just dirty, dusty rocks as far as the eye could see. And some kind of horrible stench

35

in the air. All that didn't seem to be bothering Ben too much, though. He was wandering about in a sort of daze, examining everything and laughing with a sort of insane delight she couldn't share.

Then he came to a halt, staring at a bubbling pool of what looked like mercury. 'Blimey!' he exclaimed. 'Steaming hot, ain't it?'

He was right – she could see the thick vapours seething over the surface of the mercury. She wrinkled her nose in disgust. 'Do you think the air's like this all over, Ben?'

Ben seemed to notice the stench for the first time. 'Don't want too many lungfuls of this, do we?' he asked. Then, answering her question, he added: 'It may just be around here, Duchess. Air varies a lot.' He grinned at her. 'We used to live opposite a brewery when I was a kid. You could take a walk and get tipsy all in one go.'

Ignoring this comment, Polly knelt beside the gently bubbling pool. The dim light played over the surface of the bubbles in an intriguing manner. Despite her original feelings, Polly was entranced. 'It's very beautiful.'

'Don't touch it!' Ben cautioned her.

How stupid did he think she was? 'I wasn't going to,' she snapped back at him.

Explaining his alarm, Ben gestured at the pool. 'Quicksilver gets through the pores.' Then, looking ahead of them, he frowned. 'I wonder where *he's* got to?'

Polly didn't need to ask who Ben meant. As the sailor looked around for any sign of the man who claimed to be the Doctor, there was a faint burping sound from the mercury pool. Polly gazed at the surface as a small gout of what appeared to be steam erupted. Alarmed, she was about to jump back. At that instant, a second jet flashed into life in front of her. Vapour and drops of mercury blew into her face.

She gave a cough and a cry as her nose and throat suddenly filled. Her head spun as she suddenly couldn't catch her breath. With a choking cry, she collapsed backwards into Ben's arms, unconscious.

Tapping the wallet in his palm, the Doctor was struggling to make some kind of sense out of what had happened. Obviously his initial conclusion that there was no life here was completely mistaken. The dead man had been expecting someone to meet him, somebody he didn't know, since he'd clearly mistaken the Doctor for his contact. And he was some kind of Earth official – but this was definitely not the Earth. Some kind of colony world, perhaps? Or –

'Doctor!' Ben's voice was faint, blurred by distance, but unmistakable. 'Or whoever you are!' That was Ben, all right. Not giving an inch in his convictions. 'Over here!' There was a distinct note of panic and urgency in Ben's voice now. 'Something's happened to Polly!'

The Doctor jumped to his feet and peered around, trying to judge where the voice was coming from. It was coming from behind him, back toward the TARDIS.

'Where are you?' Ben yelled again. 'Over this way!'

The Doctor started back at a run. Even if they didn't trust him, he had to help the youngsters out. They weren't as used to alien worlds as he was, and might stumble foolishly into all kinds of danger that his wiser head would cunningly avoid.

As he passed a clump of rocks, a white-suited figure stepped out behind him. The assassin's pistol had now been reversed, and he brought the butt of the weapon down with as much force as he could manage on the Doctor's head.

The Doctor crashed forward and lay still. His hat and the mop of hair had cushioned him from some of the effects of the blow, but he was dangerously close to the brink of unconsciousness. This early into his regeneration that could prove to be very dangerous. If he passed out before this new body was firmly in place, he might go through the whole process again, and he couldn't stand that.

He was vaguely aware of someone in white close by him. His hand closed about something hard, and he clutched at it instinctively. He was too busy concentrating on not losing consciousness to take in what was happening. From an immense distance, he could vaguely hear Ben's voice call out again.

The white boots ran off in Ben's direction.

The assassin was on the verge of panic and unreasoning anger. This had seemed like such a simple chore. Kill the Examiner before he could be met, then get out of the area. Now – just look at it! The Examiner was dead, all right. But that first intruder, he'd been forced to simply stun him. And now there was a second, and *this* one was yelling about a girl in trouble. How many more people were there here? The more there were, the greater the danger he'd be found out. As it was, some of the other colonists had to hear all this racket and come running. Especially the people who'd come to meet the Examiner in the first place. The assassin simply had to shut this newcomer up so that he'd have a chance to hide.

Gripping the gun tightly, he ran on.

Ben was scared stiff. Polly's face was going red, and she didn't seem to be able to breathe. Her chest was heaving convulsively, but there had to be something blocking her air passages. He knew that whatever had happened to her might well be lethal, and he felt utterly helpless. He needed help right now, even that of the bogus Doctor.

He tried to raise Polly up, bending low over her struggling body. His face was barely inches from the mercury pool as he struggled to get his arms under her.

The exploding jet of liquid-mercury caught him full in his startled face. He fought to get a breath, but his mouth and nose had been filled with the mercury vapours. Giddily, he crashed to the ground beside Polly. As he lost consciousness – the prelude to slipping into death – two things flashed through his mind.

The first was that someone dressed in white had stumbled on to the scene.

The second was that the fake Doctor had managed to get rid of him and Polly, and that there was now nobody to stop the fraud from taking over the Doctor's identity unchallenged.

5

They're Not Going to Stop Me Working on the Capsule

The Doctor was still concentrating on staying conscious when he heard footsteps approaching him and a sharp intake of breath. Then someone bent over him. The struggle of staying awake left the Doctor no energy to even open his eyes. He wasn't so much feigning unconsciousness as teetering precariously on the brink.

The man who had discovered him was completely unaware of this. He was a youngish man in his late twenties, still with the brashness of youth about his cheery face. He wore one of the white protective suits that all of the colonists dressed in when in the mercury swamps. This included a hood that covered his thick, sandy-brown hair, and goggles. Pushing the glasses on to his forehead, Quinn knelt down to examine the Doctor. His hazel-brown eyes flickered in astonishment at the clothing this peculiar figure wore. Before he could even try to feel for the man's pulse, another white-clad person stepped around the rocks.

It would have been hard to find anyone less like Quinn than Bragen. Older by more than a decade, Bragen had a cynical been-there-and-seen-it-all-before look chiselled into his hawk-like features. His dark eyes held black fires that took in all he surveyed. He looked like a wolf in almost literally sheep's clothing. His dark, swept-back hair gave him the appearance of a predatory bird, an impression strengthened by the way he seemed to hover, constantly ready to swoop down on someone or something. He constantly lived on the edge of a precipice, poised to strike.

'My men have found two more by one of the pools,' Bragen

said. His voice was level and controlled. It gave away absolutely nothing of what he felt about his discovery.

Quinn glanced up, and then indicated a discoloured area on the back of the Doctor's neck. 'This one's got a nasty bruise on the back of his head.' He sighed. 'Fallen over his feet and knocked himself out, I expect.'

Bragen shrugged. 'I suppose so.'

'Look at the way he's dressed!' Quinn said in sudden anger. 'Don't they know how dangerous this area is? Why don't they ever use the kit that we send them?'

Bragen didn't bother replying. His face said enough: *Earth never takes us seriously.* Instead, he gestured over his shoulder. 'The other two caught pretty bad doses of the fumes. Well, the girl has.'

'Girl?' Quinn asked.

'Yes. She'll need treatment back in the city. The young man with her is responding to treatment fairly well and should recover.'

As they were speaking, two more men in white suits arrived through the tumble of boulders. They could have been brothers for all that Quinn knew – they were both large, muscular blond men with absolutely impassive faces. One of them carried Polly, who had a face-mask clamped over her mouth. She was breathing regularly, but was obviously out to the world. The second guard was lending a supportive – though not sympathetic – arm to help Ben stay on his feet. Ben was a little woozy, but seemed to be aware of what was going on. His eyes kept slipping in and out of focus, but if he concentrated he could pay attention.

'These comic-opera guards of yours do seem to have some uses, Bragen,' Quinn observed, a hint of a smile on his lips.

'Yes.' If Bragen knew he was being mocked, it didn't show. 'I pick them for their physical fitness chiefly.'

'I knew it wasn't for their IQs,' Quinn answered drily. 'Give me a hand with the Examiner.'

Bragen showed a little emotion at last. He raised a single eyebrow. 'Examiner?'

Quinn picked up the wallet with the badge and card in it

from beside the Dotor. He flashed it briefly at Bragen, then slipped it into the Doctor's closest pocket.

Bragen stared at the Doctor thoughtfully. He made no move to help Quinn, instead gesturing for the guard with Ben to come forward. Ben reeled a little as the guard abruptly removed his support, but he managed to stay on his feet.

'I wonder why the Earth's sent an Examiner to Vulcan?' Bragen mused. 'Just now, I mean?' He looked at Quinn, who shrugged.

'I don't know.'

The security guard motioned Quinn back and scooped up the Doctor's still form as if it weighed nothing. Quinn moved over to see how Ben was doing.

Bragen pursed his lips thoughtfully. 'Mysterious, isn't it? We aren't due an Examiner for another two years.'

Concentrating on Ben, Quinn checked the youngster's eyes and pulse. Bit fast, obviously due to the stress he'd been through. His eyes didn't show any signs of concussion or delayed shock. Still, it would be best for the doctor back in the city to take a look at all three of them, just to be certain. Vulcan was still an alien world, with alien dangers. These three from Earth were typical – no understanding of how dangerous it could be off the Earth. 'How do you feel?' he asked Ben.

Ben could make out the words, but he was having trouble still with his throat. It felt as if he'd swallowed a bowl of molten fire. Not wishing to chance his voice, he shook his head.

'We saw your rocket overshoot the landing area. Most of the ships from Earth do overshoot. It's a steep drop, so don't feel badly about messing it up.' Ben had no idea what the man was talking about, but he'd learned from experience to keep his mouth shut until he knew what was going on.

'I'm Quinn,' the man continued, 'the Deputy Governor.'

The other man moved forward, giving Ben a hawk-like glance. 'Bragen,' he said softly, 'Head of Security.' Ben couldn't help wondering what the need for security was when meeting visitors.

'Let's get them all back, shall we?' Quinn said sharply. Ben didn't have to be psychic to realize that Quinn didn't like Bragen very much. 'I'll take the girl.' He held out his hands. The guard who carried her looked to Bragen for confirmation. Ben saw that the security man paused a moment before giving a curt nod. The sailor then saw the look of annoyance and almost hatred that crossed Bragen's face as he stared at Quinn's back.

Things were *definitely* brewing. But what?

Then Bragen assumed his impassive face again. He glanced at Ben. 'I suppose you Earth people can't wait to see Lesterson's space capsule,' he said coldly.

Ben had no idea what he was talking about, of course. It was obvious that he, Polly and – well, call him the Doctor, at least for now – had been mistaken for someone else. And the maybe-Doctor hadn't run off and left them here to die. Maybe it hadn't been a trick. It looked as if the little man was out to the world.

As Ben studied the Doctor's face, one of the bright eyes opened and winked quickly at Ben before closing again.

Strewth, Ben thought to himself, he's faking unconsciousness! But why? And . . . how much else is he faking? Still in a deeply troubled state of mind, he followed Quinn's lead as the party started off.

Alone in his laboratory, Lesterson was carefully rubbing a small triangular piece of metal with a cloth. It was shining up pretty well, all things considered. An angular, bird-like man, the colony's resident scientific genius perched on a stool, working away. He peered through his thick glasses at the metal, single-mindedly concentrating on the task before him. Lesterson considered his ability to focus on one item at a time to be one of his greatest assets. Others disagreed with him, of course, considering it his worst vice.

The laboratory was quite immense, given the scale of the rest of the city. At a time when most of the rooms were limited in size and decoration – Vulcan was, after all, a fairly new colony world – Lesterson's laboratory was over a hundred-feet long on both sides. It would have looked larger if it hadn't been so crammed.

A large mainframe computer took up a good deal of space by the main entrance. The centre of the room was filled with three long benches, on which Lesterson's electronic testing gear was arranged. The far wall held chemicals and the esoteric tubes, retorts and beakers to combine and analyse them. By Earth scales, it was a small, functional laboratory. By Vulcan standards it would almost have been an incredible waste of space and manpower.

But only almost.

Dominating the room was the bulk of the space capsule. It was about sixty-feet long and vaguely cylindrical. The front of it was blunt, the back straight. It looked like an immense bullet. The corrugated surface was broken at about ten-feet intervals by what were apparently bulkheads protruding from the ship. There were three large fins, evenly spaced about the capsule's far end. There was no sign of any way to get into the craft.

The laboratory had only two smallish windows. One looked out on to the rocky surface of Vulcan. Lesterson hadn't bothered to use it since the lab had been built. There was nothing of interest to him out there. The other window opened on to the hydroponics section next door. There the bulk of Lesterson's staff worked on acclimatizing a vast number of Earth trees, plants and crops to the fertile but odd soil of Vulcan. Once Lesterson gave his approval, the colonists would shift the thriving growths outside in an attempt to make the planet a new Garden of Eden. Lesterson might have given that approval a while ago, had he not turned all of his energy and interests to the capsule.

A stranger might have done a double take on seeing the structure. Filling a good third of the available space, there was clearly no way it could have been brought inside the laboratory. The reason for that was quite simple, really: it had not been brought to this spot. The colonists had been dredging out this section of what had been a morass to build part of the city on when a bulldozer had shattered a blade on the sunken capsule.

The plans for the city had been abruptly changed by the discovery. Lesterson had insisted that his laboratory be built around the capsule they had unearthed (unvulcaned?) so that he could examine it.

This had been done, even though they were still uncertain of the exact size of the thing. They had dug down to the rock to try and free the capsule, but it had become apparent that some of the rock had formed around part of the capsule.

How long must this thing have been buried on Vulcan before the humans had stumbled across it?

Lesterson had almost finished polishing the metal triangle to his satisfaction. Like the capsule itself, the piece showed no signs of wear. It could be a decade old, or a million years, for all that he or any of the others on his staff could tell. The only chance of finding any answers to this mystery lay in opening the capsule. Only one thing was certain: the artefact had not been fashioned by human hands. Lesterson wasn't the only one who was dying to open the capsule up.

The door opened and Janley walked in. She was Lesterson's chief assistant, though only in her late twenties. A ferociously bright and concentrated worker, she sometimes scared Lesterson with her intensity. She seemed to be unable to perform even the simplest of tasks without committing herself a hundred per cent to it. She could even turn the simple act of making a pot of tea into an act of almost religiously epic proportions. And, to top it all off, she was an amazingly attractive woman. Her open, flawless face was framed by a cascade of chestnut hair. Even the simple fatigues that all of the science staff wore failed to hide her perfect form.

Lesterson was amazed that she didn't have an ongoing relationship with anyone in the colony. He knew that most of his male staff – married and unmarried – spent almost as much time trying to chat her up as they did working. To the best of his knowledge, Janley had turned everyone down flat. He himself was married to his work, but he couldn't stop himself from sometimes staring at her beautiful features. Janley, if she noticed such glances, ignored him. Well, he could hardly blame her – he was no catch. He hadn't been even in his youth, some forty years earlier. Now he was a thin, tired man, in dire need of the thick glasses perched on his beak-like nose. His hair was still brown and fairly full, but it never behaved. Wisps constantly fell into his eyes as he worked. He had always been destined for great things – and had somehow never quite managed to achieve his destiny. When he was honest with himself, Lesterson knew he'd risen to his level of mediocrity as the chief scientist of this fledgling Earth colony. Janley could never see anything in him. It didn't stop his body and imagination from seeing an awful lot in her, though.

'Lesterson,' she began in her aggressive tone, but he interrupted her.

'Look at this,' he said, showing her the triangular piece of metal. She gave it a brief glance that seemed to categorize it instantly: *metal, polished, no obvious function. Uninteresting.*

'They've just brought in an Examiner from Earth,' she told him bluntly. 'And he's got a couple of assistants with him.'

'An Examiner?' he echoed, puzzled. 'What's he here for?'

'I thought you'd know,' Janley replied.

Lesterson nodded. 'It's the capsule. It must be! They're not going to stop me working on the capsule! I'll promise you that.'

Janley showed a little emotion at that. Her eyes crinkled prettily as she laughed. 'Could anybody?' she asked, almost mockingly.

Not for the first time, Lesterson wondered if she were trying to give him a message – that *she'd* like to distract his attention for a while. He gave her a quick, nervous look. He'd never been too interested in the opposite sex, but even he wasn't completely immune to her charms. There were only two things stopping him from following that line of research: a fear of being made a fool, since she'd never been explicit about any hypothetical interest; and the fact that he had more important things to do with his time. 'The Governor's always been difficult about it,' he said, answering her question as if it had been meant seriously. 'But surely they wouldn't come all the way from Earth just to – '

Janley clearly wasn't interested in his ramblings. 'Look,' she interrupted rudely, 'what about the meeting?'

'Meeting?' he asked, completely at a loss to understand her.

As always. He never seemed to grasp anything that she said of importance.

'I've arranged everything,' she said, not directly answering him. His eyes showed that he understood what she meant now. 'Can we still use the old rocket room?'

When the colony had begun, the room had been used to store the atmospheric sounding rockets. Lesterson's staff had utilized them to map the wind flows and weather patterns of Vulcan. Once the planet had been terraformed, the colony would disrupt the old patterns. One of the tasks of Lesterson's group was to attempt to make the changes in the weather as gradual and predictable – and safe! – as they could ever be. That was one of the reasons for the Cray mainframe computer in the lab. The Governor would have a fit if he knew how few of the memory bubbles were actually occupied with the precious weather data. And what was in the remainder. It was one of Janley's holds over Lesterson.

'Yes, I suppose so.' Lesterson sighed. Putting down the metal triangle, he took off his glasses and polished them on the edge of his lab coat. 'I wish you wouldn't get mixed up in these pressure groups, Janley.'

Pressure groups, Janley thought. How little he knew! She shook her head. They had gone through this argument dozens of times in the past. Lesterson refused to understand. Hardly the true scientific spirit. 'Somebody has to do something,' she finally said. 'The colony's running down and you know it.' She made it sound as if this deterioration could be directly traced back to him.

He put his glasses back on and picked up the silly piece of metal again 'I'm too busy,' he said.

Putting all of her powers of persuasion into her voice, Janley tried again. 'If *we* ran things, you'd have better facilities, more money.' But she'd already lost him. 'I wish you'd take an interest,' she snapped angrily. She was getting tired of his foolishness.

'I don't mind letting you use one of my rooms now and again,' he told her, 'but don't try and involve me. This is what I call important.' He held up the metallic triangle. 'This little piece of metal came out of the capsule. Just fell out, Janley.

46

Two hundred years in a mercury swamp, and look at it! Ten minutes polishing and it's as good as new.'

'Wonderful,' Janley commented without interest.

That touched a raw nerve, and he waved the artefact under her nose. 'Rain, damp, heat, mercury,' he told her. 'Nothing touches this metal. No rust, Janley, no corrosion. Think what that alone could mean!'

Janley just wanted to hurt him. She regarded the metal without interest as she turned to leave. 'Well, I hope the Examiner lets you get on with your experiments,' she said. At the door, she paused and fired her parting shot. 'Frankly, though, I doubt it. I think the Governor's brought the Examiner here to stop you opening the capsule.' She gave him a thin smile as she saw the shock and fear in his face. 'You should join our group, Lesterson,' she warned him. 'You might just need our help one day. And maybe sooner than you think.' She left the room.

Lesterson sat on his stool, the metal piece in his hand all but invisible to him. He wondered – could she be right? Is that why the Examiner is here? He glanced across at the capsule – silent, still, enigmatic and filled with promise. Humanity had reached the stars by exploiting Cyber technology. Who could even begin to guess what secrets this find might reveal? He couldn't let any stupid, obscurantist bureaucrat prevent him from exploiting his find. He couldn't!

Climbing to his feet, Lesterson set about what he knew he had to do to ensure that he was not stopped. This line of research was too important to allow any man – whether it be the Governor or even an Earth Examiner – to stop him now. He had to be ready for them when they came . . .

47

6

Why Have You Come to Vulcan?

'How are you feeling now?' The colony's Chief Medical Officer, Thane – a fortyish woman with short cropped blonde hair and a very efficient air – smiled tightly down at Polly as she unstrapped her diagnostic pad from about the young girl's arm. She was dressed in the same fatigues as everyone in the place, but she managed to make hers look like a professional uniform. She had the slightly weary, reassuring look that all of the best doctors seemed to possess. Only the tight lines about her eyes and mouth hinted at the pain and suffering she must have witnessed in her time.

'Fine,' Polly replied. 'What does all that – ' she nodded at the pad Thane had been making notes on ' – say I feel like?'

Thane's eyes twinkled. 'It says you feel fine. No aftereffects at all, I'm glad to say. Some of the first colonists weren't so lucky.'

The Doctor stopped tootling on his recorder for a moment. He was seated on the edge of another of the beds. Ben was striding up and down, casting filthy looks at the Doctor. They had less effect on the little man than rain has on ducks.

'Lose many?' the Doctor asked sympathetically.

'Six,' Thane replied, sighing. She put the diagnostic pad away. 'Wasn't that in the reports?'

'Tell us a little about the colony,' the Doctor suggested, avoiding a direct reply.

'Didn't they brief you?' Thane looked puzzled.

'I never trust briefings,' he replied. 'Second-hand information given by third-rate bureaucrats. I prefer the horse's mouth.'

Thane laughed. 'I guess that makes me the horse, then. Still, better than a donkey, I suppose.' She paused to gather her

48

thoughts. 'Well, you're in the main section – the city, we call it. Pretty small by Earth standards, I know, but we are still very new. It houses the main living quarters, the laboratories, administration and planning and the few amenities that we do possess.' She waved vaguely over her shoulder. 'The landing pad – I positively refuse to call it the space port – is just north of here. It you imagine a wheel, we're the hub. On the rim at intervals are the mining and extraction sites that make this whole venture so worthwhile.'

'Productive, are they?' the Doctor asked, giving a little toot on his recorder.

'Very.' Thane gave him a strange look. 'Surely you know all this? I mean, Earth really needs all the precious metals and trace elements that we mine here. The home world's about exhausted its own. That's the only reason this colony was approved. We're only the third ever established, and quite a way out on the frontier. If it weren't for the mines, we'd still be waiting, no doubt.'

'But there's plenty here?' Ben prompted, interested despite himself.

'It's the vulcanism, Ben,' the Doctor told him. 'It brings up the elements from beneath the crust and virtually coats the surface with them. Like the mercury pools.'

'Exactly.' Thane seemed happier now that this odd Examiner had shown a little understanding. 'And we can extract and refine the metals at low cost.'

'Are there a lot of people here?' Polly asked.

'About eight thousand, all in all.' Shrugging, Thane added: 'Admin can give you an exact figure. Most are on the periphery, in the mines and plants, naturally. There's only about a thousand of us here in the city. Mostly the technical staff and Admin.' She slapped her forehead. 'Which reminds me, I'd better let the Governor know you're awake and feeling fine.' She smiled and gave Polly a friendly pat on the arm. 'Take it easy for a bit, okay?'

As the door closed behind her, Ben rounded on the Doctor. 'That murdered man you claim to have seen must have been the real Examiner, then?'

The Doctor blew a single, high note on his recorder. *Yes*.

Ben rolled his eyes. 'And he just got up and walked away?'

'He was quite dead, I assure you.' The Doctor looked thoughtful. 'I picked up his card.' Fingering the tender area on the back of his neck, he added: 'You don't think I bonked myself over the head, do you?'

Maybe, Ben thought, but knew it was wiser not to say it. 'And you didn't see who did it?' he said.

The Doctor blew a long, low, mournful note. *No*. Then he fished in his pocket and held something out to them in his hand. It was a button, attached to a torn piece of material. 'Just after I was hit, I caught hold of the man who did it. I suppose I must have pulled this off his clothing.'

Polly examined the button, but it didn't tell her anything. 'They were all wearing shiny white suits,' she objected. She couldn't recall much about the journey here, but the image of men in white had stuck with her.

'Protective coverings,' the Doctor replied. 'This must come from whatever the man who attacked me wore under his suit.'

Ben shook his head. 'Look, I think it's pretty dull aronnd here myself. Surely this murder isn't anything to do with us? Why don't we just nip back to the TARDIS and scarper?'

The Doctor blew his low, mournful *no* again. 'We seem to have explained our presence here,' he told the two of them. 'Let's leave it like that for the present, shall we?'

'You mean that you're going to go on letting them think you're the Examiner?' Polly asked. The Doctor gave her a chirpy note on the recorder. 'But – somebody killed the last one. Won't it be dangerous?' The Doctor raised an eyebrow, and blew a high, a low and then another high note. Clearly he wasn't sure.

Ben was getting pretty annoyed by all of this. 'Why don't you stop blowing that thing?' he asked. If he were honest, what bothered him the most was that Polly seemed to be accepting him as the real Doctor. And, in the back of his own mind, he was beginning to wonder if there wasn't something in all of this renewal malarkey after all. To cover up his own confusion, he had to do something. Reaching out, he yanked the offending recorder from the Doctor's hands and then jammed it into his pocket.

'Ben!' Polly said reprovingly.

'Now, don't you start!' Ben told her. He felt he was very much on the defensive here. 'It's bad enough with him.'

'He hasn't done anything.'

'Yeah,' Ben agreed, 'that's the trouble. He – '

There was a rap on the door. The Doctor gave a small smile and called out: 'Come in!'

Bragen was the first into the room, glaring suspiciously at the trio. He was followed in by another man, again in the fatigues that all of the colonists seemed to wear like a uniform. This man was in his fifties, thick-set and with a definite air of authority about him. His hair was almost pure white, with occasional shots of grey in it, and he sported a neat beard. His eyes were deep and calculating, surveying each of the three occupants of the room. Clearly, though, he was not impressed by what he saw.

'I am Hensell,' he announced. 'The Governor,' he added, when the name didn't seem to register. 'I gather that you're all feeling better.' It was not a question.

The Doctor had recognized Hensel for what he was immediately – a minor cog in the government on Earth who had seized his chance for real power by getting the governorship of a far-flung colony world. With the vast distances that separated Vulcan from Earth, Hensell would be virtually in sole command, his orders unquestioned. People with Hensell's kind of mind would then run amuck, laying down laws as if they were paving stones and expecting implicit obedience.

Only . . . He was an Earth Examiner. The Doctor had absolutely no idea what an Examiner was, or what he was expected to do, but Hensell knew. Reading the man's challenging stance, the Doctor gauged how far he could fling his own weight around in return before Hensell would balk. 'You may assume that if you wish,' he said mildly. Rule One when working with officious idiots: knowledge is power. If you have it and they don't, they'll soon make jackasses of themselves. If he kept Hensell on the defensive and forced the man to supply information while at the same time giving nothing away himself, then –

'If Earth had seen fit to warn us that you were coming,' Hensell said frostily, 'we might possibly have been able to guide you down to a safe landing.' The Doctor caught the implication: *Don't blame us for your problems*.

'If Earth didn't inform you that an Examiner was coming,' the Doctor countered gently, 'then I expect they must have had a very good reason. Don't you, Governor?' He saw from Hensell's angry flush that this had hit him hard. The implication for Hensell was that either he was not considered important enough to bother telling – or that it was his behaviour that the Examiner was here to check up on. Either way, Hensell was losing ground here very quickly.

In an attempt to regain control of the situation, he reverted to type. When in doubt, bluster. 'I'm entitled to know these things. I'm in charge of this colony. Why have you come to Vulcan? We aren't due an Examiner for two more years yet. How does Earth expect me to get this place in shape if I'm constantly interrupted? I don't like spot checks! Furthermore, I'm going to say so! Is that understood? I am to send a message to Earth!'

The Doctor jumped to his feet. Hensell, alarmed, took a step back, but the Doctor grabbed his hand and pumped it enthusiastically, grinning like a maniac. 'Oh, I understand perfectly. You're delighted to see us and I must thank you for the warmth of your enthusiastic welcome.' He dropped Hensell's hand and marched over to the door, staring at it thoughtfully.

Hensell was now clearly so far out of his depth that he was in danger of drowning. 'Why have you come to Vulcan?' he repeated. 'What's your brief?'

Since the Doctor had absolutely no idea, he couldn't have answered that directly if he'd wanted to. 'I am the Examiner,' he said, whirling back to face the two men. His hand went into his pocket and touched the button there. 'And I intend to start my examination at once.' Whatever Hensell might imagine that meant, he was clearly taken aback when the

Doctor crossed to Bragen and began to peer myopically at the Security Head's uniform.

Bragan stared down at the odd man who was fingering the buttons on his tunic. He seemed to be upset by this. Guilt? the Doctor wondered.

'May I suggest, Governor,' Bragen began.

'You may not!' Hensell almost yelled. It was bad enough with this ridiculous Examiner challenging his command of the situation. He didn't need Bragen to start *suggesting* anything at all. As the Doctor straightened up from his examination of Bragen's tunic, Hensell glared down at him. There was only one possible reason he could think of that might prompt the arrival of an Earth Examiner. 'Somebody's leaked a report about these rebel groups, haven't they?' he demanded. 'That's it, isn't it?'

'Is it?' the Doctor asked infuriatingly. He started to look over Hensell's tunic next.

Flustered, Hensell glared down at the man. 'Internal affairs are my business,' he stormed. 'Don't interfere!' When the Doctor glanced up sharply, Hensell snapped: 'According to the charter, as defined in section nine, paragraph twenty – '

'Yes, yes, yes,' the Doctor said, finishing his examination of Hensell. He hated people trying to claim authority on the basis of some silly little by-law that made them little tin gods. It was probably the most inefficient system of government he could think of. When all else fails, quote rules by the million.

'Governor,' Bragen interrupted again, 'there is Lesterson's capsule.'

Hensell was about to reprimand Bragen again for breaking in when he considered the man's point. Maybe the Examiner wasn't here for it – but the artefact could provide a distraction, maybe even derail this meddling Examiner until Hensell could apply a little pressure of his own and have the man re-called. Hensell was not without influence back at the Colony Office in Berne . . . 'The capsule was found in the mercury swamps here while we were excavating for the city foundations,' he explained. 'It must have been here for years, long before Earth decided to colonize Vulcan. Lesterson wants to open it, but I'm not at all sure that it's wise.'

'The Governor feels it may be dangerous,' Bragen added. 'It could contain alien bacteria – start a plague – anything!'

The Doctor sighed. Typically narrow-minded bureaucrats – terrified of the unknown. The chances of an alien bacteria actually being able to infect a human being were incredibly remote. Most germs were terribly fussy about who and what they infected. And anyway, if Lesterson had even an ounce of scientific caution, he'd open the capsule in a sealed, sterile environment.

'Yes, all right, Bragen,' Hensell muttered. To the Doctor, he added: 'I suggest that you concentrate your attention on the capsule, Examiner.'

Why? the Doctor wondered. He could see in a second that this was an attempt to sidetrack him. But he had to admit that his curiosity had been roused. Vulcan had shown no signs at all during his brief investigation of having any native life forms. If the capsule wasn't from the Earth, then it was logically from some alien planet. It might be inactive now, but he'd better make sure about that. 'I shall examine the capsule later,' he promised. 'You may leave us now.'

Hensell flushed at this abrupt dismissal. Refusing to grant the Doctor the final word, he nodded curtly. 'I shall look forward to your report.' He gave the Doctor's odd clothing a look of utter disgust. 'And, Bragen, see that the Examiner and his party get some proper clothes to wear.' He swept out. Bragen, with a chilly smile towards the Doctor, followed.

As the door closed, the Doctor flopped on to the closest bed. 'What a cheek!' he exclaimed. 'I am wearing "proper clothes"!'

Ben was staring at the closed door when he heard the tootling of the Doctor's recorder again. His hand flashed to his pocket, which was empty. What a nerve! The Doctor had picked his pocket during all of that chatter. Ben almost had to admire him for it. 'You were pushing it a bit, weren't you?' he asked the Doctor. 'Seeing if that button of yours came off the Governor's tunic.'

'Yes,' the Doctor agreed with a happy grin. 'Very rude,

wasn't I? Terrible manners.' He didn't look at all ashamed; quite the contrary, he looked rather pleased with himself. He blew a few more notes on his recorder, then tucked it into an inside pocket. 'We have to have a look at that capsule.'

'You want to watch that you don't push this Examiner thing a bit too far,' Ben warned him.

Ignoring his advice, the Doctor said: 'The Examiner was killed in the mercury swamp. The capsule came out of the swamp. Could that be coincidental?'

Ben pressed on. 'At least one person isn't going to be fooled by your act.'

Looking at Polly, the Doctor said thoughtfully: 'And when Bragen found us, he distintly called it a *space* capsule.'

Exasperated at the lack of attention the Doctor was paying to him, Ben snapped: 'You ain't going to fool the bloke that did the real Examiner in!' He was happy to see the worry on the Doctor's face. He was less happy to see the same on Polly's.

The hub of the city was close to the medical wing, in the Admin Centre. Here was the Community Hall, where concerts, plays and other activities were held. Outside the Hall was a community bulletin board. Eventually, when the city was completed, everything would be on computer. At the moment, older technology still ruled. Bragen was pinning up a note under the *Personals* section when Quinn found him.

'What's all this nonsense about having to have a pass to see the Examiner?' he demanded curtly. He'd been turned back – politely, true, but obviously – by two of Bragen's goons posted in the medical wing.

Attempting to look apologetic, Bragen replied: 'It's the Governor's idea.'

'Surely that doesn't apply to *me*!' Quinn insisted.

'It isn't my order, Quinn,' Bragen explained patiently. 'Hensell said everyone. I suppose the Governor wants to stop people from bothering him.'

Quinn's eyes narrowed, suspiciously. 'It sounds to me more like one of your red-tape ideas to keep your men employed.'

Or, he added mentally, like someone's afraid that the wrong information will reach the Examiner.

Bragen spread his hands as a gesture of helplessness. 'It's really nothing to do with me.'

Quinn glared at the piece of paper Bragen had tacked to the board. It was something about wanting a partner to play chess with. Rapping the notice with one hand, Quinn snapped: 'If this is what occupies your time, you should find something better for you and your muscle-men to do!'

'We don't have any crime on Vulcan,' Bragen said, as if taking personal credit for this amazing piece of law enforcement. 'My security men –'

'Security men!' Quinn laughed scornfully. 'If brains were dynamite, they wouldn't have enough to blow their own noses!' With an annoyed snarl, he turned to stalk away. He didn't see the filthy look that Bragen gave him as he marched off. Lost in his foul mood, Quinn almost slammed into Janley as he turned the corner. 'Oh, sorry,' he apologized.

She gave him one of her devastating smiles, and Quinn's mood brightened considerably. 'My fault,' she told him cheerfully. 'Lesterson's just cleared me out of his lab.' Lowering her voice, she asked him: 'Is the Examiner going to let him open up the capsule?'

'I don't know,' Quinn admitted. 'I'm on my way to see the Examiner now – if I can push past Bragen's army of layabouts.'

Janley chuckled. Then she touched Quinn's sleeve. For a moment, he thought she was going to get personal. No such luck, though.

'You've torn your jacket,' she observed.

Quinn glanced down. The button on the edge of his sleeve was missing, along with a bit of the cloth. 'Oh, curses,' he muttered, annoyed. 'Well, it'll have to do for now. I haven't the time to fix it.'

'Want me to do it?' Janley offered.

Much as he'd have liked an excuse to get better acquainted with her, Quinn reluctantly shook his head. 'I'm late as it is,' he said. He gave her a nod and hurried on.

Janley watched him leave, thoughtfully tapping the notice she had for the bulletin board in the palm of her other hand.

7

Alien? Yes – Very Alien

The Doctor stared at the triangular piece of metal that Lesterson had polished to an impressive shine. Even to Ben's unpractised eyes, he looked very disturbed. Ben was distracted by Lesterson's incessant fiddling with items of equipment that he was setting up beside the capsule. Ben had no idea what any of it was for, but it looked quite formidable.

He and Polly were close to the maybe-Doctor by Lesterson's bench. Gathered by the door – ready to bolt in case of trouble? – were the Admin staff. Hensell and Quinn were there, along with Bragen and one of his silent security men. Over the door a lighted sign was flashing: QUARANTINE ON. It didn't make Ben feel any better to know that if there was some form of alien plague inside that capsule then only the inhabitants of this room would be infected. He might have taken the chance himself, to keep an eye on the bloke claiming to be the Doctor. He would certainly have insisted on Polly being outside, though. Neither she nor the Doctor would listen to his arguments, however, and here she was, taking her chances with the rest of them.

'Where did you get this?' the Doctor called out to Lesterson, holding up the piece of metal.

Hurrying over, Lesterson beamed at the Doctor. 'You can see why I insisted on opening this capsule, Examiner. That metal could completely revolutionize the construction of starships.'

'You cut this from the capsule, did you?' the Doctor asked.

'Cut it?' Lesterson snorted, good-naturedly. 'I haven't got anything that could cut through that stuff. Lasers just bounce right off it. No, the piece simply dropped off when we were cleaning the thing.'

58

'Dropped?' the Doctor echoed. It sounded to Ben like he didn't believe the story for some reason.

Not replying directly, Lesterson stressed: 'If that metal is so amazing, imagine what other wonders must lie inside this capsule, Examiner.'

Ben rubbed his chin. 'If you can't cut the metal, how are you going to get in?' he asked.

'Yes,' agreed Hensell, 'I didn't think you *could* open it, Lesterson.'

'I have a theory,' the scientist said excitedly. He hurried back to the capsule. The others in the room gathered around him. Lesterson showed them a thin line in the metal that had the appearance of a hatch. 'Hermetically sealed,' he explained. Then he tapped a point about halfway up, close to the left edge, and the same spot by the right edge. 'I have a theory that the opening mechanism on the other side of the door is located in one of these two spots.'

The Doctor looked at him with suspicion in his eyes. 'I'd be most interested to know how you arrived at that theory,' he said gently. For a moment, he locked eyes with the scientist. Lesterson looked away first and the Doctor smiled as if he'd won a small war. 'But for now the important thing is to open it up.'

'Open it?' Hensell echoed, as if that were the last thing he was expecting to hear. Ben gave him a thoughtful look. It was as if he'd been hoping that the Examiner would insist on it staying closed.

'Yes,' the Doctor agreed.

Hensell shrugged. 'Very well,' he agreed.

Lesterson grinned like an idiot. 'That's the first piece of sense I've heard in ages.'

Ben saw the satisfied expression on the Doctor's face. Something crystallized in the back of his mind. While the others were watching Lesterson work on the laser projector he'd set up by the capsule hatch, Ben plucked at Polly's sleeve and drew her aside.

'Duchess, I think I'm beginning to get his number now.'

'Well?' she prompted, giving the Doctor a thoughtful look.

He didn't seem to have noticed them. He was staring hard at Lesterson's triangular scrap of metal again.

'Suppose this bloke who's pretending to be the Doctor,' Ben said conspiratorially, 'just suppose he's here on purpose.'

'Here?' Polly looked around the room. 'Whatever for?'

'To make it possible for that capsule to be opened.' Ben gestured at the artefact. 'The Governor looked like he expected the Examiner to sink the whole thing. Instead, the so-called Doctor wants it opened.'

Polly stared thoughtfully around the group. 'The capsule? You may be right, Ben.'

'Maybe we'd better keep an extra-careful eye on him, then?' Ben suggested, leading her back to the others as Lesterson straightened up and tapped the barrel of the laser projector.

'My theory,' Lesterson explained, 'is that the locking mechanism is light-activated. You'll observe there's no sign of an opening mechanism. But these two patches have a very faint luminescence at night, suggesting a sensitivity. Now, if I fire a laser beam through the spots, I believe it will spread inside the lock and trigger the mechanism.'

Hensell frowned. Turning to the Doctor, he said: 'I shall have to make this your responsibility.'

'Yes, yes,' the Doctor agreed. Ben could hardly believe his nerve – as if he had any right to take such a load! 'Carry on, please,' the Doctor called to Lesterson.

Nodding, Lesterson carefully aimed the barrel at the left-hand side of the probable doorway. Then he triggered the beam. A thin red light hissed out at the hatch. Touching the metal, it spread in a small glowing web-like pattern, covering a patch of about six-inches across. Nothing else happened, though.

The Doctor leaned forward slightly, looking rather pleased with himself for some reason. 'Why don't you try the other side?' he suggested gently. 'You may have better luck there.'

Lesterson nodded and then turned the laser on its mounting to point the beam at the other side of the hatch. Again, the beam danced across the surface of the hatch in a spidery pattern. This time, the whole patch glowed.

With a sigh, the hatch slid open.

Ben held his breath. If there *were* bugs in there, they might all be dead in seconds. When nothing happened, he pressed forward with the others. Lesterson and the Doctor both moved to the entrance that had been uncovered. They seemed to be almost moving in unison as they stepped into the capsule. Ben peered into the opening.

It was only about four-feet deep. The walls were almost completely smooth. The only blemish inside was a groove of some kind. It was about six-inches long and very thin. Ben had barely noticed it himself when the Doctor slid in front of it and turned back to face the others. Ben had the distinct impression that this was to make certain nobody else saw that ridge.

'Bit disappointing,' Lesterson commented, apparently absorbed in running his hands along the shiny metal surface.

'Not really,' the Doctor said. 'This must just be the entrance bay, mustn't it?'

'I suppose so, yes.'

Hensell snorted. He had a low opinion of the whole matter, obviously. 'This hasn't really got us very far, has it?'

'Getting into the rest of the capsule is going to take time, Governor,' the Doctor replied.

Ben was absolutely convinced that the Doctor was up to something. He was stalling. Well, time to muck up his little game. 'Can't you use that laser thing again?' he asked, gesturing to the projector. 'If that's an entrance, then it stands to reason that there must be an inner door as well, don't it?'

'I'd have to measure it up,' Lesterson said, quickly. 'Find the lock mechanism . . .' He gestured vaguely. To Ben it seemed that he, too, was stalling for some reason.

'Yes, yes, yes!' the Doctor agreed, a bit too quickly. He and Lesterson were starting to look like a music-hall double act. 'I think we'll leave it for tonight.'

'Leave it?' Hensell asked, aghast. 'What do you mean *leave it*? What are we here for if not to open the thing?'

The Doctor steepled his fingers and gave Hensell a long stare. 'That is my decision,' he announced, clearly defying Hensell to contradict him. The Governor gave him an annoyed look but said nothing. He wasn't willing to challenge the

61

Examiner's authority quite yet, that much was clear. The Doctor turned back to Lesterson. 'Two hundred years you'd say this has been buried?' he asked.

'At the very least.' Lesterson led the way out of the compartment again. With one accord, everyone moved closer to the doors. Quinn glanced up at the quarantine light that was still flashing redly.

'Can't we cut that thing off?' he asked, gruffly.

Lesterson examined a series of read-outs on his instruments. 'Quite sterile,' he announced. 'No risk of infection at all.'

'Good.' Quinn hit the switch and the light died.

Looking back at the capsule, Lesterson announced: 'There must be something in the inner compartments. When we get it open, we'll be able to discover where it came from originally.'

'It's nothing to do with this planet, Vulcan?' the Doctor prompted him.

'Oh, nothing.' Lesterson was obviously certain on that point. 'That metal is quite alien to this world.'

'Alien?' The Doctor rubbed his chin as he gazed at the artefact. 'Yes. Very alien.' He glanced around as if suddenly aware that all eyes were on him. 'Well, goodnight.' He gave a cheery little wave and bolted out of the door.

Ben and Polly were just as startled by this sudden exit as anyone. They had been shown their rooms by Thane shortly before coming to the laboratory, and that was presumably where the Doctor was heading. Ben grabbed Polly's hand. 'Bet you he's up to something,' he muttered so that the others didn't hear.

'We'd better not let him out of our sight,' Polly agreed. They dashed after the disappearing figure.

Once the trio had gone, Hensell turned furiously on Lesterson. 'Well, you got your way, Lesterson. Was it really worth sending for this idiotic Examiner?'

The scientist had been packing away the laser projector. He looked up, puzzled. 'I didn't send for him,' he protested. 'I thought you did.' *To try and stop me*, his accusing glance added.

'Why don't you let me talk to the Examiner, Hensell?'

Quinn asked. He smiled grimly. 'I can find out what he's really here for.'

'No,' the Governor ordered, 'you keep away from him. Let him concentrate on working with Lesterson here. We've all got enough work to do without having some amateur critic from Earth interfering with us.'

'But I can – ' Quinn protested.

Hensell cut him off with a slashing motion of his hand. 'You heard me, Quinn.' He favoured the scientist with one of his rare smiles. He looked like a cheap politician attempting to kiss a colicky baby. 'I'm sure you don't mind keeping the Examiner busy, Lesterson. He's on your side, after all.' He nodded in the direction of the capsule. 'I don't really care what you do with him just as long as you keep his nose out of our business.'

'All right,' Lesterson said agreeably.

Hensell indicated with his head for Bragen and Quinn to follow him out. The security guard fell in step behind them, silent as ever. Quinn looked as if he were about to start another barrage, but Hensell fixed him with a glare. 'We'll talk about it tomorrow,' Hensell said.

As they left the laboratory, Lesterson turned back to the capsule. He ran his hand down the smooth metal wall just inside the hatchway. A beatific smile illuminated his face. Then he patted the artefact and crossed to his bench. The smile evaporated when he glanced down.

The triangular piece of metal was no longer there. Frantically Lesterson looked around on the bench top, and on the floor. There was no sign of it. Slamming his fist on the table in anger, he thought back.

The last person he remembered seeing with the metal fragment was that meddlesome Examiner.

8

Nothing Human, No

Ben was half-dozing on his bed. It was a knack he'd learned at sea to get some rest without actually falling into a deep sleep. Came in handy on some of the longer night watches. There was a rap on the door connecting with Polly's room and she stuck her head inside.

'Ben!' she hissed.

Blinking, Ben struggled back to alertness. 'What?'

'Quiet!' Polly insisted. 'He's in the corridor. Let's follow him.'

Still foggy from lack of rest, Ben stood up. 'Who is?'

'The Doctor, you clot!' she snapped. 'Come on!'

Fully awake now, Ben let her lead the way into the corridor. Thane had mentioned something about the colony having a similar length day to Earth's, because Vulcan's period of rotation was only an hour or so shorter than Earth's. It must be about midnight, local time, Ben guessed. Everyone else had to be in bed. Sensible people.

Everyone but the Doctor, who was vanishing around the far corner of the corridor, heading back towards the hub.

'He's going towards Lesterson's lab,' Polly whispered.

'Of course he is,' Ben agreed. 'I told you – he's after that capsule.' They trailed after him through the deserted city corridors to the science section. The Doctor never looked back, so they didn't have to hide. He seemed intent only on what lay ahead.

The lab was as deserted as the corridors, but there were lights still focused on the capsule. They were on stands, like the ones photographers used for wedding pictures. It was as if Lesterson were afraid the capsule might scarper if he didn't keep it constantly monitored. Well, for all Ben knew it just might.

As he approached the open hatchway, the Doctor pulled something from one of his stuffed pockets. Ben could just make out that it was Lesterson's triangular piece of metal. Now what was going on? He and Polly tiptoed quietly into the lab and over to the entrance to the capsule. The Doctor was bent over the far wall. As they watched, puzzled, he took the metal token and slid it into the right-hand edge of the thin slot Ben had seen him stand in front of earlier. Holding one point of the triangle, he pressed the flat edge as deeply into the groove as it would go. Then he slid it to the left.

With the very faintest of hums, the inner wall slid back.

'Ben, Polly,' the Doctor called over his shoulder without looking around, 'come and meet the Daleks.'

Ben sighed and walked over to join the little man. Polly followed, a little more reluctantly.

Beyond the now-open doorway was a second compartment. It was considerably larger than the hatchway, but its walls were almost as bare. There was also a layer of dust over the room. Not much light filtered in from the arc lamps outside the capsule, but Ben could clearly see what the Doctor had to be referring to.

Two machines stood in the room. Both were slightly smaller than he was. They tapered up from the floor to a domed top. There was a series of raised half-spheres arranged about the lower half of each machine. Above this was a band. Two appendages jutted out from what had to be the front of the thing, lifelessly pointing at the floor. Above this section was a grilled area, then the dome. Two dead bulbs and a third append-age were fitted into the dome. Both machines were identical in every respect, a dull grey colour, like the rocks of Vulcan.

'You knew they were here,' Ben said accusingly.

'You could have opened the capsule at any time,' Polly added, eyeing the metal token as the Doctor slipped it back into his pocket.

'I *guessed* they were here,' the Doctor replied to Ben's question, nodding at the Daleks. To Polly, he added: 'Didn't

that piece of metal look at all familiar to you? Think back —
the TARDIS's wardrobe . . .'

'You had one just like it!' Polly said, remembering. 'You
said something about your granddaughter, didn't you?'

'Yes. Susan took *that* piece from Skaro.' He tapped the
closet of the Daleks. 'That is their home world.'

Polly was puzzled. 'Then why did you keep it a secret?'

The Doctor was studying the Daleks carefully. 'I didn't
know whether they were alive or . . . not alive.'

Ben gave a cheery grin and slapped the metal shell. It rang
quite loudly in the compartment. 'They don't seem to be too
lively to me.'

'Never underestimate the power of the Daleks, Ben,' the
Doctor told him. He turned back to peer down at the floor of
the room next to the entrance.

Ben snorted in disbelief. Polly frowned. 'What did you
expect?' she asked the Doctor. 'Two hundred years at least in
the swamp, Lesterson said. Nothing could live through that.'

'Nothing human, no.' The Doctor seemed to be absorbed in
studying the dust on the floor. 'Ah . . .'

'What's the matter?' Ben asked. He still wasn't certain what
this odd person was up to, or if he was really the Doctor or
not. But he clearly knew something about this place that he
wasn't telling.

The Doctor rubbed his finger in the dust. It left a tiny trail.
'There were *three* Daleks in here,' he said quietly. He pointed
to an area closer to the door than the two inert figures. Peering
down, Ben could make out the outline of a third Dalek in the
dust. The Doctor looked up and met his gaze. 'So, where's
the other one?'

Ben's skin was crawling. The Doctor's tone made him shiver.
But there was nothing to be afraid of in here, surely? The
whole thing was a couple of centuries dead.

In the darkness of the shadows, it paused. There were life
forms in the capsule. Three of them, ahead of it, studying
the travel machines. But this was the night-period, when the
humans rested.

It had rested for long enough. The first, faint glimmers of

66

light had awakened it from its sleep. It had been waiting for the slightest touch of power to awaken. The photoelectric panel in the hatchway had been programmed to divert the energy of light to awaken it in its cradle. All that was needed were a few faint rays of sunlight. The capsule could have landed in forty-feet of water and still the panel would have found enough light to trigger the awakening. But that hadn't happened. The Dalek had no idea why, as yet. Instead, a short while ago, a brilliant pulse of laser light had triggered the device.

It had been wakened, but the light had died again. Still, now that the Dalek was awake, it had one clear duty: protect the capsule.

The three intruders were humanoid, and they were dangerously close to uncovering the secrets of the Daleks. It knew its duty: exterminate them.

Polly stared at the machines in front of her. 'You called them Daleks,' she said.

'Yes,' the Doctor agreed. He seemed to be very distracted.

'These machines?' she asked.

He shook his head. 'The machines are only a part of the Daleks,' he told her. 'I've encountered them before. On their home world of Skaro they were humanoid once. But a deadly neutronic war left them as stunted protoplasmic creatures, unable to survive unaided.' He tapped the machine closest to him. 'This is, if you like, their own tiny environment. Inside these machines a Dalek creature is maintained on life-support systems. It can interface with a sophisticated computer to augment its natural ferocity and skills. The Daleks are the most deadly life form that I have ever come across. They are utterly single-minded and have an implacable hatred for all other creatures.'

Ben was by now thoroughly alarmed. His eyes flickered around the interior of the compartment nervously. It was stupid, really – a grown man like him being scared stiff just because someone was telling ghost stories in the dark.

Then he heard the faint sound. It was like fingernails scraping on a board. Faint, but definitely real. Not a phantom manufactured by his fears. He glanced at the Doctor. From the

way he was standing – tense, ready to move at any second –
he must have heard the noise as well.

There was something with them in the capsule. Something
in the darkness, coming closer . . .

9

You Don't Half Make Mountains

'What's the matter?' Polly asked in a scared whisper. She didn't seem to have heard the noise, but she was nobody's fool. She had picked up the tension in the air.

'I felt something,' the Doctor said softly. 'Watching me . . .'

'Hang on,' Ben said firmly. All this talk was enough to give anyone the willies; it was time for a bit of action. 'I'll get us a light of some sort.'

He went back out of the capsule, into Lesterson's laboratory. Had he not been so intent on his task, he might have seen a stranger duck out of sight behind the far side of the capsule. Ben's attention was fixed firmly on the lab bench, however. A scan of the unfamiliar equipment there led Ben's eyes to the familar shape of a bulb on a long wire, the kind of thing an electrician uses. Plugging the end of the wire into the power outlet on the bench, Ben returned to the capsule, unwinding the lead as he went. Once inside the inner compartment, he switched on the bulb. All three of them shielded their eyes from the harsh glare.

The Doctor snatched the bulb from his hands and poked it like a weapon into the shadows. Light bounced off the walls and the two Dalek casings. Nothing out of place seemed to be there, however. 'Nothing,' the Doctor announced.

Ben had been shielding Polly – just in case. Now she sighed. 'You scared me half to death,' she told them accusingly. Ben could only hope that it had been a false alarm.

In the bright glow from the bulb, the circle in the dust was even more apparent. 'You're right,' Ben told the Doctor. 'There were three of them.'

'Then where's the other one?' the Doctor asked.

Polly frowned. 'I suppose Lesterson moved it.'

The Doctor wagged a finger under her nose. 'Ah, but we were supposed to have been present at the first opening of the capsule, remember?'

Her face fell. 'Yes, that's right.'

With an impish smile, the Doctor patted her arm. 'Nevertheless, I think you're perfectly correct, Polly. I think Lesterson did open the capsule before we arrived. I just hope he wasn't foolish enough to move one of the Daleks away to experiment upon.' He spun about, clicking off the light, and rushed outside.

Ben was in the dark for a moment before his eyes adjusted. He and Polly followed the Doctor back into Lesterson's laboratory. The tramp-like figure was examining all of the equipment on the main bench with great interest.

Polly moved to stand behind him. 'But they're dead,' she said. 'They must be.'

'There's a difference between being dead and being dormant,' the Doctor replied. He held up the bulb in his hand. 'This light is dead right now,' he pointed out. Then he switched it on, oblivious to the fact that it blinded Polly. 'The Daleks simply need power, that's all. And then they'e as dangerous as ever.'

Rubbing her eyes, Polly suggested: 'Well, warn everybody then.'

The Doctor chewed at his thumb-nail. 'But will they listen?' he argued. 'Lesterson's a fanatic of sorts. He's already lied to cover up his experiments. And the Governor's only interested in maintaining his own power. Then he mentioned "rebels".' Turning to Ben, he asked, 'What does that suggest to you?'

'I don't know,' Ben replied.

'All isn't well in this colony,' the Doctor amplified. He looked very worried indeed. 'No, I don't at all care for the idea of a Dalek on the loose here.'

'Blimey!' Ben scoffed. 'You don't half make mountains, don't you? One Dalek!'

'Yes!' the Doctor cried. 'One! And I assure you that one Dalek is quite enough to wipe out this entire colony.'

Quinn slipped into the room that Thane had assigned to the

Examiner. It was pitch-black inside. 'Examiner!' he hissed. 'Examiner!' When there was no reply, he moved to where the bed was and reached out to shake the man awake.

The bed was empty.

With a muffled curse, Quinn switched on the bedside lamp. The bed was still made, and had obviously not been slept in. This was going to set his plans back. But where *was* the man?

The door opened. Quinn looked up, expectantly, but his face fell when he saw who it was in the doorway. 'Bragen! Dont you ever knock before you enter a room?'

The Head of Security gave a sanctimonious smile. 'I'm sorry if I . . . startled you,' he said, clearly lying. 'I expected to find the Examiner in his room – not you, Quinn.'

'Well, he's not here,' Quinn snapped back. He didn't care for Bragen's smugness at all. 'You'll no doubt want to snoop under the bed and in the closets looking for him, so I'll leave you to it.' As he tried to push his way past, Bragen grabbed his arm.

'Just a minute,' Bragen said coldly.

Angrily, Quinn jerked his arm free. 'Don't try your luck with me, Bragen,' he warned.

'On the contrary,' the security man said, 'I'm attempting to *avoid* trouble. The Governor gave you explicit instructions that you were not to talk with the Examiner alone. Yet here you are, alone in his room.' He gave a mocking smile to Quinn. 'I'm sure you can offer a suitable explanation.'

'I can,' Quinn agreed. 'But I don't have to answer to you for anything, Bragen.' He jerked open the door. One of the silent security guards was waiting there. 'And don't try and block my way again,' he called over his shoulder before walking off down the corridor.

Bragen slammed his fist angrily against the door frame. He winced with pain, then managed to gather the tattered edges of his temper together. Glaring at the guard, he snapped: 'The Examiner is missing! We must search for him. He must be found – immediately.'

Ben sat on one of the lab stools, watching the strange little man examining the equipment. From time to time he would jot down a reading or two with the nub of a pencil on his shirt sleeve. 'Of course,' Ben said carefully, 'the real Doctor was always going on about the Daleks.' He gave the little tramp a thoughtful stare. 'You wouldn't be trying to convince us of something, would you?'

The maybe-Doctor gave a loud sigh. 'I had hoped you'd got over those suspicions of yours by now.'

'I'll bet you had,' Ben agreed. 'Well, you're wrong then. It's just a bit of a truce at the moment, isn't it? That's all.' He nodded across at Polly, who was nervously playing with a spatula, turning it over and over in her hand. 'I mean, we're stuck with these people here thinking you're this Examiner from Earth, aren't we?'

'I see.' The little man glanced at him from under his shaggy fringe. 'But the glue isn't very permanent, is that it?'

Polly gave him an almost apologetic glance. 'It *was* very convenient that you happened to find the real Examiner's papers, wasn't it?'

'I did find them,' he insisted. 'He was murdered. Someone must have moved the body after they hit me on the head. It *was* there.' A sudden realization dawned on him. 'You think I faked this ID?'

'It does make sense, mate,' Ben replied. 'Didn't Hensell say that they weren't expecting an Examiner for two years yet? What's wrong?' he asked. 'Couldn't get the TARDIS here in the right year?' Then he looked at the open capsule. 'Or is this the right year after all, eh?'

'I *am* the Doctor!'

Ben shrugged. 'Yeah, well, that proves everything then, doesn't it?' He rolled his eyes.

The Doctor was almost dancing about with poorly contained impatience. 'We're just wasting time,' he complained. He stared at the two Daleks, barely visible through the hatch in the capsule. 'Of course, as the Examiner I could always order them to destroy the Daleks.'

'Can you?' Polly asked eagerly. That would at least remove one of their problems. Whoever this person was – and Polly couldn't decide whether she believed him or not – if those creatures were Daleks, then they had to be destroyed. Mind you, if this stranger was lying about being the Doctor then he might just be lying about those things being Daleks as well. Maybe he only wanted them to believe that those machines were Daleks so they'd help him to destroy them. For all she knew, that could be why he was here. In which case, it was up to her and Ben to stop him from doing that. Her head was aching from all of the suspicions and uncertainties.

'I can try,' the little man answered. 'I must try.'

Ben grinned. 'Tell you what I think,' he offered.

The Doctor smiled back. 'I'd be most interested.'

'You wouldn't have done some funny kind of switch with the Doctor?' Ben asked. 'Just so you could get on this planet and make some sort of trouble here? Like over that?' He gestured at the capsule.

The stranger sighed and shook his head. 'Ben, for goodness sake, get your priorities right! The Daleks are more important than your childish suspicions.'

Ben grinned again, as if he'd proved his point. 'Yeah, but you see if I'd said a thing like that to the real Doctor, he'd have bitten my head off.' He shook his head. 'You're a phoney and you know it. Why not just admit it?'

The little man stared at Polly. Gently, she added: 'Tell us the truth. Please.'

'The truth is,' he replied crossly, 'the truth is whatever you choose to believe. But I *am* the Doctor.'

Before Ben could say anything else, the door slammed open. Lesterson strode in, his hair in a mess. He'd obviously been wakened from his rest. Beside him walked his assistant, Resno, who'd spotted Ben in the lab and had seized his chance to alert his boss.

'What do you think you're doing?' Lesterson snarled. 'Who gave you permission? You've no right to be in here, no right at all!'

The Doctor pulled the Examiner's ID from his pocket and virtually slapped it against the lens of the scientist's glasses. 'On the contrary, I have every right, and shouting doesn't help. Read this. Aloud.'

'Accord every access,' Lesterson read, reluctantly.

'Exactly,' the Doctor agreed. 'And it doesn't say "except for Lesterson's laboratory", does it?' Then, looking vaguely worried, he started to examine the pass. 'Unless it's in the fine print.'

Knowing that he'd lost that battle, Lesterson tried a different tack. 'I should have been asked first,' he complained.

The Doctor gave an incredulous grunt. 'Why? So that you could hide the other two Daleks?' Without waiting for a reply, he rounded on Ben. 'What did you notice first when you looked in that capsule?' he demanded.

'Eh?' Ben hadn't been expecting this. 'Er, well, the Daleks.'

Sounding like a lawyer in a bad TV show, the Doctor asked, 'And you were astounded?'

'Well, yes.'

'Intrigued?'

'Er – '

The Doctor whirled around to point an accusatory finger at Lesterson. 'Yet *you* haven't even given the capsule a second glance! The inner door – which you claimed not to know how to open – is now open and you can see right in. But you didn't even look! Why? Because you've already been in there and seen them. Where's the third Dalek?'

Lesterson tried to look innocent. He didn't do a very good job of it, however. Ben thought he could take lessons from the so-called Doctor. 'I don't know what you're talking about,' Lesterson said.

'You opened the capsule without permission,' the Doctor said. 'You found that second door and opened it. You discovered the three Daleks. You took one of them away and hid it. I want it back!'

'Those are all lies!' Lesterson protested.

'They're not lies,' the Doctor insisted. The door to the laboratory opened and Bragen strode in, accompanied by one of his inevitable guards. The Doctor didn't seem to even notice the intrusion. His whole attention was centred on Lesterson. 'You knew how to open the capsule too easily. Because you'd already done it.'

'Oh, thank you!' the scientist said sarcastically. 'It doesn't seem to have occurred to you how much time it took me to measure every single inch of the surface and – '

'Stop it, stop it, stop it!' the Doctor cried, like a baby having a tantrum. When Lesterson fell silent, the Doctor glared at him. 'I want the third Dalek. Where is it?'

Bragen stepped forward, determined to control whatever was happening here. 'May I ask what this is all about?' he asked coldly.

Polly gave him her very best smile. 'We opened the inner door to the capsule only to discover Lesterson had already been inside.'

For the first time Bragen looked across at the capsule. His eyes widened as he saw the inner door now open.

The Doctor pointed to Bragen's astonished look. 'That's how you'd have reacted if you were telling the truth,' he informed Lesterson. 'You're playing about with things you don't understand.'

Realizing there was no further point in lying, Lesterson said defiantly, 'All right. I admit it, I was in there.'

'And you nicked a Dalek!' Ben accused.

'Dalek?' Bragen was rapidly losing his grip on the situation, which was doing little to improve his temper.

'Do you know what Daleks are?' the Doctor asked, almost in tears. He couldn't come right out and ask them what year this was. That would ruin any credibility he had in their eyes. He had been hoping – almost praying – that it was some time after the Daleks had invaded the Earth.

'I presume it's the name you've given to those two metal creations,' Lesterson replied, deflating the Doctor's hopes completely. Humanity on Earth had not yet met the Daleks.

'Yes,' the Doctor agreed. 'And they're worse than anything you can possibly imagine in a million years!'

'Lumps of metal,' Lesterson scoffed. 'They're quite inactive.'

Recalling the scratching sounds that he'd heard in the capsule made Ben shudder. 'That's what you think, mate,' he said.

'They're dead,' Lesterson insisted.

The Doctor caught Ben's eye before he could blurt out what

they had been searching for. He gave a slight shake of his head and a mournful *no* note on his recorder. Knowing Lesterson's passion for this thing, news of a living being inside it would only spark further foolish attempts to research it. 'Dormant, not dead,' he said, gesturing at the two Dalek machines. 'I want them broken up or melted down. Up or down – I don't care which. Just do it!'

Lesterson reared back, furious. 'I refuse to allow it!'

'You're very pig-headed!' Polly snapped, unable to control herself any longer. 'You must listen.'

'Polly,' Ben said, plucking at her arm and trying to get her to quieten down. But it was to no avail. Only Polly got started, she was harder to stop than a battleship.

'No, Ben.' She nodded at the Doctor. 'He may well be right. Those . . . things give me the creeps.'

'The creeps!' Lesterson scoffed. 'How terribly scientific. Keep out of this.' He turned his back on her, treating her like a stupid child intruding on the talk of adults. He rammed his finger almost into the Doctor's face. 'I'm warning you – all of you – keep away from my laboratory. Keep your hands off my experiments.'

Bragen tried once again to regain charge of things. 'Gentlemen,' he said winningly, 'please! Shall we just – '

'I'm the Examiner,' the Doctor yelled at Lesterson, completely ignoring the security man. 'I demand that those Daleks be destroyed!'

'You're exceeding your authority,' Lesterson snapped back.

'Perhaps we should let the Governor decide that,' the Doctor replied, and rounded on Bragen. 'I want to see the Governor immediately.'

'That won't do you any good,' Lesterson said.

'I'm afraid he'll be asleep,' Bragen explained, glancing at the clock on the laboratory wall. It was, after all, the middle of the night.

'Then we'll wake him up,' the Doctor said. 'I'm going to wake you all up. You don't know the danger of the Daleks – and I do!' Spinning on his heels, he marched straight for the door. Like a procession, Ben and Polly fell in behind him.

Bragen directed a glance at Lesterson and Resno and then followed. The silent security guard was the last to leave.

Resno closed the door and turned back to his boss. 'Could he stop the experiments?' he asked.

'I don't know!' Lesterson snapped. He was polishing his glasses again, a sign of great agitation. 'Anyway, that's none of your concern.' He thought feverishly. If that idiot did convince Hensell, there might be trouble. Hensell hadn't actually given his approval for what Lesterson had done so far, and he was angling for a solid reason to reprimand him publicly. This could be all the excuse he'd need. Lesterson glared at Resno, as if it were somehow all his fault. 'Go and get Janley and come back yourself. We haven't got much time left.' Resno nodded and opened his mouth. 'Hurry up, Resno!' Couldn't he see that this was an emergency? 'Quickly, man, quickly!' The urgency in Lesterson's voice finally seemed to sink in. Resno set off at a trot down the corridor. Lesterson locked the door behind him. Then he crossed to the capsule.

The compartment containing the two . . . Daleks? Why on Earth did this idiotic Examiner call them that? Giving these machines names, like they were pets or something! They were robots, that was all – alien robots, granted, but they could represent an incredible breakthrough for him.

Reaching into the right-hand side of the hatch, Lesterson triggered a small panel that the Doctor hadn't spotted. The right-hand wall slid quietly open to reveal another chamber.

Inside it rested the missing Dalek. As the Doctor and Polly had guessed, Lesterson had already begun his work on it. He'd opened the lid of it to discover a computer inside of incredible complexity and built to some alien system of logic. It hadn't taken him more than a few moments to realize that all it needed to bring the machine on line was power. He'd begun to connect cables to recharge the Dalek when he'd been forced to hide the machine away and pretend he'd never been inside the capsule.

Lesterson was utterly convinced he was doing the right thing. Scientific progress could never be served by listening to the rantings of Luddite fools like the Examiner, or the silly superstitious fears of the girl who assisted him. Small steps, carefully taken, were what was required. And he was being forced to take the next step before he'd had time to fully evaluate his previous stages.

'He won't stop me experimenting,' Lesterson promised the machine. 'There must be a way to bring you back to life. And I'm going to find it.'

He had very little idea that he had in fact already partially succeeded in his quest. The Dalek machine was still completely inoperative. But inside the still-hidden compartments of the craft, the single living Dalek creature was very active indeed.

10

Plenty of Nuts

Bragen ushered the Doctor politely but firmly back into the room he had been assigned. Ben and Polly stuck with him, determined to have a council of war as soon as Bragen vanished. The security head was doing his best to be charming. It wasn't his fault that he wasn't very good at it.

'Of course you do have the right of any access,' he told the Doctor, who promptly whipped out the Examiner's badge and waved it in front of Bragen's eyes.

'I don't need you to tell me that,' he said peevishly. 'It's right here in black and white.'

'But Lesterson watches over his ideas like a mother hen, you know,' Bragen continued, fighting to keep his temper. This little man really irritated him.

'So you're advising me to be discreet? Is that it?' The Doctor glared up at Bragen. 'If you knew there was a bomb under this floor set to go off in five minutes, would you ask my permission to rip up the floor boards to get at it? I doubt it.' His eyes narrowed as he realized there was something different about the room since he'd sneaked out earlier. They fastened on a bowl on the bedside table. It contained bananas, nuts, apples, cherries and a small bunch of grapes. 'Ah! Fruit!' He dashed across to the bowl and picked up a banana. After polishing it on the shabby edge of his coat, he then replaced it and repeated the actions with an apple.

Bragen seemed at a loss, watching the Doctor buffing the fruit. 'It's up to you, of course,' he said, 'but I would counsel a low-key approach in your investigations. Of course, if you were to tell me why you're here and what it is you are examining, then I could offer my help.'

The Doctor didn't even bother to look up from the bowl as

he started work on the cherries. 'Yes, I'm sure you'd love to help.'

'Well, it's not a very good time at the moment,' Bragen snapped. 'What with all of these disturbances.'

'Disturbances?' Polly asked. People like Bragen had a whole dictionary of euphemisms – such as *nuclear device* when they meant *atomic bomb*. Or *disturbances* when they meant things like *murders*.

The security head waved his hand dismissively. 'Oh, little acts of sabotage. Secret newspapers. Rebel cliques. Nothing important, you understand, but it does keep the Governor busy. I expect he'll tell you about it himself if he thinks that it's important enough.'

Cocking his head to one side, the Doctor gave Bragen a thoughtful stare that seeemd to unnerve the man. Hensell had already alluded to rebels, and here was Bragen – the man responsible for stopping such activities – carefully drawing attention to them. There seemed to be some kind of power play going on, as well as some not-too-subtle attempts to guide his investigations. Not for the first time, the Doctor wished he knew who had called the dead Examiner here, and why.

Bragen took the Doctor's scrutiny for silent criticism. 'The Governor's going off on a tour of the perimeter in the morning,' he explained. 'He has to check up on the progress in the mines and extraction centres, as well as with the shipments back on Earth. I'm sure you understand that he's a very busy man. But I'll check if he can see you before he goes, shall I?'

The Doctor was busily shaking an apple up and down in the air. 'Oh, please do,' he said. Bragen gave him a rather wintry smiled and then left the room.

As soon as the door was shut, Ben rounded on the Doctor and snatched the apple angrily out of his hand. The Doctor looked puzzled for a second, as if he had no clue as to where the apple had vanished to. Then he grabbed the grapes and began shaking them, showering the tiny fruits all over the room.

'You know, it's little things like this,' Ben told him angrily, 'that make it hard for me to believe you're really the Doctor. The other one, I mean. The proper one.' Unable to find the right words, he slammed the apple back into the bowl. 'Oh, nuts!'

'Plenty of nuts,' the impish little man said, snatching up a selection. 'Want one?'

Ben stabbed a finger at the Doctor. 'You, my old china, are an out and out fraud!'

'China?' the Doctor asked, whipping out his 500 year diary. 'Went there once, I believe.' He began to flick through the pages, then stopped, pointing at the unintelligible script there. 'Told you! Met Marco Polo.'

'China!' Ben couldn't believe this idiot. 'It's rhyming slang – china plate, mate. Friend.'

'Yes, I believe Marco Polo was a friend,' the Doctor agreed, returning to his examination of the fruit. Ben threw his hands up in disgust.

Polly moved over to the odd figure. 'Don't listen to him, Doctor. I believe you.'

To her surprise, this announcement didn't please him. He looked alarmed and then held a finger to his lips. Intrigued, Polly watched as he groped in his pocket. Pulling out a pen-knife, he unsnapped the rather dull blade, and then used it to slice open one of the apples.

In the core was a small metal pill. With a fiendish grin, the Doctor dropped it on to the floor and jumped on it with both feet. Then he gave his companions a shooing gesture. Ben nodded and started looking around the small room. Polly followed his lead. A moment later, Ben gave a small snarl of triumph, and pulled another of the tiny devices from under the windowsill. As he broke it, the Doctor stuck up two fingers, then added a third.

One more to go . . .

'This is like hunt the thimble,' Polly said. 'Why don't we give them something for their troubles?' Smiling at Ben, she said, 'You could give them one of your old sea shanties.' Rather off-key, she started to sing: 'Blow the man down, bullies, blow the man down . . .'

Ben put his hands over his ears. 'Do you mind?'

Polly found the final bug, under the base of the table lamp. Ben stomped it to death.

'Blimey, they believe in making us at home, don't they,' he commented.

'That'll be the last one,' the Doctor told him. 'One for the job, a back-up, and a backed-up back-up in case the back-up fails.'

'You guessed they were there,' Ben accused him. 'That was why you were talking all that nonsense.'

The Doctor looked hurt. 'I never talk nonsense,' he said. Then, in a sudden fit of honesty, he felt compelled to add, 'Well, hardly ever.' Then he smiled. 'Yes, I knew they were there. I mean, why else deliver a bowl of fruit at two in the morning? They would have been afraid of waking me up. So someone knew I wasn't here.'

'I'll bet you Bragen did it,' Ben said.

Polly nodded. He *was* Head of Security, and had the equipment to do it. 'Do you think it was his own idea? Or was he doing it under orders?'

'The Governor?' Ben considered the matter. 'Dunno. Both of them seem to be up to something, don't they?'

'Maybe I should ask Quinn,' Polly suggested. 'He seems like a nice man.'

'Get her!' Ben scoffed. 'You just want an excuse to chat him up! I caught you eyeing him over.'

Polly blushed; Quinn *was* rather good-looking. Ignoring Ben's gentle laugh, she went over to the Doctor. She was convinced now that he was who he claimed to be. It didn't make sense, perhaps, but what else about the Doctor ever had? Still, he did seem to have made enemies of Lesterson and Bragen. The pair of them were villains if she'd ever seen any, which meant that this man had to be one of the good guys, surely? He was studying the button he'd been grasping when he was hit in the swamp. 'What about that?' she asked him.

'This is the only clue we've got to the murderer of the real Examiner,' he told her. 'I was just wondering about motives.'

Polly frowned. 'Who asked him to come, or who had reasons to kill him?'

'Both.'

Ben joined them, munching on the ruins of the apple the Doctor had mutilated. 'Lesterson's absolutely crackers about his capsule. Nothing else matters to him. He'd never have called in the Examiner, who might have got in his way.'

Polly said, 'But he might have had to kill the Examiner for exactly the same reason.' She sighed. 'Then what about the rebels? Bragen said the Governor's been having trouble with them.'

'Yeah.' Ben rubbed his chin. 'Funny that he should mention that so obviously, ain't it? Especially since it reflects so badly on himself, if you catch my drift. Anyway, I reckon you can rule the Governor out about calling the Examiner. He'd never have done that. It would have been just as good as admitting he couldn't run this place properly. No official would ever own up to that! I don't care what planet we're on or time we're in, politicians are all the same.'

'I think we should put a little pressure on Lesterson,' the Doctor suggested. 'He's the weakest link. The more we lean on him, the more he'll tell us to try and get rid of us.'

'I don't know why we should bother,' Ben said. 'We should just let them all sink in their own muck and nip off back to the TARDIS.'

The Doctor shook his head. 'But what about the Daleks, Ben?'

'I still don't see what you're worried about,' Ben replied. 'I mean, all right, I'll buy it that those tin cans could be dangerous. They look like they mean aggro and all. But they're not up to much right now, are they?'

'Ah, but what would it take to reactivate them again?' The Doctor pulled his recorder from his pocket and ran through a few bars of 'On Top Of Old Smokey'.

'Besides, what about that thing you and the Doctor saw in the capsule?' Polly asked.

'Well, I can't explain that,' Ben admitted.

'I can,' the Doctor replied gravely, but didn't. 'That's why we *must* stay.'

11

They'll be too Frightened to do Anything Else

Lesterson was competely absorbed in his work. The third
Dalek now stood in the middle of his laboratory. He'd finished
connecting the computer in the dome to his Cray mainframe,
ready to monitor any changes. Now he was laying out the
connections from a thick power cable that scrolled across
the floor. He'd sharply refused Janley and Resno's offer of
help. Both his assistants stood by the main bench, waiting for
further instructions.

'Ugly-looking brutes, aren't they?' Resno grumbled, staring
at the Dalek. 'What's he want to muck about with them for?
Leave well enough alone, I say.'

Janley laughed scornfully. Even though it was the middle
of the night, she looked gorgeous. Resno could think of better
places to be with her than here. Unfortunately, she'd made it
perfectly clear in the past that she was definitely not interested
in him. Or in anyone else that he'd ever noticed. He felt it
was a terrible waste of such beauty.

'You're a fine one to be a research assistant,' she mocked
him. ' "Leave well enough alone"! You'll be saying "there are
things man wasn't meant to know" next. There'll be no progress on this planet with people like you around.'

'We're doing very well as we are,' Resno snapped back,
stung by the venom in her voice. 'Or we were, until you lot
came, stirring things up. You won't get anywhere, you know.
The Governor knows all about you rebels. He'll smash the lot
of you when he's ready.' His revelation that he knew she was
in the rebel camp didn't seem to bother her in the least.

'The Governor?' she laughed. 'He couldn't smash – '

'Be quiet!' Lesterson yelled. He was trying to concentrate
on his connections. 'Where do you think you are? This is a

scientific laboratory, for goodness sake! Leave politics at the door. Resno, get on with checking the power output. It's got to be rock steady. We haven't got all night. We'll have the Examiner down on our backs again if we don't get this thing working.' He gestured. 'He's got some phobia about these . . . Daleks!' He bent back to his work, driven by his own scientific greed.

The Doctor was sitting cross-legged on his bed, staring at his diary. He was turning the pages at a furious rate. 'I know the Daleks,' he told Ben and Polly. 'I know the destruction they cause. The misery. I *have* to know what else I know!'

Polly was almost getting used to these odd references by now. 'Did the Daleks destroy your planet?' she asked.

The Doctor shook his head. 'I don't think so. But I did leave in the TARDIS. Susan and I.' He frowned, obviously concentrating hard. 'I wish I could remember what happened to Susan. It has something to do with the Daleks.'

'She gave you that Dalek key,' Polly said gently.

'There's more than that. I just can't quite recall.' He shook his head.

Ben was quite fed up with this conversation. 'What I don't get,' he told the Doctor, 'is what these Daleks are doing here? I mean, you said that they invaded the Earth once, but they could hardly have come here to take over this place, could they?'

'Not hardly, Ben,' the Doctor agreed. 'They arrived long before the humans did. It may have been an accident. Even the Daleks make mistakes.'

'Well, if they didn't mean to come here, wouldn't they just move on if they were revived?'

'Undoubtedly.' The Doctor favoured Ben with a very bleak look. 'But remember, they have an intractable hatred for all other living species. They would move on, all right – after they had sterilized the whole planet!' He could see from the shocked expression on his travelling companions' faces that this had hit home. 'I wish I could remember my history!'

'History!' Ben's aggressiveness had resurfaced quickly. 'This is the *future*!'

'All time is relative,' the Doctor told him. Before he could elaborate, there was a knock on the door and Bragen entered. 'Well?' the Doctor asked. 'Where's Hensell? What did he say?'

Bragen shrugged. 'He sends his regrets, but he can't see you now. He asks that you meet with him first thing in the morning.'

The Doctor remembered Lesterson's expression. He was not a man to wait about while his precious experiments were in danger. 'It won't wait till then!' he snapped.

'It must,' Bragen insisted.

'No.' The Doctor uncoiled himself from the lotus position and leaped to his feet. His lithe actions were marred when he almost fell over as he stood on a trailing shoelace. 'Action must be taken immediately. I'll go and see him myself right now.'

Bragen stood in front of the door. The meaning of his action was clear enough. 'I'm afraid you can't do that. Once his door is closed, no one is allowed into his room.'

The Doctor wagged a finger under Bragen's nose. 'Then how did you talk to him, um?' For a second, Ben could almost see some of the old Doctor's fire in him. Maybe, just maybe, he was telling the truth.

'The Governor has been working non-stop recently,' Bragen said coldly. 'He really is dog-tired.'

The Doctor knew he would get nowhere like his. Bragen's officious little mind wasn't subject to alteration by mere reason. 'Very well,' he sighed.

Giving them all a final curt nod, Bragen left.

'What will you do now?' Polly asked the Doctor. She doubted that he would simply give up.

'Contact Earth,' he replied. 'Hensell will have to listen to them. I'll get Earth to back me up.'

'Will they believe you?' Ben asked. Ater all, he wasn't certain just how much of the man's story he believed himself.

'By the time I'm through with them,' the Doctor promised, 'they'll be too frightened to do anything else!' He suddenly jumped for the door, jerking it open. The corridor was empty.

He frowned. 'I could have sworn . . .' he said softly. There was no guard posted to make certain they stayed in their rooms. Why not? Surely Bragen didn't trust them that much? 'Oh well. Wait here, I won't be long.'

Polly half-closed the door behind him as he hurried off. She glanced at Ben and saw the puzzled look in her friend's eyes. 'You're beginning to believe that he is the Doctor, aren't you?'

The sailor shrugged. 'I dunno. But he's got to do a lot more to convince me.'

In Lesterson's laboratory, the scientist was finally ready to begin. He stood beside the generator, watching the read-outs on the computer. Resno was around the other side of the computer, his back to the wired Dalek, scanning his board. Janley was by herself, at the main testing bench. In her lap she had a small pad computer for taking notes.

'Ready to introduce power,' Lesterson announced. He was unable to keep the required scientific detachment in his voice: he was as excited as a child on Christmas morning.

'Noted.' Janley seemed to have absolutely no problems keeping her voice level. She jotted down the time as well.

'Connecting,' Lesterson announced. He powered up the generator, then switched on the buffer he'd placed on the line in case of problems. If there were an overload, he couldn't chance damage to the alien machine. The barest whisper of a reading registered.

'All connections responding,' Resno reported from his panel. He swivelled about and looked at the Dalek. It was still as lifeless as ever.

'Nothing at all?' Lesterson snapped.

'No.'

'Are you sure?' Lesterson had a momentary vision of this entire thing being a waste of time; of the Governor sending him back to Earth, scorn heaped on his head, tail between his legs. That even more than the thought of failure scared him silly.

'Of course I'm sure.' Resno sounded very irritated by the

question. 'There's nothing wrong here and nothing registering.'

'Let's see.' Lesterson stalked around the computer.

Resno gave him an angry look. 'Really, if you don't trust me to read a dial – '

'Shut up,' Lesterson said coldly. He could see that Resno was correct: there was absolutely no power absorption by the Dalek. It meant that the machine was either as dead as a lump of rock, or else the power levels were too low to bypass any corrosion or systems failure. 'We'll try again,' he decided. 'This time we'll increase the power by one fifth. Got that, Janley?'

'Yes,' she confirmed. 'One fifth.'

Lesterson returned to his station and tapped the bar controlling the power outflow. He watched the flicker of digital numbers until it achieved the precise level required and then gently let go of the bar.

'I'm getting a reading,' Resno reported. 'Slight, but definite. There's some loss of power.' He swivelled around again.

One of the appendages – the one with what looked like a sink plunger on the end of it – was twitching slightly. 'It's moving!' Resno exclaimed.

Lesterson looked across at the Dalek. He felt a wild surge of joy. 'Janley, note this,' he said quickly, as if afraid that the movements would vanish if they were too slow. 'Number one attachment with sucker responding to power.' As he spoke, the uppermost appendage began to rise slightly. 'Number two attachment not moving. Number three attachment with lens responding.'

'Noted.'

Lesterson glared at his other assistant, who was still staring at the Dalek. 'Watch those meters, Resno!'

Resno whirled back around, scanning his panel. 'All connections still responding,' he reported.

Crossing to the Dalek, Lesterson examined it thoughtfully. Janley brought her pad and joined him. 'Of course we can't be sure,' Lesterson told her, lecturing, 'but it is reasonable to suppose that the sucker stick operates like some kind of hand.'

Even as he mentioned this, the appendage rose slightly. Acting on some sort of internal piston, it extended a few inches towards Janley. Nervously she jumped back.

Lesterson smiled slightly. 'Don't be alarmed. We've merely introduced temporary power into it. There's no danger.' He tapped the dome. 'We'll have to open this up and do a lot more work inside here to know how to work the device permanently.' He bent to study the second, unmoving appendage. 'Can't imagine what this short, stubby arm is for.' He peered down the hollow tube, but couldn't see anything within.

Janley pointed her stylus at the upper appendage. 'Could this lens attachment be some sort of an eye?'

'Oh, undoubtedly,' Lesterson agreed. 'You know, I think this thing is some sort of a probe. The eye records the external world, the sucker-hand can collect samples. The other one – maybe it's some kind of a delivery system for chemicals! Yes, yes! The capsule delivers these devices to some alien world, where they can spread out and collect data for the people who built them!'

Janley noted the hypothesis on her panel. 'Could it be intelligent?'

'Intelligent?' Lesterson shrugged. 'Doubtful. Certainly not as we would recognize it. There may be some equipment within for it to transmit information back to the capsule. There's probably a computer in there geared for analysis and transmitting the data home. These remote units certainly have some kind of directing influence. Perhaps a crude positronic brain, I suppose.' He tapped the dome. 'Can't wait to open this thing up and get to work!'

As he spoke, the two appendages dropped listlessly back to their rest positions. Frowning, he turned to face Resno. 'Now what?'

His assistant shrugged. 'Everything still reading the same over here.'

Lesterson thought for a moment. 'Maybe the power's leaking away somewhere,' he said. 'We'll try and raise the power level again.' He and Janley returned to their places for their next attempt.

As they did, the Dalek's eye-stick slowly moved to follow

them. Within the machine, the guiding intelligence concentrated on focus. It could make out images of three humans. It was vital to learn where the power was coming from . . .

'The eye-stick!' Resno called. Lesterson and Janley whirled around, but the appendage was in the same position as it had been when they had last looked – flopped down. Resno frowned. 'It was watching us!' he said. 'The lens was changing shape.'

'Don't be absurd, man,' Lesterson said.

'It was, I tell you,' Resno insisted. 'I saw it.'

Lesterson glanced across at Janley and shook his head slightly to indicate that she should not record this conversation. 'You can't use the phrase "watching us",' he told Resno. 'Good heavens, you'll be trying to convince us that thing has intelligence next. Get a grip, man, and let's get on with the experiment if you don't mind.'

Resno, obviously seeing that there was no point in arguing, gave a short nod and returned to monitoring.

The Dalek had no way of issuing a sigh of relief. But it had been greedy and had demonstrated a startling lack of caution. It had to be more careful from now on. The human named Resno was already suspicious of it, and that was not good.

Still, he was only one problem. One that could be removed. The Dalek had to discover the source of power – that was all that mattered.

And then . . .

12

It's Watching Me, Lesterson

The Communications Room was close to the centre of the hub. It was by the Admin Offices, naturally. The Doctor paused at the door. If his memory served him correctly, the ground station would be linked to a series of satellites in synchronous orbits of the planet. Each one would have the power to punch holes through the sub-ether and allow the colony to comunicate directly with Earth. There would be some transmission delay, of course, but nowhere near as long as it would take a message at light-speed to travel back to Terra. In perhaps five or ten minutes, he might be speaking to someone with both authority and sense. Gently, he pushed open the door.

There were no signs of life in the large room. Banks of computers lined the walls, and a screen at the far end showed the positioning of the satellites above Vulcan. There were an awful lot of dots, far too many simply for communications. Maybe they represented the remains of the original probes that had discovered Vulcan, or even weather and research satellites. At any rate, unimportant.

In the centre of the room was a console. The chair in front of it was lying on its side and there was no sign of the technician. He'd hardly have knocked over his chair and left it like that. Fearing the worst, the Doctor hurried across.

The young man was under the console, a bad bruise on the back of his neck. The Doctor rubbed his own neck thoughtfully. It hurt in exactly the same place as the young man's bruise. It looked as if there were a rash of people getting banged on the head. At least the technician was still alive. The Doctor could see his chest expanding and contracting.

He could also see that there was going to be a rather more substantial transmission delay than he had feared. The underside of the panel had been ripped open. Dozens of wires trailed out of the panel, many showing evidence of being sliced through. The Doctor examined the wreckage more closely. Several of the tubes had been brutally smashed, and someone had poked a heavy object inside the casing to break as much as possible.

His acute ears caught the faint sound of a man shifting his weight from one foot to another. He gazed around the room, but there were a lot of potential hiding places in the banks of computers.

'I know you're there,' he said gently.

Quinn stepped out from a gap between two of the instruments. In his left hand he was holding a pair of three-foot long pliers as a club. 'Examiner!' he said, sounding relieved. 'Thank goodness it's you. I've been trying to talk to you alone ever since you arrived.'

The Doctor wasn't at all certain that being alone with Quinn was a very good survival tactic. Those pliers were almost certainly the instruments that had done the damage to the console – and, probably, to the back of the technician's head. The Doctor had suffered enough blows – physically and emotionally – for one day and was not at all eager to give Quinn a chance to add to his woes.

Luckily, he didn't have to take chances. The door opened and Bragen marched in, accompanied by one of the guards. His eyes quickly took in the scene. 'What's happened here?' he demanded.

Quinn sighed. 'What do *you* want?'

The Doctor gestured to the technician. 'I just found this man unconscious.' Both he and Bragen stared at the pliers in Quinn's hand.

'So did I,' the Deputy Governor explained. 'I was just examining him when I heard someone approaching, so I hid. It must have been you, Examiner.'

Bragen glowered at him. 'So you hid, eh?' He snatched the pliers from Quinn's hands. 'And what about these?'

'I picked them up. They were beside the tech.' Quinn seemed finally to realize that everyone was looking at him in a very suspicious fashion. 'What is this all about?'

The Doctor pointed to the console. 'The cables have been cut.'

'The cables?' Quinn frowned. 'Where?' He joined the Doctor and Bragen. The Doctor bent down and pulled at a handful of the severed wires. 'This is serious,' Quinn said. 'It's not just the internal communications system that's been disrupted. We're cut off from the Earth, too.'

As the Doctor straightened up, his eyes flickered over the torn patch on Quinn's jacket. Interesting . . .

Bragen scowled at the wires as if they were somehow responsible for their own predicament. 'The only people who'd want to do that are the rebels,' he growled.

Quinn jerked an angry thumb at the silent guard. 'If these muscle boys of yours had any brains, they'd stop things like this!'

Fishing in his pocket, the Doctor pulled out the button he'd been carrying with him and offered it to Bragen. 'I was attacked just after I arrived here,' he said quietly. 'This was a souvenir I collected.'

The security head took the button. Then he grabbed Quinn's sleeve and jerked it up. The button and the ragged gap matched exactly. Bragen's eyes sparkled triumphantly. 'This button belongs to you, doesn't it?'

Quinn shrugged. 'I expect so. I only recently noticed that I'd lost it.'

'I vaguely recall holding on to the man after he hit me,' the Doctor explained. 'I may have pushed back his protective suit and pulled that off him.'

Obviously realizing that the way the conversation was going was hardly helping him, Quinn said, 'When you two are quite finished – '

'Be quiet!' Bragen snapped.

Quinn flushed with anger and glared right back at the security head. 'Don't speak to me like that,' he said icily. 'I am the Deputy Governor.'

'All I know,' Bragen retorted, 'is that you're a man the Examiner believes to have attacked him.' He held up the button. 'With some proof, I might add. And a man found sabotaging the communications equipment – '

'That's a lie!'

' – having attacked one of the engineers first,' Bragen finished, with some contempt. 'Still holding the pliers when the Examiner and I arrived.' He smiled tightly. 'I'd detain the Governor himself on evidence like that.'

'I hope you're not thinking of detaining *me*,' Quinn said softly.

'Thinking? I'm doing it.' Bragen gestured to his guard. 'I could hardly let you run around after doing this, could I?'

Shaking the guard's restraining hand off his arm, Quinn glared at Bragen. 'You fool!'

'I'd be a bigger fool to let you go.'

Quinn backed away from them. 'I'm warning you for the last time, Bragen. You'd better keep your ridiculous police away from me.'

Bragen gave a short nod. The guard pulled a squat pistol from his belt and pointed it at the Deputy Governor. 'Do they still look ridiculous to you, Quinn?' he asked dangerously.

The fight went out of Quinn. 'You win this round, Bragen,' he agreed. 'But we'll see how this looks in front of the Governor in the morning.' The guard jerked the pistol and Quinn preceded him out of the door.

Bragen turned to the Doctor. 'The Governor will want an enquiry. May I ask what *you* were doing in here, Examiner?'

'I was going to radio the Earth,' the Doctor told him honestly. 'To get them to order Hensell to destroy the Daleks.'

'Lesterson's discoveries?' He raised an eyebrow. 'I see. Well, I'll include that in my report to the Governor.'

The Doctor was under no illusion that it would be a report to flatter anyone but Bragen. 'You believe the cables were cut by these rebels of yours,' he said, 'but there may be another reason. Perhaps someone wants to make certain that I don't interfere with Lesterson's experiments.'

Bragen nodded slowly. 'You're right, that is a possibility that had not occurred to me. Do you believe that Lesterson is up to this?' He gestured at the mess.

'I think that Lesterson is so narrow-minded that he could well endanger us all,' the Doctor told him earnestly. 'This damage may well be the least of it if he gets those Daleks going again. Believe me – I know!'

Bragen gave him a faint smile. 'Then we should all be glad that he doesn't have permission to continue, shouldn't we?'

'We should,' the Doctor agreed, 'if I were certain that he was willing to wait.'

Lesterson was busily rerouting the circuits in the generator system. He'd reached the limits of the portable one and was now forced to tap into the main city circuits. The power drain he was contemplating would normally have shown up on the instruments in the central station. He'd been craftily using his computer net to shut off some of the unnecessary power drains. It was four in the morning, so he could divert the power without risk of being discovered.

Of course, this wouldn't be a state that would last very long. It was important to get results before someone discovered his tampering. But he was utterly convinced that he would soon have the results that he desired.

While he did this, Resno was busy setting up a camera to record the rest of the experiment. Lesterson wanted it all on video as a back-up. If the machine lost power again, he wanted to be able to prove he had made it move.

'Right,' Lesterson finally announced, 'I've redirected the power. We can go up another fifth now.' He glanced at his male assistant. 'You'll have to dodge between your meters and the camera, Resno.'

'Right.' Resno wanted to ask: *And what about Janley? Can't she do some of the work?* But he knew that Lesterson hated having his orders questioned. 'Ready.'

The scientist nodded. 'Connecting – now.' He gripped the bar and eased it upward again. The panel showed the flow of the diverted power as it surged into the Dalek machine. In the background, he was vaguely aware of a resonant humming from the generator.

From his station, Resno reported, 'All connections are responding.'

'It's working!' Janley said.

As they watched, the eye-stick and sucker-stick both moved slowly back to their horizontal positions.

'Excellent!' Lesterson crowed happily. 'Film it, man, film it!' As Resno moved over to the camera tripod, Lesterson turned to Janley. 'Note all of the input and output readings. I have to know precisely how much power that machine is absorbing, and what degree of movement conforms to the power drain.'

As the three humans worked, the Dalek's eye slowly swivelled around to point directly at Resno. As the lab assistant stared into the camera viewfinder, he was shocked to see the eye staring back at him. Resno straightened up slowly.

The body of the Dalek moved soundlessly to align with the eye. The unidentified third appendage rose to point towards Resno.

'It seems interested in you, Resno,' Lesterson commented. He became aware that Resno was staring back at the Dalek almost in shock. 'Whatever's the matter with you, man?'

'I tell you, it's intelligent,' Resno said, panic in his voice. 'It's watching me, Lesterson! Weighing me up! I can sense it!'

Lesterson snorted. 'Don't be a fool, man. You're starting to sound like that stupid Examiner's superstitious female assistant.'

'Well, maybe she was right!' Resno said. He was backing slowly away from the camera. 'I don't like it, I tell you. We don't have any idea what these things are capable of!'

Lesterson held him gently from behind. 'We'll never find out what they can do unless you take a film of every reaction, will we? Now, please get on with your job.'

Resno reluctantly nodded. He bent back to the camera. Lesterson moved back towards his post at the generator and computer, ready to begin the next phase of tests.

There was a sudden electrical clattering sound, like an intense discharge of electricity. Resno gave a scream, collapsing over the camera. Parts of it had begun to melt from some intense reaction. Lesterson and Janley both spun around in time to see the Dalek's third appendage react slightly as the noise cut off.

Resno fell the rest of the way to the floor and lay very, very still.

The Dalek started to move again. This time it was swinging around towards Lesterson and Janley. With an incoherent cry of horror, Lesterson fell on the power lines. He literally tore his connectors apart, heedless of the sparking. As the power cut off, the Dalek's appendages went limp once more.

As Lesterson dived back to his controls to kill the power drain, Janley went carefully over to where Resno had fallen. Her eyes burned, but not with sympathy for the drowned man, or anger at the Dalek. She was filled with much darker emotions.

This experiment was becoming much more interesting than she had ever expected.

Finishing the shut-down, Lesterson rose to come over. Janley quickly waved him back. 'It's all right,' she said, 'he isn't dead.'

'I'll never forgive myself,' Lesterson said, on the verge of tears.

'It was some sort of shock wave,' Janley informed him. 'It seems to have stunned him.'

'What are we going to do with him?' Lesterson was almost babbling in his shock. 'We must get him to the hospital.'

'I'll look after him,' Janley promised. She crossed the room and put a gentle, protective arm about Lesterson's shoulders. 'Don't feel so badly. He's only stunned.'

'Are you sure?' He was almost begging for reassurance. 'He's very still.'

'Yes, of course I'm sure,' Janley told him drily. 'I trained in biology, didn't I? It's not hard to tell the difference between alive and dead. Now, what about the Dalek?'

Lesterson looked into her eyes, seeming to draw strength from her. 'Yes, yes, of course. I have to remember what's most important here.' He shook his head to clear out the remainder of his panic. 'I shall have to get it ready for the morning, even if it means working all night.'

'If you don't,' Janley agreed, 'the Examiner will stop the whole thing.'

'I could work inside the capsule,' Lesterson said. 'Close off

97

the door. Yes. That's best, I think.' He turned back to her. 'I'll leave you to look after Resno. Please make sure he's all right. I'll never forgive myself if anything's happened to him.' He went across to the capsule and then entered to prepare it for his work.

Janley went to the communications panel on the wall and punched in a code. To her surprise it stayed dead. She examined it quickly, one eye on the capsule in case Lesterson came out. No carrier signal – odd. Well, she'd have to improvise. It wouldn't be hard to dupe that idiot Lesterson. Only one thing was really important to him. It had now become very important to her, also. Nothing could be allowed to stand in the way of his experiment.

Especially not that fool Resno's body.

Crossing the room, she grabbed Resno's arms and then dragged his dead body behind the farthest of the lab benches. There were boxes of supplies under it that would hide it from a casual viewer. Over some of them was a tarpaulin. Janley jerked the edges of this down to completely hide the body. Returning to the door, she studied her handiwork. Excellent! No one would see the body there before she could arrange for its disposal.

There was a footfall from inside the capsule. Janley jerked the lab door open, and stood in the gap. 'Fine,' she said to the far wall, 'I'll check in first thing.' She closed the door as Lesterson came out of the capsule.

'Yes,' he told her, 'there's room to work inside it. I'll have to relay the power lines, of course.' He stared at the door. 'How's Resno?'

'Thane came for him herself,' Janley assured him. 'He'll have the best of care. He's really going to be all right.'

'You're sure?' he pleaded.

Grief, what a pain! 'He just needs a long rest,' Janley said. 'I had to promise we'd not bother him for a few days. And he'll be kept in isolation. After all, we don't want anyone else to hear about this little accident, do we? They might get worried and stop your experiment.'

As she'd expected, this hit all the right buttons. 'No, certainly not,' he agreed. 'Quite right. As long as he'll be fine.'

Then he turned back to the Dalek and patted the lifeless machine. Janley rolled her eyes in disgust at his gullibility.

'Got to get you ready for the morning,' Lesterson told the Dalek. 'When the Governor and that meddling Examiner arrive, you'll be waiting for them.' He gently touched the gun-stick. 'We'll both be ready.'

13

What Have you Done, Lesterson?

And then it was morning. The Doctor sat by his window, staring out as the fledgling sun illuminated the stark surface of Vulcan. The rocks, so grey and featureless in the harsh light of day, were glowing in the soft intensity of dawn. In many ways, the surface of this planet was beautiful.

'You've got to defend Quinn,' Polly insisted. Though she'd had only two or three hours' sleep, she still seemed to be both bright and full of energy. The Doctor suspected that it was her indignation and innate sense of justice that were fueling her.

Ben, with typical bluntness, was having none of this. The Doctor could see why his previous self had decided that Ben would be an admirable companion. Once he was on the scent of trouble, there was absolutely no side-tracking him. Of course, if he was on the wrong scent . . .

'I know it's "innocent until proven guilty",' Ben said, 'but – well, he's *guilty.*'

Polly, in her turn, was having none of this. Her intuition had kicked into high gear. The Doctor respected this, knowing it was not the titter-behind-the-hand sort of thing most people assumed it to be. 'Oh, don't be silly, Ben,' she said. 'He's the Deputy Governor.'

'So what?' Ben asked, aggressively. 'I had a headmaster once who got pinched for riding on a bus and not paying his fare. Rank don't prove anything at all. A crook's a crook, whether he's a peasant or a king. Besides, maybe he's got the motive.'

'Like what?' Polly asked, scornfully.

'He's the *Deputy* Governor, right?' Ben smirked at her. 'Maybe he doesn't like playing second fiddle.'

'That's just supposition,' Polly argued.

Her obstinacy seemed to bring out the worst in Ben. The Doctor suspected that Polly's obvious attraction to Quinn wasn't helping Ben's attitude, either. For all of his pretence, Ben was quite clearly taken with Polly.

'His jacket button isn't supposition,' Ben said. 'And the Doctor caught him red-handed in the Communications Room with a pair of pliers, didn't he? And don't tell me he was just plucking his eyebrows with them!'

'I thought you didn't believe he was the Doctor,' Polly countered. 'You can hardly call him a credible witness then, can you?'

'She's got you there,' the Doctor put in, which earned him a black look from Ben.

'Look,' Polly persisted, 'there are some people you just know are all right. Know just by looking at them.'

The Doctor gave her a cheery smile. 'Does that mean that you believe I'm the Doctor, then?' He looked at Ben, who still appeared unconvinced. 'Or are you saying that my looks are against me?'

Before either of them could reply, there was a knock at the door. Bragen, looking as if he'd had a perfect night's rest, strode in and gave them all a chilly smile.

'Good morning,' he said briskly. 'The enquiry is ready to begin. I've come to escort you.'

The Doctor leapt to his feet, placing an arm around each of his companion's shoulders. 'Now we shall see who's right – shan't we?' he asked.

Lesterson didn't seem in the slightest bit fatigued, despite his hours of work. Janley had to admit that she rather envied him. Running her hand through her hair, she thought, God, I must look a sight! She felt tired and messy – an unusual feeling for her. Then again, she'd never had to nursemaid a dead body and a live and seriously out-of-kelter scientist before.

Rubbing his hands eagerly together, Lesterson said, 'Well!'

Stifling a yawn, Janley glanced at her watch. 'Is it time?'

'I think so.' He looked almost drunk. 'I feel quite excited.'

Grow up! Janley thought. Aloud, though, she said, 'So you should. It's a wonderful achievement.'

'The wonderful part of it is,' Lesterson replied, 'that we have no real idea of the scope of this experiment, Janley. Who knows where we may go from here?' He moved across to the hatchway of the capsule. The Dalek stood in the doorway, covered by another of his tarpaulins. With a flourish, he tore the covering from the machine, rather like a magician producing a rabbit from his hat. Janley almost expected a drum roll. Lesterson smiled affectionately at the machine. 'Who knows what this Dalek, as the Examiner calls it, can do?'

'And it's harmless now?' Janley asked.

'Completely. I've removed the gun-stick.' Lesterson gestured at the gaping socket in the Dalek's body. His face clouded as the reference to the gun reminded him. 'Resno – have you been to see him today?'

'Yes,' Janley lied, avoiding glancing at the far end of the room. 'Thane's giving him her complete attention as she promised. He's going to be all right.' Her eyes narrowed. 'Nobody must hear about that accident! It could give the Examiner the leverage he's seeking to halt the whole project.'

'Yes, of course,' Lesterson agreed. Then he looked back at the Dalek and his smile reappeared. 'Come on, let's go and surprise them all!'

Hensell's office came as no surprise to the Doctor. The colony was laid out well, but with the usual spartan touches. None of the rooms was larger than necessary, nor were they over-decorated or ostentatious.

Except Hensell's.

Naturally, it had to be fit for his dignity as the colony Governor. Which meant that it was about six times as large as it needed to be. The huge picture window gave a panoramic view of the surface of Vulcan. One day, it would probably be impressive. Right now, the view was no better than one any citizen of Earth could get from the top of a quarry. When the terraforming was completed and there were trees, grasses and plants outside, it would be like looking over the Garden of Eden. Hensell probably aimed to stay in power long enough to see the view. The Doctor was mildly impressed – he hadn't credited Hensell with so much foresight.

The room itself was mostly bare. Hensell's large desk dominated the far end of the room. It was placed in front of the window, the natural focus for any visitor's eyes. Hensell's chair was large, plush and undoubtedly expensive. The guest chairs were some plastic and extruded aluminium affairs, shoddy and cheap, especially when compared to the Governor's – well, 'throne' wasn't too strong a word for it. Apart from the chairs and desk, the only decorations in the huge room were a small coffee table and a minute filing cabinet. The latter had to contain all the work at Hensell really did.

Hensell was seated at his desk when one of Bragen's men ushered the Doctor, Ben and Polly into the room. The Doctor rolled his eyes – such an obvious ploy to let them know they were being granted a tiny fraction of Hensell's valuable time. Never one for kowtowing to pointless displays of authority, the Doctor wandered across to the desk and adroitly plucked the paper from Hensell's hands. The Governor looked shocked at this liberty.

'You seem to specialize in trouble, Examiner,' he growled.

'If you'd seen me last night when I needed you,' the Doctor replied, dropping the sheet of paper on to the desk, 'none of this would have happened.' He didn't elaborate on whether he meant his behaviour or the sabotage.

'I have to tour the perimeter today,' Hensell said rather defensively. 'It's an arduous job, and I really required my sleep.'

'So I was told,' the Doctor agreed drily.

'Bragen followed my instructions,' Hensell said. 'We've had eleven – incidents – that you would probably feel like reporting back to Earth.'

Ah! So there it was: Hensell was afraid that the Examiner had been called in to report his incompetence. The Doctor smiled inwardly. Hensell was no worse, though sadly no better, than most officials given power without supervision. And he was terrified of losing his moment of glory. The Doctor moved on to Plan B. Soothe the ruffled fur. 'Not if I'm satisfied you can deal with your own difficulties, Governor,' he replied carefully, giving a slight upward curl to his lips.

Hensell's eyes widened as he realized what the Examiner

103

was saying: that none of this *had* to be reported back to Earth. Perhaps he'd been a trifle hasty in judging this fellow, after all. Maybe there was no need for them to be antagonists.

The door opened again, and the guard returned. This time he was leading Quinn, who looked rather the worse for wear after a night in detention. Accompanying them was Bragen, who was having difficulty keeping the smugness out of his face.

Hensell glared at his deputy. 'What the devil have you been up to, Quinn?' he growled.

'Nothing,' Quinn replied. 'Absolutely nothing.'

Hensell slapped the file folder on the edge of his desk. 'What about Bragen's report, then? These are facts, Quinn. What have you got to say for yourself?'

Quinn didn't even look at the thick file. 'Does the engineer *say* I hit him?' he asked mildly.

'He was hit from behind,' Bragen snarled.

Shrugging, Quinn said, 'Then there's only circumstantial evidence.'

'The Examiner was also attacked in the mercury swamp,' Bragen reminded him. 'We have a button from your jacket, which was found in the Examiner's own hand.'

Quinn refused to flinch under Hensell's stare. 'I can't explain that,' he admitted.

'I'm sure you can't,' Bragen retorted sarcastically.

'Somebody put it there,' Polly said. She felt that someone had to stick up for Quinn. She had been favourably impressed by the man, and was certain that he was being railroaded in this hearing.

Flashing her a grateful smile, Quinn nodded. 'It's the only logical explanation.'

Hensell looked to the Doctor for help, but he seemed absorbed in some mental gymnastics. 'Examiner,' he said, 'you seem to be in two minds.'

'Yeah, and two bodies,' Ben muttered to himself.

'You had mentioned to Bragen that Lesterson's machines . . .' Hensell continued, then paused. Should he look in the file, or admit a momentary lapse? Well, he was a busy man and could be expected to forget minor details. 'What do you call them?'

'I call them what they are,' the Doctor told him. 'Daleks.'

'Yes,' Hensell said. 'You claim that they could be a motive for destroying our communications.'

'I do,' the Doctor agreed.

Hensell was about to add to his comment when his face clouded. He stared at the door, and the others with him turned to see what was happening – all but the guard, who kept his own eyes on Quinn.

Lesterson was standing in the doorway, a look of triumph on his face.

Annoyed, Hensell said, 'This is a special enquiry, Lesterson. I must ask you – '

'This won't wait.' The scientist didn't seem to realize that he was committing the worst possible offence in Hensell's book: interrupting Hensell's display of authority. 'You won't be disappointed,' he promised.

'Didn't you hear what I said?' Hensell demanded.

Lesterson was too excited to care. 'Governor,' he said, almost leaping and dancing, 'I've completed an experiment that is going to revolutionize the colony. Please, bear with me.'

The Doctor jumped to his feet, his eyes darting around. 'Lesterson!' he cried, clearly on the verge of panic. 'What have you done?' He stared at the still-open door behind the scientist. 'Just what have you done?'

'I'll show you,' Lesterson said eagerly. He seemed to be totally oblivious to the Doctor's obvious display of shock and fear. 'All right!' he called out of the door. 'Janley – now!'

The Dalek glided through the doorway and into the room.

For a moment, there was a stunned silence. The enquiry was completely forgotten as all eyes focused on the Dalek.

All but one. The Dalek's own eye turned to examine the Doctor.

The Doctor backed away from it. He stumbled over one of the plastic chairs and fell into it, gripping the back for support. Ben stared from the Doctor to the Dalek, instinctively moving

105

to protect Polly. From what? He wasn't sure. There were only three things he was absolutely certain of at this moment.

The first was that the Doctor had been correct: this Dalek was a menace of incalculable extent. The second was that Lesterson had to be one of the biggest fools in the entire universe. The third . . .

'It recognized him,' Ben whispered to Polly. 'The Dalek – it recognized the Doctor!'

Polly stared at the Doctor. He was ashen, in a state of almost total collapse in the stupid plastic chair. He hadn't even looked this bad before he'd undergone the strange renewal. 'What's the matter, Doctor?' she asked. To her, the Dalek was simply some mechanical monstrosity, malign certainly, but not over-powering. She couldn't understand either Ben's sudden chills, or the Doctor's quite obvious terror. 'Are you all right?'

'The fools,' the Doctor breathed. He clearly meant Lesterson and Janley. 'The blind, unthinking fools!'

Ben stared at the Doctor. 'You're terrified,' he said, and felt more than an echo of the same emotion in his own soul. There was no rational reason for it, but it was there. It was the same kind of chill, clean through to the bone, that he'd felt when the Cybermen's unemotional gazes had bored into him. Then his innate practical nature resurfaced. 'What can it do?'

The Doctor realized somewhat belatedly that the gun-socket was empty. A Dalek without the power to kill was still a formidable foe, but it was also out of its element. 'Nothing,' he told Ben, '*yet.*'

'It knew who you were,' Ben hissed. 'I know it sounds crazy, but it did!' He looked scared and apologetic at the same time. 'Well, if a Dalek can recognize you as the real Doctor, then I suppose I can too.'

The Doctor couldn't even manage a weak smile at this. Though he was very pleased that Ben had finally surrendered the last of his suspicions, he was too frightened by the other events to really care. It wasn't so much that one unarmed Dalek was such a formidable foe, it was the problem that if one Dalek could have been repowered without his knowledge, then what else was occurring right at this very second that he

106

didn't know about? When dealing with the Daleks, ignorance was not bliss, it was inevitably fatal.

Somehow, Lesterson was completely oblivious to this exchange. All of his attention was concentrated on Hensell, the one man who had the power to stop his experiment. 'This creation is called, I understand, a Dalek,' he explained, seeming almost intoxicated by his success. 'Look at it! I have simply given it electric power. And do you know what?' He grabbed the Governor's hands, completely obviously to his breach of etiquette. 'It's capable of storing it!' He laughed, drunkenly. 'Furthermore, it responds to orders!' He clapped his hands to get its attention. 'Turn around,' he ordered.

The Dalek tore its gaze away from the Doctor. Slowly, but unmistakably, it began to swivel to face Lesterson.

The scientist pointed at one of the plastic seats. 'Move that chair,' he ordered.

The Dalek glided across the floor. The sucker-stick rammed out, and the chair went sliding across the floor.

'You see?' Lesterson cried exultantly. 'Imagine what this is going to do to our mining programme, our processing, packaging – dozens of tedious labour-intensive jobs, Governor! It can end all of the colony's problems.'

This had gone on more than long enough, the doctor thought, and pushed past Janley to address Hensell. 'It will end the colony's problems,' he agreed, 'because it will end the colony!'

The Dalek's eye-stick swivelled to examine the Doctor again. Lesterson chuckled. 'It seems to be having a good look at you, Examiner.'

'Yes,' the Doctor agreed warily. 'Unlike a human being, a Dalek can always sense its real enemy.'

The Dalek's dome swivelled until the eye-stick was pointing at Lesterson once more. In the silence, it suddenly grated in a mechanical tone: *'I am your servant!'*

There was a thunderstruck silence from all of the humans in the room. Then Lesterson turned to stare in rapture at his assailant. 'It spoke!' he said. 'Janley, did you hear it? It can talk!'

'It can do many things, Lesterson,' the Doctor replied bitterly. 'But the thing that it can do most efficiently is to extermi-nate human beings. It destroys them without mercy. Without conscience. Destroys them!' He glared at the scientist. 'Do you understand me? It destroys them!'

While the Doctor was speaking, the Dalek simply ignored him. It continued to intone mechanically: '*I am your servant! I am your servant! I am your servant!*'

The Doctor pressed his hands over his ears, but there was no drowning out the horror of the inhuman intonations. '*I am your servant! I am . . .*'

14

I Obey

Lesterson stared at the Dalek in absolute fascination. 'I had no idea it could talk.'

The Doctor glared at him. 'There are a lot of things you have no ideas about, Lesterson.'

Ignoring him, Lesterson turned to his assistant. 'Janley, did you hear it?'

'More to the point,' the Doctor interrupted, looking from one to the other, 'do you believe it?'

Janley turned to the Doctor. For a fleeting second there seemed to be something in her expression that was almost as horrifying as the Dalek. Then it was gone. 'Why are you against this project?' she asked.

'I'm against the Daleks,' the Doctor replied. 'I'll tell you all again: one Dalek poses more threat to this colony than a string of armed atomic missiles would!'

'Rubbish!' Lesterson snorted.

Hensell clearly felt that it was more than high time he took control of the discussion once again. 'That's a bit strong, isn't it, Examiner?' he asked.

The Doctor looked around the room. Ben and Polly were the only ones showing any sensible fear. Lesterson was completely consumed by his precious experiment. Janley and Bragen both wore calculating looks. Hensell appeared to be determined to mine the whole fiasco for his own benefit. And Quinn looked bored. 'Do any of you know the Daleks?' the Doctor asked. Then he answered his own question: 'No, of course you don't. I do.'

Lesterson smirked at him. 'We've only got your word for that.'

The Doctor turned on him in anger. 'I order you to immobilize this Dalek and to halt any further experiments.' As soon as he had spoken the words, the Doctor realized that he had made a grave error.

Hensell bristled at this usurpation of his authority. 'You can't give orders like that!' he snapped.

'That's perfectly true,' Bragen agreed, backing up his superior. 'You have the authority to examine, to make recommendations – and to report back to Earth.' He didn't have to bother adding: *When you can*.

The Doctor stared at them. 'So you're all against me?'

Lesterson stuck his finger under the Doctor's nose and waggled it about. He had no idea how close he came to having it bitten off. 'We've discovered these Daleks,' Lesterson crowed. 'Oh, you may have named them, but I'm the one who's made them operate. And I know you don't like one of the mere *colony worlds* having anything that the Earth hasn't got.' The Doctor could see by the surprised and happy expression on Hensell's face how well that little crack had gone over. One more nail in his coffin – and theirs.

'They're capable of speech,' Hensell said thoughtfully.

'And why not?' Lesterson asked. 'After all, they clearly have a certain amount of rudimentary intelligence – but it is an intelligence that we can control.'

Hensell stroked his beard thoughtfully. 'So what you want is permission to continue your experiments?'

Janley stepped in. Turning on all her considerable charm, she smiled at him and said: 'Governor, do you have any idea of the work that this single unit can do?' She didn't know herself, but promising the moon and stars could hardly hurt at this stage. 'Why, if we set it to work in one of the mines it could double our production – overnight!'

The Doctor twisted from Lesterson to Janley to Hensell. 'Are you blind?' he appealed to them. 'Why can't you understand?'

'Pay no attention to him, Hensell,' Lesterson urged the Governor. 'Janley was perfectly correct about the work that this robot can do for us.'

The two scientists were acting like twin demons tempting a willing soul into hell. Janley gently stroked the Governor's hand. 'Think what *that* will mean to the annual production figures,' she breathed.

'And the effect of that on Earth,' Hensell agreed. He was already experiencing fantasies of promotion and wild acclaim from the bureaucracy of the home world. 'Yes, yes – they would be very grateful . . .'

The Doctor could see that Hensell's empty head was becoming filled with visions of being re-called to Earth to be crowned with glory. Chances of victory in this fight were slipping through his grasp faster than mercury would. Glaring at the silent Dalek, he hissed: 'I shall stop you. I shall!'

Rubbing his hands in satisfaction, Hensell turned to Lesterson. 'All right, Lesterson, permission granted.'

'Permission?' the Doctor. 'Permission for what?'

Lesterson flashed him a smug smile. 'Permission to finish my experiment, Examiner.'

'Didn't you hear a word I've been saying?' the Doctor cried. 'The Daleks must be destroyed!'

'Never!' Lesterson replied.

'If not by my order, then by the Earth's,' the Doctor said. He spun around to glare at Hensell. 'You know perfectly well that if I recommend to Earth that you destroy this Dalek then they'll pass on the official order.'

Hensell spread his hands in mock helplessness. 'If you can bring me such an official order, I shall naturally follow it.'

The Doctor scowled. 'Communications with Earth have been severed. You know that perfectly well. That's what this hearing was supposed to be about.'

Hensell tried to look sad, but failed by several orders of magnitude. 'Then we shall just have to wait until it's restored, won't we?' He came to join the Doctor. 'Examiner, perhaps if you could tell me *why* you are so much against this project?'

Realizing that the battle was lost, the Doctor turned bleak eyes on the Governor. 'I told you. I realize I can't prove what I say, but you have no idea of the danger.' Lesterson snorted in contempt. The Doctor threw him a filthy look. 'Yes, danger. I shall contact the Earth for the required order of destruction just as soon as communications have been restored. Come along, Ben, Polly.'

Throughout the whole discussion, the Dalek had stood silently by. Now the Doctor marched across and tapped it on the dome. 'You're my servant, are you?'

There was the barest of pauses, then: 'Yes.'

'Very well then: I order you to immobilize yourself – immediately!'

The Dalek seemed to lock gazes with the Doctor. Then the eye-stick and the arm both drooped towards the floor.

'What do you think you're doing?' Lesterson cried. Despite his gangling build, Lesterson was stronger than he looked. He almost picked the Doctor up bodily and swung him around. His right fist flashed back and he looked ready to kill. Ben grabbed his fist, twisting it until Lesterson moaned.

'Take it easy, mate,' Ben advised him. As soon as the scientist let the Doctor go, Ben released his wrist.

'The trouble is,' the Doctor told Lesterson, 'I can't let you find out the magnitude of your folly for yourself. Too many other people would get hurt. I have to stop you before it's too late.' He started towards the door, then called over his shoulder: 'Meddle with the Daleks, Lesterson, and you're a dead man.' He marched out of the room, Ben following behind. Polly paused in the doorway and looked back.

'You must listen to him,' she told them all. 'Believe him. He knows what he's talking about.' Seeing that her words were having no effect, Polly sighed and trailed her friends out of the room.

Her face darkened with anger, Janley stepped forward to examine the dead machine. As she did so, the eye-stick rose to stare back at her. 'Lesterson!' she exclaimed happily.

Lesterson stared at the Dalek as it came back to life. 'You didn't obey the order!' he said, shocked.

'He has gone,' the Dalek responded.

For a second, Lesterson was chilled. 'Then you obey only as long – '

'His order was wrong,' the Dalek replied. 'I serve human beings. I cannot serve if I am immobilized. You are the one who gave me back my power. Your orders are right. I serve you. I am your servant.'

'You tricked him!' Lesterson said, laughing. 'Oh very well done! I like that.'

Quinn studied the Dalek carefully. 'I thought you said the Dalek was *everyone's* servant, Lesterson. Now we discover it's picking and choosing who its masters are. It's got very advanced brain power, hasn't it?'

Hensell finally looked a little concerned. 'It reasons, Lesterson,' he pointed out. 'Just how extensive is its intellience?'

'It's a damn sight more cunning than you think it is,' Quinn added. He seemed to have forgotten that he was here on trial.

Lesterson looked at both men. 'There's really no cause for concern, Governor,' he replied. 'There is no need to look for bogeymen. You just wait until you see how much work it can do! Then you'll be satisfied. Trust me.'

The Governor was still not completely convinced. As a man accustomed to giving orders, he knew how important it was that his orders be carried out, not questioned. And the Dalek was apparently questioning the Examiner's orders. Where would this line of logic lead the machine? Now, look here, Lesterson,' he said. 'I'm perfectly willing to back you up over this, but you have to give me plenty of proof that it won't backfire in my face!'

'I shall indeed,' Lesterson agreed.

'Well, be quick about it,' Hensell added. 'As soon as the communications room is restored, the Examiner is going to get in touch with Earth. We need some good solid facts to win them over to our side.'

'I understand,' Lesterson told him. Turning to the machine, he said, 'Follow me, Dalek. I'm going to put you through your paces.'

'I obey,' the Dalek agreed, falling in behind him. Janley, a thoughtful expression on her face, followed them both from the room.

Polly was having second thoughts. 'I think we should have stayed and tried to help Quinn,' she called.

Ben looked back and shook his head. 'We wouldn't have helped him, Pol. I've seen farces like that before. The Governor's already tried, convicted and sentenced him. The whole fiasco's just for show.'

'But he didn't murder the real Examiner,' Polly said. 'I'm sure I didn't.'

'The way I see it,' Ben told her, 'this lot's too busy arguing amongst themselves to do much about anything. First things first, and the Daleks are the important thing.'

The Doctor stopped dead with a cry of delight. He grabbed the startled Ben's hand and began to pump it up and down with terrifying enthusiasm. 'Congratulations, my boy!'

Snatching his hand back before some vital part was shaken loose, Ben shook his head. 'What did I do?'

'You used your brain,' the Doctor told him, 'that's what you did. The Daleks have a very dangerous ally in this colony: human stupidity. It's probably the only thing in the universe that's killed more human beings than the Daleks have.' Then he set off again. Ben shrugged and followed.

'I still think Quinn's innocent,' Polly muttered before dashing off after them.

It was quite apparent that neither Bragen nor Hensell shared Polly's view of their colleague. Now that the interruptions had been dealt with, the hearing was underway once more. The Governor looked at Quinn and shook his head. 'I don't understand you, Quinn,' he said.

'How can I be in league with the rebels?' Quinn asked him.

Bragen slapped the file. 'The evidence confirms it!'

'Nothing of the sort,' Quinn shot back. He looked at Hensell, hoping he'd show some reason. 'It was I who warned you of their dangers.'

'Yes,' Bragen interrupted again. 'As part of an overall plan, no doubt.'

Quinn glared at him. '*You* wouldn't even take the matter seriously.'

'If I was wrong then,' the security man replied, 'I have a chance to rectify the mistake now.'

'So that's your attitude?' Quinn asked.

Seeing that the hearing was degenerating into a shouting match, Hensell rapped his fist loudly on his desk. 'Quinn! I suggest that we continue this enquiry in an orderly fashion. Do I need to remind you that this is a very severe charge? The Examiner *was* attacked, there is no question about that.'

'And the button that the Examiner grabbed from his attacker was missing from your suit,' Bragen added.

Hensell tried to look reasonable. 'Look, man, if you have anything useful to add, then I suggest that you say it now.'

His deputy was clearly struggling to make a difficult decision. Finally, with a dark look at Bragen, Quinn said, 'I didn't attack the man. I had no reason to. After all, I was the one who sent for him.

Hensell reeled back as if he'd been punched in his ample stomach. 'You did *what*?'

'It was necessary,' Quinn said coldly. 'In the circumstances, I would hardly be likely to damage the communications either. I had every reason to want the lines to Earth to stay open.'

Hensell was still having trouble fathoming out why his assistant had gone behind his back in this manner. 'Why, Quinn, why?'

'Because of the rebels,' Quinn said.

'Rebels!' Bragen exclaimed. 'They are nothing more than one or two foolish fanatics. Unless . . .' His eyes bored into Quinn. 'Perhaps your purpose was to publicize the existence of these rebels. The Governor and I know the truth about the whole affair: that these acts of petty sabotage are nothing more than the work of one or two embittered, frustrated maniacs.'

'You know better than that, Bragen,' Quinn shot back.

'However,' the security man went on smoothly, 'you sent for an Examiner from the Earth. Why? To prove that there's trouble here – when there isn't? To prove that the Governor can't handle things – when he can?'

That alarmed Hensell, as Bragen had obviously meant it should. 'What? Explain yourself, Bragen.'

'If you're removed, Governor,' Bragen amplified, 'then who will take your place?' He swung around, pointing his finger at Quinn. 'The Deputy Governor, of course. And that's the real reason you've made all this trouble, isn't it, Quinn? To take control of the colony. You attacked the Examiner to make him think that the rebel situation is so desperate here that he isn't even safe. Then you wreck the communications systems to make the rebels look better organized than they really are. Admit it, why don't you?'

Quinn looked helplessly from accuser to accuser. 'Governor, you should have listened to me,' he said. 'Bragen, I swear I'll break you for this!'

Bragen leaned down on the desk to stare Hensell in the face. 'I tell you, he's blown one or two tiny incidents up to make them look like there's a full-scale revolution in progress here – against which you are incompetent!'

Hensell glared at Quinn in utter disgust. 'Get him out of my sight!' he ordered.

Triumphantly, Bragen turned to gesture to the guard. The man grabbed Quinn's shoulder. The Deputy Governor tried to shake free of the restraint. 'Don't believe him!' he begged.

The guard drew his gun, swinging it in a short arc. The butt slammed into Quinn's head, dazing him. Before he could recover, the guard dragged him from the room.

Hensell climbed unsteadily to his feet. 'Chose him myself,' he said dully. 'Trained him . . . He'd have had my seat in a few years anyway!'

Bragen nodded sympathetically. 'For some ambitious men, a few years is too long to have to wait.'

The Governor banged his fist on his desk in anger. 'As if I don't have enough to do! Now this happens!'

Bragen inclined his head again. 'If there's anything I can do to help, Governor, you only have to give the word. If I might go now?' He started to withdraw.

'Bragen,' Hensell called. The security head's back was to Hensell, so the Governor couldn't see the look of hungry anticipation on Bragen's face. 'Loyalty must be rewarded. Since I seem to have lost a deputy, from this moment you shall assume his duties. As of now, you are officially Deputy Governor of Vulcan.'

Bragen managed to control his exhilaration enough to turn and give a short, formal bow. 'I'll do the best I can.' Then, before he could betray himself, he spun around and marched out of the room. Once the door was closed behind him, he laughed aloud.

Everything was going perfectly, just as he had planned. Now for the next step.

15

You've Done Nothing But Meddle

The Doctor sat in his room, staring into nothingness. Ben and Polly stood by, trying hard not to fidget. Suddenly, the Doctor leapt to his feet, grabbed one of the omnipresent plastic chairs and slammed it down hard on to the communications unit that was built into the wall. Then he tossed the chair aside and brushed shards of plastic from the shattered unit.

'I don't care who you think I am,' he said over his shoulder as he examined the exposed circuits, 'we *must* work together against the Daleks. These people here are already fighting amongst themselves. We mustn't.'

Ben stared over the Doctor's shoulder at the mess. 'I just hope you know what you're doing.'

'So do I!' the Doctor agreed fervently. He rummaged around in his pockets until he found the Swiss army knife again. This time he pulled out the screwdriver blade and began to disassemble the broken unit.

Ben threw Polly a despairing glance. 'He's a regular delinquent, isn't he?' Privately, he felt that this latest action was one more reason to accept this odd little man as the real Doctor. The old man would have destroyed *anything* in his path to get at what he needed. Ben began to see that though this strange person acted in very different ways from the old Doctor, there were definite areas where the two personalities overlapped. Both, for example, had a deep-seated hatred of the Daleks. And for officiousness. Now there was this tendency to ransack what was available to create what was needed. Ben's resistance to the idea that this *was* the Doctor stood in severe danger of crumbling entirely. 'Look,' he said to – to the *Doctor*. 'I don't want to appear dim, but how's this bit of vandalism going to do the Daleks in?'

118

'They believe Lesterson's the driving force,' the Doctor said, ignoring Ben's question, 'but I don't. The Daleks are simply using him. Now, if we can destroy the Daleks, then the people here will either lock us up or kill us. If we leave the Daleks alone, everyone will be killed.'

Ben weighed this up and found the logic severely lacking. 'Either way, we're for the chop,' he said glumly.

Quinn walked quietly along, slightly ahead of his guard. He knew that he was being taken back to the detention cells, which were quite close to the Medical Wing. Where the Examiner had been placed. As he walked, Quinn tried to estimate his chances. Bragen's goons were all chosen for their strength, not their brains. His own strength lay in intelligence, not brawn, but he had been on the university ju-jitsu team in his day . . . True, it had been a while since he'd felt the need to work out, but it had to be like riding a bicycle, didn't it? After a while the moves must be ingrained.

Or, at least, he hoped so.

At the corridor intersection leading to the Examiner's quarters, he suddenly rounded on the guard. The man was good. He tried to block the attack, but Quinn was moving on instinct now. His foot lashed out, and he hooked it around the back of the guard's knee, jerking the man off-balance. A swift chop to the neck sent the poor unfortunate sprawling, almost unconscious. Quinn spun around in a tight circle, noting with satisfaction that nobody else had seen the fight. Then he set off for the Examiner's room, a hard and determined expression on his face.

He breathed a silent prayer of relief when he saw that the door to the room was unguarded. Bragen's arrogance hadn't gone that far, then. Fighting to compose himself, Quinn pushed open the door. 'Examiner!' he said, urgently. Then he halted and stared.

The Examiner sat in the centre of a pile of electronic components. There was a gaping hole in the wall where the comm unit had once sat. The portable radio and even the digital alarm-clock from the side of the bed were both strewn about the cross-legged figure. He had a jeweller's lens screwed firmly into one eye and popped it out to glance up at the intruder. 'What do you want?' he asked. 'Can't you see I'm busy?'

Quinn shook his head to clear the haze. 'It's imperative that I speak with you,' he said. 'I was the one who sent for you.'

'Really?' The little man didn't sound convinced.

'Yes. You *must* investigate the rebels. Don't let Bragen or Hensell fool you about their importance. You must discover where they hold their meetings and – '

The guard jumped him from behind, dealing Quinn an agonizing blow to the kidneys. The ex-official gave a stunted cry of pain and collapsed. The guard, unsatisfied with his easy victory, promptly gave the fallen man a savage kick to the ribs.

'Stop that!' Polly cried, leaping across the room. The surprised guard quickly changed his mind about inflicting more injuries on his prisoner. Instead, he grabbed the gasping Quinn by the scruff of his neck and hauled him to his feet. It probably wasn't a coincidence that Quinn was now between him and the wild-eyed Polly.

'No, Polly!' the Doctor snapped. There was a tremendous amount of strength in his tone, and his companion slowly came to a halt. She didn't take her eyes off the guard, however. 'Don't interfere,' the Doctor added, more gently this time. 'There is nothing we can do at the moment.'

'But . . .'

The Doctor leaped to his feet and joined her by the door. Ben fell in behind the two of them. Looking up into the burly guard's face, the Doctor said softly: 'You will take him directly to his cell, won't you?'

'Of course,' the startled man agreed.

'Good.' Turning away, the Doctor waved his hand casually. 'Off you go, then.' As soon as the door shut behind the two men, he returned to his tinkering as if there had been no interruption.

'Is that all you're going to do?' Polly asked, on the verge of an explosion of emotions.

Ben gently laid his hand on her arm. 'He's right, Pol. One thing at a time.'

'So we let them take Quinn off to jail?'

The Doctor spoke as he worked. 'Quinn may well have been framed.'

Polly stared at him, confused. 'Then if you think that – '

'The operative word,' he interrupted, 'is "think". We don't know it for a fact. There *is* proof against him, but – well, it seems rather contrived, don't you think? But that will work itself out in time. We've more important things to occupy our minds.'

Polly was like a dog working at a bone. She refused to give up. 'It's wrong what they're doing to him. You only have to look at him to know he's innocent!'

'Oh, aye,' Ben said, with a pang of jealousy. 'And you've done more than 'look' at him, haven't you?'

Polly rounded on him. 'And what's that supposed to mean?'

'Stop it, both of you!' The Doctor held up his hand like a teacher restoring order in class. 'As I said before, let's not fight among one another, shall we?' As his two companions looked contrite, he gave them a cheery grin. 'That's much better. Now, Polly, this is one occasion when a little injustice is better than wholesale slaughter. We have to concentrate all our efforts on the Daleks.'

'Yes, all right,' Polly agreed. With a sigh, she buried her concern over Quinn for the moment. 'But what can we do? They won't listen to reason.'

'Yeah' Ben agreed. 'They're a right load of berks, if you ask me.'

'No, Ben,' the Doctor replied, nearing the end of his work. The device he had assembled looked like the inside of a television tube after an unfortunate encounter with an axe murderer. It was small, only about six inches square, but he hoped he'd recalled all his wave theory properly. Not only was it a long time since he'd studied the subject, but his recent renewal had left his brains in something of a scrambled state. 'I don't think that you're being fair. They're intelligent men in the normal run of things, but this is far from normal. They are simply blind to the danger. I'm not. You mustn't underestimate any of them. Hensell isn't the Governor for nothing.' He considered that point for a moment, then continued. 'And Lesterson's a first-rate scientific genius. He worked out how to open that capsule without any prior knowledge of Dalek mechanisms. And he managed to repower that Dalek. He simply cannot see the end result of the logical chain he has set into motion.' He gave both of them a bleak look. 'Unfortunately, I have the benefit of experience to go by. I've seen all too much of what the Daleks are capable of doing.'

'Maybe that's the answer?' Ben suggested brightly. 'How about kidnapping Lesterson and hiding him away for a bit?'

Polly gave him a look of revulsion. 'And what good would that do?'

Ben's face fell. 'Well, it would stop him from bringing the Daleks back to life,' he said, realizing that his suggestion had fallen rather flat.

'Would it, Ben?' The Doctor jumped to his feet, slipping the device he'd just finished into one of his oversized pockets. 'That would be true if Lesterson was still the driving force. But that's no longer the case. Now the Daleks are in control and they are using him. And all the time they are feeding his ego, making him all that much easier to manipulate.'

Polly realized that the Doctor, for all his jovial appearance, was quite frightened. 'But they aren't armed,' she said.

'And neither are we,' the Doctor replied.

'We could go back to the TARDIS,' she suggested. When Ben snorted, she glared at him. 'I know it sounds like I'm advocating running away, but I didn't mean it like that! I meant for us to find a safe and quiet place to think. While we're here, we're being used for some sort of power struggle. Things are happening around us that aren't connected to the Daleks.'

'So we're back to Quinn's rebels again, eh?' Ben asked.

'Yes,' the Doctor agreed, 'and Polly's quite right. The Daleks are not the only trouble here. But they are definitely the most important one.'

'So, what do we do?' Ben said, looking at the Doctor for a plan of action.

The significance of this was not lost on the Doctor. He favoured Ben with a grateful look, knowing he was now accepted for who he claimed to be. 'I think it's time we took another look at Lesterson's Daleks. Come along.' He led the way into the corridor, then turned towards the laboratory. 'And while we're going, consider a few points. First, if there really are rebels, what are they rebelling *against*?'

'Hensell,' Ben replied promptly. 'He's a pompous little jack-ass, if you ask me.'

'He's a politician,' the Doctor observed. 'It's a common failing. But that's not enough of itself. People draw cartoons or write parodies of people like Hensell. They don't start revolutions.'

'Why do you think they're rebelling, then?' Polly asked.

'Ben,' the Doctor said, evasively, 'you've got a good, practical eye. From what you've seen of this colony, how much would you say it cost to build it?'

'Crikey, you want me to be a regular Arthur Negus!' Ben moaned. But there was a faint smile on his lips. 'Hard to say, isn't it? Billions, at the very least. And they'd need a good merchant marine of space just to bring in supplies.'

'Exactly.' The Doctor nodded happily. 'The sort of thing you'd expect a government to fund, right?' Then he stopped abruptly and tapped the side of his nose. It was a gesture that they'd seen the old Doctor perform many times. 'So where are the flags?'

'The what?' Ben asked, bewildered once again.

'The flags,' the Doctor repeated, gesturing at the spartan walls. 'Surely you remember from the South Pole – all the spaceships, all the men, all the equipment had little flags and stickers plastered to them. So, if this place is run by some country or other, why haven't we seen any evidence of it?'

Polly shook her head. 'Now that you mention it, there hasn't been anything like that. But if this place isn't American, or British, or whatever, who does fund it?'

The Doctor smiled. 'Don't dawdle,' he said, and set off at a brisk pace again. Polly set off after him, with a final shrug of her shoulders at Ben.

Lesterson was in heaven. He and Janley were in the laboratory, the disarmed Dalek in front of them. Janley held a small computer note-pad at the ready, jotting down observations as fast as Lesterson could make them. The Dalek stood watching and waiting. It shifted back and forth very slightly, as if impatient, eager to be doing other, more interesting, things.

He couldn't blame it. The tests he'd been running were child's play to this magnificent robot. But, scientific method was called for here, and he had to stick to it. Even if both he and the Dalek wanted to run faster and further ahead.

'Test fourteen,' Lesterson announced, as Janley tapped the keys of the pad. He couldn't keep the excitement from his voice.

'I am ready,' the Dalek answered. Its voice showed no emotion at all. Naturally not – what use would a machine have for emotions?

'When sodium acts on ethyl alcohol, what is the derivative?' Lesterson glanced at the stopwatch he clutched in his hand. The question wasn't as simple as it sounded. The Dalek had a remarkable grasp of chemistry, but it had been necessary for Lesterson to feed it information on the human notations involved. The Dalek not only had to work out the answer to the question, but had to translate it into whatever frame of logic it had been programmed with, solve it, and then translate it back into English.

'Sodium ethoxide,' the Dalek responded. 'C-two-H-five-O-Na.'

'Incredible,' Lesterson sighed, happily. 'Five seconds!'

Janley, ever the more practical, glanced down at her notes. 'It's right, too.'

'Of course it's right!' Lesterson leaned across and patted the dome of the Dalek. 'Can you imagine what kind of positronic brain this robot has, Janley? Imagine the vast store of facts it must carry.' He smiled down at the machine. 'Sulphuric acid?'

'H-two-S-O-four,' the Dalek grated promptly.

'You see?' Lesterson said.

There was a sudden knock on the door, and the Doctor popped his head around it. 'May I come in?'

The scientist's good humour evaporated instantly. 'What do *you* want?' he snarled.

'Just to see how you're getting on,' the Doctor said, cheerfully. He dashed across the room and stared at the Dalek. The eye-stick stared right back at him. Whipping a handkerchief from his pocket, the Doctor brushed at an imaginary speck on the Dalek's lens. The Dalek quickly moved back several feet.

'If you imagine – ' Lesterson began. He was a thin, wiry man, but his blood pressure was starting to rise. For the second time with the Doctor, he was almost tempted towards the use of his fists, a feeling he hadn't indulged since he was seven.

'Please!' the Doctor tried to look shocked. 'I'm not here to make trouble. I'm interested, that's all.

Lesterson wasn't about to take that remark at face value. 'You've done nothing *but* meddle and interfere ever since you arrived on Vulcan!'

The Doctor gently took his arm and smiled innocently into his eyes. 'Ah, but I did give you permission to open the capsule, didn't I? Why don't you just carry on, and I'll sit here and watch.'

Peering at the strange man through his glasses, Lesterson appeared uncertain. 'And you won't try and stop me?'

'Stop you? Good heavens, no!' The Doctor gave Lesterson his most winning smile. 'I know we got off on the wrong foot, but I'm a reasonable man. I've been thinking it over. Perhaps I was a bit hasty, let my emotions carry me away on the spur of the moment.' He winked conspiratorially. 'You know?'

'Well . . .' Lesterson didn't want to appear to be a stumbling block in the way of peace. 'If you really want to call a truce?'

'A truce?' The Doctor almost jumped up and down with joy. 'My dear fellow, I hope we'll become friends.' He shook the amazed Lesterson's hand vigorously.

'Yes,' the scientist agreed. 'Er, possibly.' He managed to reclaim his hand before the Doctor shook it loose at the shoulder. 'Very well, you may stay.'

'Oh, thank you, thank you!' The Doctor reached for Lesterson's hand again, but the scientist promptly snatched it out of harm's way. As if lost, the Doctor glanced around. He appeared to notice Ben and Polly for the first time. 'Amuse yourselves for a while, will you?' he asked. 'I'm likely to be rather busy here.' With his back towards Lesterson and Janley, they couldn't see him when he winked at Ben and Polly and waved an imaginary tiny flag.

Polly caught on immediately. 'Right,' she said briskly. 'I rather fancy a stroll around the colony.' She offered Ben her arm. 'Shall we?'

'Let's shall,' he agreed, matching her grin. He carefully closed the door as they left.

The Doctor sidled over to Lesterson. 'So, what are you doing now?' he asked, peering over his shoulder.

'Running tests to evaluate the Dalek's mental abilities,' Lesterson said. As the comm unit chimed, Janley moved to answer it. Lesterson grabbed her pad as she passed, and then held it for the Doctor to look over. 'It's showing a remarkable grasp of chemistry.'

'That's not all it can grasp,' the Doctor replied. 'Not by a long chalk.'

Janley cleared her throat, and both men looked at her. The Dalek's eye-stick never wavered from the Doctor. 'Something's come up,' she said apologetically. 'Is it all right for me to slip out for a few minutes?'

'But – the tests,' Lesterson said, looking down at the pad.

'That's all right,' the Doctor said quickly, snatching the pad. 'I believe I can work this.' He smiled at Lesterson again. 'I'd like to think I can offer a little help.'

'Well, in that case . . .' Lesterson shrugged.

The Doctor tapped on the pad quickly. If Janley left, it would leave only Lesterson in his way . . .

As soon as she was unobserved, Janley slid a small bundle from under the nearest bench. Hunched over it, she hurried from the room.

'May I start?' the Doctor asked, cocking his head to one side. He crossed to the Dalek and rapped on its dome to centre its attention. 'If Z is M, then what is UUB?'

'H-two-O,' the Dalek replied, almost instantly. 'Water.'

'Isn't that brilliant?' Lesterson exclaimed.

The Doctor gave him an odd look. 'I'm doing this for your benefit, not mine. I already know how clever they are.' He slipped a hand into his pocket and started to edge his way towards the laboratory's power unit.

Lesterson gave him a disappointed glance. 'I thought you had changed your mind about the Daleks.'

'Never!' the Doctor told him fiercely. 'I *know* what they are. But at least you've had the good sense to remove the gun-stick.' He gestured at the hole in the Dalek's casing.

Lesterson lowered his head slightly, as if from guilt. 'Yes,' he said softly.

It was the opening the Doctor had hoped for. Instantly, he snatched the small device he'd made earlier from his pocket and slapped it on to the power unit. Then he adjusted the small dial that had once worked the radio and clicked the on switch.

Instantly, the laboratory was filled with a high-pitched whine. Lesterson moved to cover his ears, and even the Doctor grimaced at the bone-shaking squeal. The Dalek began to spin where it stood, faster and faster. Its arm and eye rotated wildly.

Though the Dalek was disconnected from the power unit now, it was still capable of picking up power transmissions. The Doctor knew this from his past encounters with the creatures. He had simply built a small standing-wave generator to constantly change the electrical field generated by the power unit, giving the Dalek what effectively amounted to electronic seizures. With luck, they would be powerful enough to burn out the core memory of its computers and kill the Dalek embryo that lived within the casing.

'What are you doing?' Lesterson screamed. He flung himself at the Doctor, exerting astonishing strength.

'Trying to save your life!' the Doctor yelled back.

Lesterson sent the Doctor sprawling and snatched the device from the power unit. Snapping off the switch, Lesterson threw the device on to the floor and ground it under his heel. Then, white-faced with fury, he rounded on the Doctor. 'Get out!' he screamed. 'Get out!'

The Doctor began to move, still defiant, for the door. As he passed the Dalek, it ceased spinning. The eye-stick zeroed in on the Doctor again.

'I – have – sustained – no – damage,' it said slowly. It wasn't clear if it was addressing the Doctor or Lesterson.

The Doctor glared back at it. 'Perhaps I'll have better luck next time,' he said softly. Then, turning his back deliberately on the Dalek, he marched for the door.

Shaken as he was by this explosion of events, Lesterson didn't miss what happened next. The Dalek spun to cover the Doctor's back, the empty socket of the gun barrel centred on its target. There was a series of clicks as the Dalek attempted to fire the missing gun.

Lesterson staggered back against the bench for support. The robot did have emotions! It was reacting in anger and fury! If it had possessed the means, it would have killed the Doctor. Wiping his sweating forehead, Lesterson stared at the Dalek. For the first time, he began to wonder if there *was* something in the mad ramblings of this stange Examiner.

16

Keep Her in a Safe Place

Janley glanced quickly around to make certain she wasn't being observed as she quietly entered Hensell's office. Her plans had gone too far now to be jeopardized by accidentally being seen here, of all places. But the corridor was deserted. With relief, she quickly closed the door behind her with her free hand. Then she shifted her burden into both arms as she hurried across the acres of carpeting to the Governor's desk and the man awaiting her there.

Turning from the view he had been studying from the window, Bragen looked at Janley with deep satisfaction glowing in his hawk-like eyes. 'You were able to get away, then?' he asked.

Janley nodded, depositing her bundle on the mirrored surface of the Governor's desk. 'Yes. Lesterson's occupied with his experiments. The Examiner is with him.' She glanced around the room. 'Where's Hensell?'

Bragen smiled thinly. 'He's called a meeting of the production managers. The all-important monthly statistics beckon. He'll be occupied there for hours yet.' He moved to the far side of the desk and eased himself into the chair there. 'He left me in charge.'

And he was clearly enjoying the feeling of power. He wore the mantle well. That was what had drawn her to him immediately. Janley knew the power she had over men: her looks and poise had been drawing admirers to her like flies to honey since she was in her teens. She liked the power she had over men, but craved *real* power. When she had arrived on Vulcan, she had carefully studied all the heads she had turned, sizing up her best chances of achieving her goal. Quinn had made a gentle play for her, but she had dismissed him almost immediately. Even though he was the Deputy Governor, he was more interested in genuinely serving than in controlling. That wasn't what she was after. It wasn't until she had met Bragen that she had seen mirrored in his eyes the lust for power that she felt so strongly. And he had a sharp mind, one that crafted delicate plans to achieve his goal.

The first stages had played out, and Quinn was now in jail, awaiting a trial. Janley had as little doubt about the verdict as Bragen. And now Bragen held Quinn's post.

'We could take over the colony now,' she suggested. She licked her lips in anticipation of the event.

'No,' Bragen said flatly. 'No, it has to be absolutely right. Do you think I want to take over a colony full of rebels, Janley?'

'I don't understand,' she confessed. 'Why put me in with the rebels, then, and get me to help them?'

He smiled coldly. 'It's perfectly simple. With your skills and – appeal, you've been able to build up the rebels. Not too much, just enough to stir them up so that they can create the right amount of trouble to get rid of Hensell. And then,' he said, swinging his feet up on to the polished desk, 'then we crush them. Without your leadership their backbone will crumble and it will be a simple matter for my men to crush them – publicly. The colony will be grateful, the corporation will be grateful, and I'll be the new Governor.'

Janley smiled. It sounded perfect. 'And we will rule the planet,' she said softly.

'Precisely.' Bragen returned her smile. 'So you just carry on encouraging our ignorant friends.' He nodded at the wrapped bundle. 'Is that the thing you told me about? Can you persuade the rebels that this will help them?'

'I'm sure of it.' Janley unwrapped the device, revealing the gun-stick that Lesterson had carefully removed from the activated Dalek. 'Valmar thinks that he can work in a switch that will turn this Dalek weapon on and off.'

Bragen laughed. 'It's amazing what people will fall for,' he sneered. Valmar was the driving force behind the rebels – a brilliant, creative engineer. He had made only one mistake:

falling in love with Janley. He believed her implicitly. Lying convincingly was one of Janley's greatest talents.

'It really works,' Janley replied. She tapped the sleek barrel of the gun. 'It killed Lesterson's assistant Resno.'

Bragen swung his legs from the desk and stood up. He eyed the gun with new respect. 'Did it, indeed?'

'Yes. But if we attach a switch, we'll be able to control its power.'

'Excellent. A real weapon will make the rebels more of a threat, and cement your position with them.' He considered for a moment. 'And does Lesterson know how powerful this device is?'

'No. Lesterson believes that Resno's simply shaken up, that he's taking a few days off under Thane's care, and is resting.'

Bragen nodded. As ever, Janley had planned well. 'And the body?'

'Valmar disposed of it in one of the mercury pools. It won't be found unless we wish it.' Janley gave a tight-lipped smile. 'Lesterson was the indirect cause of Resno's death. It's a good hold to have over him if he makes trouble.' She rewrapped the gun. 'I'll give this to Valmar, then?'

'Yes.' Bragen dismissed the matter, his mind clearly on other things.

'When do we move?' Janley asked. Power was so close to being in her grasp, she was getting greedy for action.

'Not quite yet,' Bragen replied. Seeing the disappointment in her eyes, he added: 'I need another card in my hand. The Examiner bothers me.'

'That ridiculous man?' Janley scoffed. 'I thought Quinn was the only danger to our plans.'

'Not any more.' Bragen rubbed his chin, deep in thought. 'And don't dismiss the Examiner as a fool. A lot of that's merely an act to disarm suspicions. He wouldn't be where he is today if he were really that idiotic. What we need is something else, some other card in play . . .' Then the answer came to him. A wolf-like smile slowly spread across his features as he carefully told Janley what she had to do.

131

'I told you they wouldn't let you see Quinn,' Ben grumbled, following Polly down the latest corridor. The place was beginning to get on his nerves, it was so bleak. Every corridor looked like the last, without individuality or interest.

'Then we'll have to talk to somebody else, won't we?' Polly replied firmly. 'The Doctor is relying on us to get him the background information he needs about the rebels while he concentrates on the Daleks.'

Ben hated it when Polly got into one of her moods. Sometimes she could get quite bossy, especially when she was on one of her crusades. She was quite determined to vindicate Quinn and get him freed, that much was obvious. 'So, who else is there?' he asked. 'We can hardly ask Hensell to tell us. And Bragen's the Security Chief – *he* won't admit that there's any problems he hasn't solved.'

Polly gave him a cheerful smile. 'Then we'll have to talk to Thane, won't we?'

'The medic?' Ben considered the suggestion. 'You may have something there, Duchess. People tell all their aches and pains to their doctors, don't they? But do you think she'll see us?'

Polly halted beside the community notice board. 'I know she'll see us,' she replied brightly. She tapped a piece of paper on the board. 'I spotted this last time we walked past. It's a note from her asking you, me and the Doctor to stop by for a check-up.'

'Blimey, Pol,' Ben said in admiration, 'what sharp eyes you have.' He frowned at the board. 'You know, there's something that puzzles me about this place. On the one hand, it's on an alien planet, light-years from Earth, with starships coming in and all this electronic whiz-bang stuff all over. Then, on the other hand, they use a message board and drawing pins to leave each other notes. Odd, ain't it?'

'It is a bit strange,' Polly agreed. 'A mixture of the ultramodern and the primitive. Well, maybe Thane will have some answers for us.'

The blonde doctor did at least have a friendly smile for them. 'I see you got my message, then.' She stood up. 'Don't worry, it's nothing serious. I just like to check upon some of my successes now and then to make certain I'm not deluding myself.' She came to a halt beside a machine that looked like a weighing machine. It had a base joined to a five-foot long handle. Atop this were two hand-grips, and two digital read-out screens. 'Right, who's first?'

'Me, I suppose,' Polly volunteered. 'What do I have to do?'

Thane sighed. 'Yes, I suppose it's a bit of an antiquity by Earth standards, isn't it? Like most things here. Just stand on the platform and grip the handles, please.'

Polly did as she was instructed, picking up on Thane's bitter comment. 'You get a lot of – out-dated equipment here?' she asked.

'As much as the Company feels it can get away with to cut costs,' Thane replied. She began tapping buttons on the panel.

'The Company?' Ben prompted her.

'Yes.' She gave him a quick, puzzled look. 'They really didn't brief you very much, did they? Surely you know that this planet is owned and operated by International Mining Corporation?'

'As a commercial venture,' Polly said. 'So they provide only what they have to in order to keep you going and cut corners where they can.'

'Precisely.' Thane sounded angry. 'If they'd given me the medical facilities I was promised, we'd have had a lot less deaths. They're not interested in people, just output.'

Polly began to understand some of the older woman's anger. 'And they say it isn't economical to give you better technology or more supplies.'

'And that's why the place looks so barren and you have to leave messages on a bulletin board,' Ben finished off triumphantly.

'Exactly.' Thane jotted down the readings from the dial. 'It looks like you're in good shape, Polly. No after-effects from the mercury poisoning at all. Right, off you get.' She nodded at Ben. 'Your turn now.'

Polly was beginning to understand the situation much better. Here was the reason for the discontent, and the fuel that kept the rebels going. This IMC company was bleeding the planet dry to make itself rich, and keeping the colonists dependent on it for whatever supplies they did get. She could hardly blame some of them for wanting to change things. It also explained why Hensell wasn't well-liked – as mouthpiece for the Company, he was distrusted by the colonists. And as a good company man, he probably worked to keep production up and costs down. And he no doubt had a fat retirement pension waiting for him back at home on Earth when he was finished here. It was definitely a poisonous situation here, and not just from the mercury, either.

As Ben took his turn on the diagnostic machine, Thane asked Polly: 'Where's the Examiner? He must have his tests done too, you know.'

'He's with Lesterson in the laboratory,' Polly answered. 'I'll ask him to stop by and see you as soon as he's finished, shall I?'

'I'd appreciate that,' Thane said gratefully. 'I can close his file then. I'd hate to see any drastic changes in his health.'

'Yeah,' Ben muttered in agreement, 'the last change was bad enough.'

'Oh?' Thane raised an eyebrow. 'Having medical problems, is he?'

'Not exactly,' Ben hedged. 'More like he's giving *us* medical problems.'

'Ah, I see.' Thane smiled. 'There must be a lot of stress in your line of work.'

'More than you'd think,' Ben assured her.

Polly slipped out of the room while Thane was conducting her examination of Ben. She was glad of the excuse to go looking for the Doctor. Now she had some facts to give him about the rebels. Maybe this would help the Doctor somehow to free Quinn. Absorbed in her thoughts, she almost bumped into one of the colonists who was pinning a note to the bulletin board. 'Oh, sorry,' she apologized. She was about to back off when she recognized the girl. 'You're Lesterson's assistant, aren't you?'

'That's right,' Janley agreed. 'You're not looking for the Examiner, are you?'

'Well, yes,' Polly replied. 'Isn't he in the laboratory still?'

'No, they finished their tests,' Janley replied. 'And we just received the word that the Communications Room is now operational, so the Examiner went there to send a message to Earth. About the Daleks, I believe.'

Excitement surged in Polly: it looked like both of their problems were about to be solved. 'Great,' she said happily. 'Thanks. I'll catch him while he's there, then.'

'You'll find it easily enough,' Janley told her. 'It's on the right, down the next corridor spoke.'

Polly nodded and hurried off in the indicated direction. Janley watched her leave, a nasty smile playing about her lips. It was all going exactly according to plan.

As Janley had predicted, Polly found the Communications Room within moments. She tapped on the door, then opened it and entered.

She frowned in puzzlement. Despite Janley's claims, the Doctor wasn't in the room. Nor, apparently, was anyone else. That was odd, because there were supposed to be some technicians working on repairing the smashed units.

'Doctor?' Polly called. 'Hello! Is there anyone here?' Then, as she moved forward, she realized that Janley had definitely lied to her: the main computers were dead, and the central panels were still in pieces, electronic parts and wiring scattered about the floor. The room was certainly not operational, as the other woman had claimed.

Worried now, Polly turned back to leave the room. As she started to move, a strong hand clamped about her mouth, and a second about her chest, pinning her arms to her sides. Polly struggled to free herself from this unseen assailant. Then, as she fought, there was a sickly smell as something cracked beneath her nose. She couldn't help breathing it in, and then she collapsed in her attacker's arms.

Janley hastily replaced the shattered ampule of tranquilizer into her jacket pocket. She would dispose of it later, where it wouldn't be found. then she smiled up at the man holding Polly's limp form in his strong arms. 'Well done, Valmar. That should keep her quiet for a while.'

Valmar glanced down at the woman again. His craggy face creased into a frown. Then he looked up at Janley from under his long, dark fringe. He was a slender man, nervous, but intense. His dark eyes seemed to absorb information as he looked around. A genius with all things mechanical, he constantly allowed his curiosity to override his judgment. 'I've got no idea who she is, but she was snooping about. She may have understood what I'm doing with the comm units.'

'I sent her,' Janley told him. 'She's one of the Examiner's assistants. We want her kept safely out of the way for a while. Get a couple of your men to keep her in a safe place.'

Valmar nodded, then let Polly's unconscious body drop cruelly to the floor. He stepped over it to look at the bundle that Janley clutched under her arm. 'Is this it?'

'Yes.' She unwrapped the Dalek gun-stick and held it out to him. 'This is what I told you about.'

Examining the weapon made Valmar's eyes gleam. It was beautifully constructed, with a single purpose in mind. 'Should have quite a good range,' he said in admiration. 'Workmanship, this is.'

'Can you fit a trigger?' Janley asked.

'Easily.' Valmar's face split into a grin of pure pleasure. 'This little beauty should win us the revolution.'

Janley's smile echoed his. 'Splendid. Then, very soon, we shall throw off the shackles of slavery and become a free people.'

'And Hensell will be first against the wall,' Valmar said with satisfaction. Originally one of the senior engineers, Valmar had been demoted by the Governor after an industrial accident. Hensell had blamed Valmar for the four men who had died, even though it had not been Valmar's fault. But it looked better on the Governor's report to lay the blame at the feet of an individual, rather than where it belonged – with the IMC board of directors. Now Valmar aimed to have his recompense.

'All of our oppressors will be dealt with as they deserve,' Janley told him. 'And any who side with them. Those who are not with the revolution are against it!'

'Freedom!' Valmar replied happily. He bent to examine the Dalek gun again, and thus missed seeing the mocking smile on Janley's lips.

Fool, she thought. So easily manipulated by stupid phrases and idiotic desires. Soon there will be change all right, but there will be precious little freedom for you idiots.

17

When I Say Run, Run Like a Rabbit

Ben glanced about the empty medical room blankly. 'I don't understand it, Doctor,' he said. 'Polly was definitely going off to look for you.'

The Doctor looked about with little interest. 'Well, I was with Lesterson all the time till you came and got me for this silly medical. Polly never came for me.'

Ben nodded. 'So I was sure she must have come back here. But there's no sign of her, is there?'

'Nor of Thane, either,' the Doctor said. 'I do so hate being kept waiting by doctors. Still, maybe we can make the best of a bad situation. Why don't we run the tests on me ourselves and leave Thane a note of the results?'

Trying to ignore his worry about Polly, Ben led the Doctor over to the diagnostic machine. 'It's quite simple,' he explained, demonstrating it. 'You just stand on the platform and hold the handles. The instruments monitor your heartbeat, breathing and the rest.' He nodded at the small panel in the centre of the machine. 'It all shows up there.'

The Doctor peered at the read-outs with interest. 'Oh, this looks like fun.' He raised an eyebrow. 'Judging by these figures, you're in excellent condition. Almost as fit as I am!'

'I should think so,' Ben laughed.

'Come on, get down,' the Doctor said, waving his hand. 'Let me have a go.'

'Anyone'd think it was a toy,' said Ben, relinquishing his place.

The Doctor hopped up on it and gripped the handles firmly. 'Does it have a kick-start?' he asked.

There was a howl from the central panel, and Ben bent to

examine it. 'No, but according to these figures, you should have! It looks like you're dead!'

'Don't be silly. I haven't felt this fit in five centuries.' The Doctor peered rather myopically at the read-outs. 'Oh, of course! It's calibrated for humans, isn't it? I must be giving it something of a mechanical nervous breakdown.'

'I'll say.' Ben shook his head. 'Well, we can't leave *those* readings for Thane. She might want to have you buried. We'd better make some up.'

The Doctor glared at the machine as he clambered off it. 'I assure you, Ben, I'm as fit as a man of a tenth of my age.'

'Yeah, but if you're over seven hundred and fifty years old, that's not saying much, is it?' Ben finished making his notes, and then his mind went back to his primary worry. 'I wonder what's happened to her?'

The Doctor's mind also returned to the subject that was causing him the most concern. 'Ben, if you were a Dalek, what would your next move be?'

'What about Polly?' Ben insisted.

'Polly?' The Doctor shook his head. 'No, she's a bright girl, but I don't think she could predict – '

'She's *missing*,' Ben said, sighing.

'Oh, I hardly think so,' the Doctor replied. 'She's probably looking for more information to get Quinn out of jail. You know how single-minded she can get.'

'Then she should be simple to find,' Ben answered. 'Come on.' He grabbed the Doctor's arm, dragging him towards the door.

'Where are we going?'

Ben held up his fake readings for the Doctor. 'To leave this on the bulletin board for Thane. Then to report Polly as missing. I don't care if we do make fools of ourselves and she's fine. I'll feel better if we report it.'

Before he could protest, the Doctor was dragged out of the medical room door by Ben and they started off down the corridor.

In his laboratory, Lesterson had finally calmed down. 'I managed to stop that fool Examiner just in time,' he muttered to himself. Thankfully, the Dalek had suffered no ill effects from whatever the infernal meddler had done to it. It was now following Lesterson as he performed his daily monitor of the orbital instrumentation. Lester couldn't help but feel that it followed him around like a dog might – a very intelligent dog.

'What is that reference?' the Dalek asked, as Lesterson jotted some figures down.

'It's amazing,' Lesterson marvelled, 'you have an almost human interest and curiosity.'

The eye-stick focused on him. 'A Dalek is not the same as a human.'

'No,' Lesterson agreed slowly. 'Well, there are some people here, you know, that believe you're the enemy of human beings.'

'I am your servant,' the Dalek grated. 'What is that reference? If I am to help you, I must understand.'

'Yes. Yes, of course.' Lesterson tapped the glowing screen with his stylus. 'This is a machine I built myself. It computes the paths of meteorite storms that cut across the orbital path of our weather satellites. They can get quite intense. There's some speculation that they may be the shattered remains of an old moon.'

'Speculation without facts is useless,' the Dalek stated. It looked down at the screen. 'How accurate is it?'

'Fair.' Lesterson shrugged. 'About seventy per cent. It helps us to cut down our satellite losses.'

'Daleks can build computers with one hundred per cent accuracy.'

'A hundred per cent?' Lesterson echoed. 'But there's so much data, so many potential – '

'One hundred per cent,' the Dalek repeated. 'If you provide materials and a separate power source, a computer will be built.'

Lesterson could hardly believe his ears. He had wanted his Daleks to be of use to the colony, but he had never expected anything like this! Still, they had positronic brains, so they should be able to build better computers than a human could. Yes, it made perfect sense. And this was the opportunity he had been seeking: a chance to show how much good the Daleks could do for the colony. Replacing even a single destroyed satellite cost millions of credits; he could just imagine what IMC on Earth would say if they could eliminate those expenses completely. They'd never listen to that fool Examiner and allow his Daleks to be taken apart for scrap!

'I'll go and see Hensell at once,' he promised. 'I know that this will be of great interest to him.'

'Good,' the Dalek said. 'I will be ready to dictate the blue-print when you return.'

Lesterson nodded, barely able to contain his excitement. He hurried out of the laboratory, closing the door behind him.

The Dalek glided across the floor, listening at the door. Enhancing its audio pick-ups, it could make out the sound of the scientist's feet moving away down the corridor outside. Satisfied that it would not be observed for a while, the Dalek spun about and returned to the power unit. There it raised its manipulator arm. The interface rod in the centre of the suction 'hand' slid out a few inches, entering one of the unused ports. There was a second of inactivity, then the Dalek withdrew from the machine.

The sequences of lights on the power unit changed their pulsing. The output was rising, and the hum from the generator with it. The Dalek turned away and glided across the floor of the laboratory. Then it entered the Dalek capsule to continue its hidden work.

As Ben pinned his note for Thane on the bulletin board, the Doctor stood beside him, staring off into space. His lips and fingers were moving, and he looked for all the world like a schoolchild attempting to solve a difficult sum. Ben started to move off, then realized he was on his own.

'Hey!' he called back at the Doctor. 'I thought we'd agreed to go and see Bragen.'

'Did we?' the Doctor asked absently. He began rummaging through his pockets, eventually turning up the stub of a pencil. Snatching a piece of paper from the board, he licked the point of the pencil, then began to scribble away furiously. 'Given the linear coefficient and assuming the . . . No, no, no, that won't do! You can't *assume* anything with the Daleks!' He started again, then broke off once more. He chewed the end of the pencil almost down to his fingers. Then, frustrated, he pinned the note back on the board. 'It's useless. I'm working in the dark. Without the proper information.' He glanced at Ben, then sprang on him. Grabbing his arm, the Doctor pulled him down the nearest corridor. Before the startled Ben could say anything, the Doctor hissed: 'Sshhh!'

Obeying the order, Ben glanced back into the corridor hub. He saw the lanky shape of Lesterson stride past. From the smile on his face, something major had happened to make him so cheerful. As soon as Lesterson had passed out of sight down the Admin wing, the Doctor released his tight hold of Ben's arm.

'What was that all about?' the sailor complained, rubbing his arm to restore its circulation.

'Didn't you just see Lesterson go by?' the Doctor demanded. 'I didn't want him to spot us. Right now, he's obviously left the Daleks on their own in his laboratory. This may be our chance to destroy them. I wanted Polly to be our look-out, but we'll have to trust to luck. Come on!'

They hurried down to Lesterson's laboratory, which at first glance was empty. Then, from inside the Dalek capsule, there came a bright flash of light. The Doctor chewed at his lower lip as he traced the newly laid power cables that snaked across the floor and into the open capsule hatchway.

Ben's face clouded over. 'Somebody's in there,' he muttered.

The Doctor nodded. 'Short-circuit the generator, Ben,' he ordered. As Ben moved towards the power couplings, the Doctor began to edge his way over towards the capsule. He wanted a better look at what the Daleks were doing in there. The cables they had laid were very high-duty sizes. They had to be draining every spare erg of energy that the colony was providing. Before he could reach the capsule, a Dalek moved out to block his path. It swung its empty gun socket around to cover him.

'What are you doing here?' it demanded.

'What's that to do with you?' Deciding that his best course

141

of action was attack, he assumed his most imposing manner. 'Stand aside!'

'Entry here is restricted,' the Dalek stated.

'Not for me it isn't,' the Doctor answered. 'Accord every access – I've got a badge here somewhere that says so.'

'That is an order!' the Dalek insisted.

'A *Dalek* order,' the Doctor said softly. 'Daleks can't give orders. You are our servants.' He raised an eyebrow. 'Or had you forgotten that bit?'

'Servants to some,' the Dalek granted. 'You are our enemy.' The eye-stick whirled around to centre on Ben, who had been edging his way towards the power unit. 'Stand back!'

'Don't be afraid of it, Ben,' the Doctor said evenly. He peered out from under his heavy mop of hair at the lone Dalek. 'It isn't armed. Disconnect the generator. I want to find out what it was doing in the capsule. Screwing up all of his own courage, he brushed past the unarmed Dalek.

Then he halted. In the hatchway of the capsule were two further Daleks. Both of these retained their weapons, which were swinging around to cover the Doctor and Ben. The Doctor stumbled backwards, almost falling over Ben in his rush to retreat.

'So that's what it was doing in there,' he said.

Ben's eyes were fixed on the two guns. 'You don't think Lesterson repowered them?'

'No. He's not such a fool as to leave them with their guns.' The Doctor lowered his voice, hoping that the Daleks wouldn't hear him. 'When I say run, run like a rabbit!'

Still, the Daleks hadn't attempted to kill. This was so unusual that the Doctor was tempted to push his luck and stay a little longer. If it were only his life, he might do it. But he couldn't risk Ben's as well. The unarmed Dalek glided back across the floor to join the other two in the capsule. As it did so, it momentarily blocked their line of fire.

'Run!' the Doctor yelled, and followed his own advice. His arms and legs moving as fast as they could, he shot for the door and out. Ben was a split second behind him, and slammed the door to keep the Daleks inside the laboratory.

The unarmed Dalek turned to the others. 'I have sent the scientist human for further materials.'

'And power?' asked a second Dalek.

'Yes,' the first Dalek confirmed. 'Power we can turn into static. Then we will conquer.'

'We will conquer,' the three of them chorused together. 'WE WILL CONQUER!'

The Doctor stormed into Hensell's office, disrupting the planning session that the Governor, Lesterson and Bragen were having. Hensell looked up, a scowl crossing his face as he saw who the intruder was.

'What the blazes do you want now?' he snapped. 'We were discussing what to do with Lesterson's Daleks.'

'I suppose it's too much to hope that you've come to your senses and are making plans to destroy them?' The Doctor's gaze swept across three inflexible faces. 'I didn't think so. Well, you've got more problems than you know about. There are now *three* activated Daleks in Lesterson's lab.'

'What were you doing in there?' Lesterson yelled angrily. 'You were trying to destroy them again, weren't you?'

'That isn't important,' the Doctor shot back. 'The Dalek used your power supply and brought the other two Daleks back to life again.'

'So?' The scientist shrugged. 'I was going to do that anyway.'

'Are you off your rocker, mate?' Ben demanded. 'These two are armed!'

Lesterson sighed heavily. 'You're simply being difficult, both of you. We simply turn off the electricity for a while, disarm them and everything will be safe again.'

The Doctor shook his head in despair over this lack of understanding. 'They're dangerous,' he explained again. 'Deadly. And they are incredibly brilliant. They will devise a way to rearm themselves!'

'You're right about one thing, Examiner,' Hensell cut in. 'They are brilliant. The Daleks have a plan that will enable us to cut millions of credits from the costs of our satellite surveillance systems.'

'Confound your infernal satellite programme,' the Doctor yelled. 'The whole lot can be melted down for scrap all I care!'

This was heresy to Hensell. Faced with the opportunity to save the Company millions, he could not afford to back down now. 'I've lost my patience,' he told the Doctor coldly. 'I'm sick and tired of all this wrangling over the robots.'

'Then do something,' the Doctor replied.

Hensell pushed a thick, shaking finger under the Doctor's nose. 'Now you just listen to me, Mister Examiner. Don't try and run my colony for me. Lesterson has *carte blanche* with the Daleks from now on.'

The Doctor fell back a step, appalled. 'What?'

'You heard me.' Hensell moved to sit down again. 'I've got quite enough to do running the colony without having to settle these petty scientific disputes the two of you are having.'

'*Petty disputes*?' the Doctor howled. 'This isn't a minor thing, you idiot! The Daleks will take over this colony and destroy you all unless you act now.'

Deliberately turning his back on the fuming Doctor, Hensell addressed his new second-in-command. 'Bragen, I have to visit the perimeter. The mine workers are proving to be – reluctant to agree to the new schedules that the company wants implemented. I think a personal visit is called for. I'm putting you in direct charge here until I return. See to it that Lesterson has everything he wants.' Then, with a nod to Bragen and Lesterson, he marched out of the room.

The Doctor stared after him in shock. How could even Hensell be so blind? What did he hope to gain from all of this that could possibly explain the incredibly stupid chance he was taking with the Daleks? And as for Lesterson –

'Admit you're beaten,' the scientist said, not unkindly. 'You know something about these Daleks. Join with me.' He held out his hands beseechingly. 'Help me.'

'The best help I could give you, my dear Lesterson,' the Doctor told him just as kindly, 'would be to put a loaded pistol to your head and then pull the trigger.' Spinning on his heels, he stormed out of the room. Ben darted after him.

Lesterson stared at the open doorway thoughtfully. 'I'll need a permanent guard on my laboratory, Bragen,' he said finally.

'Very well,' Bragen agreed. 'But I think I have another way to keep the Examiner quiet.'

The Doctor was pacing about the room he had been assigned like a caged tiger. He was muttering to himself darkly. 'Greed and ambition, that's all it is!' he finally burst out, startling Ben, who was deep in his own black thoughts. 'Wait until they find out what their precious production figures will cost them!'

'But what about Polly?' Ben asked him. The Daleks were still something of an abstract menace to him; unlike the Doctor, he had never seen them in action. On the other hand, Ben understood the human potential for evil pretty well. He'd seen it from his youth on the London streets, through his experiences in both English and foreign ports, and from his few travels to date with the Doctor. To him, there were only two possible explanations for Polly's disappearance: kidnapping and murder. Not knowing which to expect was tearing him apart. As he watched the Doctor pacing, he suddenly became aware that there was a square of paper protruding under the edge of the door.

Rushing to the door, he flung it open. There was nobody in sight in the corridor, and no way of knowing how long the paper had been there before he'd noticed it. As he closed the door, Ben picked up the folded sheet of paper. Before he could read it, the Doctor snatched it from his fingers.

'Listen to this, Ben,' he said. 'The girl is safe. She will remain so as long as you leave the Daleks alone.' He glanced up, worried.

Ben took the note back and read it for himself. 'Who sent this, Doctor? Any ideas?'

The Doctor shook his head as he peered at the paper over Ben's shoulders.

'You don't seem very concerned,' Ben muttered angrily. 'We've got to get Polly back.'

'And if we can't?' the Doctor asked gently, as he snatched the paper back again and held it up to the light. The door opened behind him and Bragen strode into the room. Without looking around, the Doctor said: 'I didn't hear you knock.'

'Perhaps because I didn't, the Deputy Governor responded.

'I wanted to see you,' Ben told him.

'Really?' Bragen cocked his head to one side. He looked at Ben with a bored air. 'And what about?'

'It's Polly,' Ben said angrily. 'She's missing. We can't find her anywhere.'

Bragen sighed. 'Very well. I'll have one of my men begin a chain of enquiries. She can't have gone far, so it shouldn't take long to find her.'

'It may take longer than you think,' the Doctor informed him. 'Read this. Do something about it.' He thrust the letter into Bragen's hands.

After a cursory scan, Bragen looked back at the Doctor. 'Interesting.'

'Is that all you've got to say?' Ben demanded.

'What else can I say?' the Deputy Governor spread his hands helplessly. 'I suggest that while my men look for her, you do exactly what this letter demands, to avoid placing her in any further danger.'

'And that's it?' Ben asked incredulously.

Bragen stiffened. 'I do have other concerns,' he replied, irritated. 'For example, some of my men have discovered a body in the mercury swamps. Quite close to where we found you, in fact. It was the body of a middle-aged man . . .' He let his voice trail off significantly.

The Doctor assumed an air of boredom. 'And why should that be of interest to me?'

'No one has been reported missing from the colony,' Bragen replied.

'Really?' The Doctor pulled out his recorder and tootled a couple of shrill notes on it. Then he pointed the instrument at Bragen. 'What about my assistant, Polly?'

'She's not a middle-aged man, is she? And she's not my main concern at the present.'

The Doctor glowered at him. 'You forget yourself. I am the Examiner and – '

'If you *were* the Examiner, of course, I'd have every man I have out looking for her.' Bragen smiled nastily at the startled Doctor. 'But you're not the Examiner, are you?'

Ben stepped forward, his fists bunched. 'Don't try that on, mate,' he advised Bragen.

The Doctor placed a restraining hand on the sailor's arm. 'Wait, Ben.' He studied Bragen carefully. 'And on what do you base that assumption?'

'Who are you?' The Deputy Governor smiled again. It wasn't a pleasant sight. 'Friends of Quinn's? Saboteurs come to build up the rebellion? Is it just a coincidence that all of these events have happened since you arrived?'

Ignoring the accusations, the Doctor pointed again with his recorder. 'There's only one possible way you could be certain that I'm not the Examiner.'

'Oh, really? And what's that?'

'Simple.' The Doctor played a couple of low notes.

Ben caught on. 'Right!' He pointed an accusing finger at Bragen. 'You must know what the real Examiner looked like.'

'And only two people met him after he landed here,' the Doctor finished. 'Myself – and the man who killed him. That's how you knew about the body and who it is.'

'Doctor,' Ben said urgently, 'we've got to tell the Governor that Bragen's the killer.'

Bragen laughed derisively. 'Do you think he'd believe you? I'd soon convince him that there's a much more likely suspect – the stranger who showed up with his badge and claiming his authority.' He smiled at the Doctor. 'Which could put you in a serious amount of trouble, couldn't it? Unless you can account for yourself?'

'Then why don't you arrest *us*?' the Doctor demanded. 'Because there's just that spark of doubt, isn't there? That we might – just might – be able to convince Hensell that you're the one to blame and that you're the one who's framed Quinn.'

Bragen looked at the Doctor with grudging respect. 'All right. So neither of us can afford to make a move right now. But I'm warning you, leave Lesterson alone. And his Daleks.' He moved to the door, then looked back. 'After all, we don't want to lose a second Examiner, do we?' He slammed the door behind him as he marched out.

'Blimey!' Ben sat down on the bed with a thud. 'Now we know who the killer is, and we can't do a thing about it.' A sudden thought struck him. 'Here, Doctor, that letter said to leave the Daleks alone. And so did Bragen. You don't think he's behind her kidnapping, do you?'

'It's hard to be sure, Ben,' the Doctor replied. 'There are plenty of others who want Lesterson free to work.' He looked at his young friend bleakly. 'It seems our hands are being tied more and more tightly.'

Ben could see in the Doctor's face that he didn't have an answer to their problems. It was beginning to look more and more as if this were one fight that they were almost bound to lose.

In his laboratory, Lesterson was staring at what lay on his bench. Two Dalek guns. He picked one up, and then turned to face the Dalek he had repowered. 'You disarmed the other two?' he asked, amazed.

'Yes,' the Dalek grated. 'We are your servants. We do not need weapons.'

'I'm very glad,' Lesterson told it, relief flooding through him. 'I knew the Examiner had to be wrong about you.' This simple act should convince even that hard-headed critic.

'Did you get our materials?' the Dalek asked.

'Yes,' the scientist told it, replacing the gun on the bench. 'Everything you need you can have.'

'And a power plant?' the Dalek persisted.

'Everything.'

The Dalek spun around and glided across the floor towards the capsule. As it did so, two more Daleks emerged. Lesterson noted with satisfaction the gaps where their gun-sticks had once been sited. They moved to join the first Dalek.

'We will get our power,' it reported.

The three Daleks spun to face Lesterson. 'We will get our power!' they chorused.

As he watched the Daleks, a nagging doubt flickered across Lesterson's mind. Again, that concern for more power. Was it really to use it for the benefit of the humans? Or did the Daleks have some more personal – and sinister – reason for wanting it?

'We will get our power!' they said again.

Lesterson couldn't repress a shudder. There was, for all the inhuman quality in the Daleks' electronically generated voices, a definite satisfaction in their chant. As if something were being planned by them.

149

18

Insanity

Disturbed by his thoughts, Lesterson crossed to the generator. He stood there for a moment, his doubts warring within him. Finally, he came to a decision. He reached out, twisting the power output from full to half.

Instantly, the three Daleks were affected. Their eye-sticks and arms drooped. One managed to twist its top section about slightly. Its eye-stick quivered up to the horizontal position, trying vainly to focus on Lesterson.

'Turn – back – the – power – supply,' it begged, its voice slurred.

'I will, I will,' the scientist agreed. 'But I want you to understand that I control you.'

'We – are – your – servants,' the Dalek agreed weakly.

'I know,' Lesterson said. 'Remember that.' He surveyed the three Daleks carefully. 'I give you all a special charge, just as I have the first Dalek I brought back to life. Any further power you need must come through this generator. And I control the power you need. Is that perfectly clear?'

'We – obey,' the Daleks chorused.

'Very well.' Certain that he had now impressed them, Lesterson restored the output to full strength. The waning appendages of the three Daleks immediately returned to their normal positions. Two of the Daleks spun around and glided back into the capsule. The third moved towards Lesterson. He frowned at it. 'Where are they going?' he demanded.

'To await your orders – master.'

'Good.' Lesterson liked the sound of that word. It was all to the good that the Daleks understood and acknowledged the hold he had over them. 'Did you prepare the blueprint on your new satellite programme idea?'

'It is ready,' the Dalek reported. It slid over to the work-bench, its arm indicating a small pile of metal.

Lesterson joined it there. The pile turned out to be a number of thin sheets of some form of flexible metal he'd never seen before. Etched upon the surface were drawings and circuit diagrams. He began to scan them. As he did so, his excitement level rose: it looked as if the Daleks had some very sophisticated understanding of both computers and scanning methods. The sheets outlined a system that would indeed simplify the orbital mechanics of meteor detection. As soon as it could be implemented, his opinion of the Daleks would be justified before the Governor. 'This is marvellous,' he said happily. 'I'm glad that we understand each other.' Needing more light to examine the prints in detail, he moved to another bench, switching on a reading lamp.

The Dalek's eye-stick followed his movements. 'We understand the human mind,' it said softly. Lesterson didn't hear it.

Bragen sat behind Hensell's desk, carefully reading through the reports that had accumulated. It was astonishing how much paperwork even a small colony like this could generate. If IMC supplied enough money for a good computer net, then a lot of this tedium could be abolished. But that was unlikely. Still, unlikely things did happen.

His new uniform as Deputy Governor had finally been delivered to him. He wore it now, proudly, but with an eye to its temporary nature. Soon he wouldn't be *Deputy* Governor . . .

Looking up from his work, he scowled at Valmar. The engineer had the comm unit built into the desk scattered about the floor in pieces. Some sort of diagnostic equipment was plugged into the gap. 'Isn't that finished yet?' Bragen snapped.

Valmar looked up, fire in his eyes. He was obviously struggling to control his temper. 'Nearly,' he finally said, returning to his work. Tapping out the codes on the disassembled pad, he spoke into the microphone. 'This is Valmar. Test call, please.'

From the far end of the huge room came the sound of

raised voices. Both Valmar and Bragen looked up as the door slammed open. The Doctor and Ben entered, while a frustrated guard tried to drag them back out again.

'You can't go in there, I tell you!' the guard snapped. Then, aware that they were already in the office, he looked up and caught the Deputy Governor's glare. 'I'm sorry, Bragen. I tried to stop them.'

Bragen jumped to his feet, leaning forward on the desk. 'What is the meaning of this intrusion?'

'Intrusion?' the Doctor asked innocently. 'What intrusion? We're just returning all of your various calls. This is just a social visit. This guard – ' he indicated the man, whose face went crimson ' – tried to tell us you were too busy to see us. But we knew better, didn't we, Ben?'

'I tried to stop them, Bragen,' the guard interjected sullenly. 'I did my best.'

'All right,' Bragen said. 'Your best is obviously not good enough. And don't call me by name. I've told you that before.'

The guard glowered. 'Yes. *Sir.*'

Bragen ignored the insolence. 'Dismissed.' He watched the guard until he had marched out and closed the door before turning to the Doctor. 'Well?'

The Doctor smiled back at him. 'Oh, what a nice new uniform,' he gushed. 'Smart, very smart. I wish I had one like that.'

From his place on the floor, Valmar picked up the handset to the comm unit as it bleeped. 'Terrace.' There was a faint burst of sound. 'I can hear you clearly. Good. Now try and patch in the connection with the interior, then the perimeter stations.'

Bragen moved away from the desk, blocking the Doctor from interfering with Valmar. 'As you can see, *Examiner*,' he said, laying stress on the title, 'I'm having some repairs done.'

'So I see,' the Doctor replied. His expression grew puzzled. 'Funny. I'm certain that Janley received a call earlier in Lesterson's lab. And his communications wouldn't be repaired before yours, would they?' Before Bragen could reply, the Doctor

152

added: 'And this is the reason why you've refused me entry for the last half-hour?'

Bragen drew himself up to his full height. 'I do not have to give you reasons any more.'

The Doctor nodded thoughtfully. 'So that's the way the wind blows now, is it?'

Having taken as much of this verbal fencing as he could, Ben could keep silent no longer. 'We want to know what you're doing about Polly!' he yelled. 'She can't just have disappeared. What are you doing about finding her?'

'You are doing something, presumably,' the Doctor added.

Bragen gestured at Valmar, who was in the process of reassembling the comm unit. 'Now that our interior communications are working again it should be easier. I have had men out asking questions. You really mustn't expect miracles, you know. Even if you *are* the Examiner.' He smiled at his private joke.

Finishing his work, Valmar began to gather his tools together. 'There we go,' he told Bragen. 'There shouldn't be any further trouble now.'

'Good,' Bragen said coldly. 'It's about time, too.'

The Doctor stepped forward. 'When do you expect to regain communications with Earth?'

Valmar glanced at him. 'As soon as I can,' he snapped. 'Interior communications were the priority, you know. Bragen's orders.' He looked at the Deputy Governor. 'Is that all?'

'Yes,' Bragen replied. 'Get out.' As Valmar turned to leave, Bragen held up his hand. 'No. Wait.' The technican looked back, stifling a staged yawn. 'Don't be insolent with me!' Bragen snarled. 'You're lazy and inefficient. The work should have been completed long before this.'

'I did the best I could,' Valmar said sullenly.

'I know your work record,' Bragen responded, slapping one of the files on Hensell's desk. 'If you really did the best you could, perhaps we should assign an able-bodied man to your position and reassign you to work you *can* manage. Cleaning out the garbage, for example.'

Valmar's face flushed. Clenching his fists threateningly, he took a step forward.

153

Bragen's face twisted in a sneer. 'You're one second away from prison, my friend,' he said softly. 'Be very careful.'

The two men locked gazes. Valmar was the first to look away. Then he turned to leave once more.

'Remember,' Bragen called after his retreating back, 'in future I'll be watching you, Valmar. Now, get out.'

The door slammed behind the technician. The Doctor studied the Deputy Governor with interest. 'Finding your feet, are you?'

'What do you mean?' Bragen demanded, annoyed.

'Wearing a new uniform – and a new attitude?'

'There's too much of an easy-going attitude in this colony,' Bragen snapped back. 'Quinn fostered one. But I'm bringing in new methods. Smartening things up. That means a certain amount of control.'

Ben grunted. 'You won't get better work out of people by bullying them.'

'People need leadership,' Bragen said.

'Indeed,' the Doctor agreed. 'But it all depends on what *kind* of leadership. You may discover that your brand is more unpopular than Hensell's.'

Bragen sat down at the desk and picked up the next file. Then he forced a smile on to his face. 'If you wish to criticize the Governor, you had better save it for your report – Examiner.'

At that second, a Dalek moved smoothly into the room. The Doctor and Ben stared at it in a mixture of astonishment and confusion. It was disarmed, and attached to its sucker-stick was a metal tray. On the tray was a glass of some liquid, with ice cubes chinking in it.

'So,' the Doctor breathed, 'you've given the Daleks the run of the colony, have you?'

'Why not?' Bragen asked. 'They're harmless, and I assure you that they make splendid servants.' Ignoring the Doctor's snort of derision, Bragen reached out and took the drink from the tray.

The Dalek's eye-stick swivelled to take in the Doctor and Ben. 'Shall I bring liquid for your visitors?' it asked.

'No,' Bragen replied. As the Dalek moved smoothly back

across the room, Bragen smiled at the Doctor. 'I know you won't be here much longer.' He took a sip from his drink.

'I wouldn't count on that if I were you.' He slumped down into one of the chairs, then glanced thoughtfully at the Dalek. 'I wonder how long they can keep moving around on these floors? They're not metal . . .'

Ben stared from Bragen to the Doctor anxiously. 'We can't stay here,' he said. He nodded at Bragen. 'If this character won't help us, we've got to look for Pol ourselves.'

Rather than taking offence, Bragen smiled. 'That's good advice,' he told the Doctor. 'Especially since there appears to be no evidence.'

This was too much for Ben. 'No evidence?' he yelled, leaning across the desk dangerously. Bragen jerked sharply backwards. 'What about that letter, then? What more do you want?'

Bragen dismissed the subject. 'Only you saw it delivered. Only you claim that your friend is missing. Naturally, I'm supposed to take your word for it that this isn't some sort of scheme to keep my men occupied while the rebels act.' He gave them an insincere smile. 'I'm doing all that I can under the circumstances.'

'Why, you – ' Ben looked as if he were ready to launch himself across the mirrored surface of the desk and straight at Bragen's throat. The Doctor grabbed hold of him hastily. 'No, Ben,' he hissed in his companion's ear. 'This isn't the answer.'

Calming, Ben gave a curt nod. 'You're right. He isn't worth it, Doctor.'

Bragen glared at them both. 'Goodbye – *Doctor*,' he said.

'*Examiner*,' the Doctor corrected. He led Ben away from the desk.

Understand this,' Bragen called from behind them. 'The only reason you're not in prison as suspects is because the rebels have to be dealt with and I haven't the time to bother with you. But make trouble and you'll get trouble.'

'Thank you,' the Doctor replied, without turning. To Ben, he added: 'Interesting isn't it, that now he's Deputy Governor the rebels have suddenly become worth bothering about?'

'I don't care about the rebels,' Ben said. 'I just want to find Pol right now.'

The Doctor gave him a thoughtful look. 'The two might not be as far apart as you seem to think, Ben.'

As Bragen tried to compose himself after the Doctor's visit, his comm unit buzzed. Trying to mask his annoyance at the further interruption, Bragen scooped up the handset and flicked on the screen. An image of Hensell flickered at first, then settled down. It was obvious from the background tunnel that he was at one of the mine sites.

'Ah, there you are, Bragen,' Hensell snapped. Clearly the talks were not going well. 'Thank heavens the communications are working again. Let me have your report, man; I'm very busy here.'

Bragen buried his anger and managed a smooth smile. 'There's nothing to report, Governor. Internal communications are back, but we're still isolated from Earth.'

'And that meddling Examiner?' Hensell asked. 'Is he still poking his nose into our affairs?'

A genuine smile touched Bragen's face. 'We're managing to keep him – occupied.'

'Interfering busybody,' Hensell muttered. 'I'll be glad to see the back of him. Well, I'm going to be stuck here another day or two at the very least. You can manage until I return, can't you?'

'Yes,' Bragen replied. As the picture faded away, he looked up from the desk. He gave a slight start. The Dalek waiter had returned silently, and was watching him. 'What do you want?' he snapped, angry with himself for showing shock.

'Have you finished your liquid?' the Dalek asked.

It was just trying to be efficient, that was all. 'No,' Bragen told it. The Dalek spun about and moved smoothly away again. As he watched it leave, Bragen wondered if it had been listening to his conversations. Then he dismissed the idea with a snort. These Daleks could have no possible interest in what he was up to. He was just suffering from a touch of paranoia while he waited for his plans to mature.

There was no way the Daleks would interfere with his mastery of the colony. No way at all.

The Doctor's path led them back towards the hub of the building, and the bulletin board. As he and Ben approached it, they could hear voices. The Doctor held a finger to his lips for silence. Puzzled, Ben followed his lead. They peered around the corner together.

Lesterson's assistant, Janley, was at the board. With her was a slightly plump, short man that Ben had not seen before. He had thinning dark hair, carefully combed over the rotund skull to attempt – unsuccessfully – to hide his spreading baldness. Ben was willing to bet he dyed his hair to mask the grey in it. He seemed the sort who'd do anything to cover his weaknesses. He was apparently just arriving as Janley was leaving.

'Kebble,' Janley said, nodding her head at the board. 'Better check the agenda.'

'I'll do it right now,' Kebble agreed. He scanned the notes as Janley left. After a moment, he moved on.

The Doctor had found a magnet in one of his pockets and seemed very absorbed in studying it. He tapped it against the wall and the floor, but it refused to stick. 'Non-magnetic,' he said to himself. 'Then the Daleks can't be transmitting power. They must be storing their energy internally for now. I wonder how good their batteries are?' He sat on the floor, thinking, his back against the wall, his legs stretched out. Pulling out his recorder, he began to play a little jig.

'Doctor,' Ben hissed. He pointed down one of the side corridors. The Doctor stopped tootling and followed Ben's gaze.

Three Daleks, all minus their gun-sticks, glided down the corridor, and into a second.

'Insanity!' the Doctor said firmly, clambering back to his feet.

'Eh?'

The Doctor gestured at the retreating Daleks. 'Allowing the Daleks to move around like this.' He gnawed at his lip, deep in thought. 'Ben . . .'he said slowly. 'Surely . . . Look, we've just left Bragen. He had a Dalek acting as his servant . . .'

'Yeah.' Ben shrugged. 'Bit creepy, but so what?'

'It was stationary outside the office when we left.' He stared down the corridor the three Daleks had emerged from. '*That* is the corridor leading to Lesterson's laboratory.'

'So?'

'Ben,' the Doctor said carefully, 'think! We're supposed to have one Dalek behind us. Yet three have just gone past. *Three*, Ben.' He rubbed his chin. 'There were only three in the capsule – so where did the fourth one come from?'

Ben shrugged. 'Maybe the first one scarpered around quick to join his mates.'

'They're fast, Ben, but they aren't invisible.' The Doctor's face contorted as he struggled with the question. 'Unless . . . No. No. Lesterson couldn't have manufactured more. Maybe there was another hidden chamber in the capsule.'

Ben was losing interest in the matter. 'Look, you're making a big deal out of nothing. The one we left behind just nipped down a side corridor to join the other two, that's all. It's Polly you should be thinking about, not Daleks. Who cares if there's three or four of the things?'

The Doctor nodded. 'We'll go and talk to Lesterson. I want to show him the note. It tells us to leave him alone, after all.'

'You think he wrote it?' Ben asked. His fists clenched. 'I could . . . ask him.'

'Well, perhaps he might have an idea about where Polly could be, at any rate.'

'Or that assistant of his,' Ben suggested. 'Janley, I mean. There's something about her . . .'

'Yes,' the Doctor agreed. 'That girl interests me. She received a call on the comm unit before it was repaired. And she put up a notice on the board just now. One that Kebble found very interesting.' He moved over to stare at the note on the board. As he did so, a woman came around the corner, apparently heading for the board. She stopped as she saw the Doctor there, apparently trying to decide whether to pause or not. Intrigued, the Doctor nodded at her.

'Come along, Ben,' he said. 'We'd better see Lesterson right away.' He led Ben off down the corridor away from the board, then stopped. Turning, he saw that the woman was standing beside Janley's note, jotting something down. Somehow, she seemed to realize she was being watched. She glanced around and saw the Doctor. Quickly she snapped her pad shut and hurried off.

'Interesting,' the Doctor murmured. 'I frightened her off for some reason. I wonder what the fascination of this board is?'

'You remember what Thane said,' Ben replied, irritated at the delay. 'It's the only way they've got to put out messages for each other.'

'What about the comms units?'

Ben shrugged. 'General messages, then. Who cares? We're going to see Lesterson – *now*. We have to find Polly!'

'Yes, all right,' the Doctor agreed. He started off again with Ben, but the bulletin board was clearly on his mind. He glanced back as he walked, and saw someone else at the board. It looked like Thane, and she was also jotting in her pad. The Doctor decided that he'd better take a much closer look at what was so appealing about Janley's note. But, first things first: right now they had to have words with Lesterson. About a disappearing assistant, and an appearing Dalek.

19

These Things Are Just Machines

Janley was hard at work with her notes when a shadow loomed over her. Startled, she looked up. Lesterson, his face drawn and tired-looking, was there, a piece of the Daleks' flexible metal in his hand.

'You startled me,' she said. 'What is it?'

'The Daleks,' Lesterson replied, waving the sheet at her. It hummed softly as he shook it. 'They've made up a new list of materials that they want.'

Janley tapped the SAVE function on her pad, then held out her hand. 'Let me see.' Lesterson handed her the metal the Daleks used instead of paper. She quickly scanned the list, then shrugged. 'We've got all these things in stock.' A slight frown marred her perfect features. 'They've rebuilt the satellite computer already.'

'I know that,' Lesterson snapped. Something was clearly vexing him.

'They need material to work with,' Janley told him in their defence.

'But why these quantities, Janley?' he asked. 'Why? *Why?* How could they have used up all the materials I gave them – when was it?' He glanced at the clock. 'Good heavens, it was only a few hours ago!'

'They're building new things for us,' Janley told him soothingly. It wasn't easy, stroking his ego like this, but she knew she had to do it. 'Wonderful things.'

'I don't want them to do anything without consulting me,' Lesterson snapped. He ran a hand through his hair. It came away sticky with sweat. He looked like a man subject to nightmares. His gaze came to rest on the capsule. The door

160

to it was closed. 'They've even locked themselves in there now. What are they doing inside there?'

'You're worrying too much.' Janley had never seen Lesterson this agitated before. But it was imperative that he didn't discover what *her* plans for the Daleks were. 'They're probably just working on ideas for the mining systems they planned.'

'*They* planned,' Lesterson said. 'Not us.'

'Don't worry so much.'

Lesterson gave her a panicky look. 'That's the sort of remark I've been making to a lot of other people,' he mumbled. 'The Governor, the Examiner . . . Don't you see, Janley?' He seemed to be begging for her understanding. 'The Daleks are proving that they have a dangerous amount of original thought!' He almost ran across the laboratory floor to the capsule. Hammering on the locked door, he yelled: 'What are you doing in there?' There was no reply. Almost frantically, he threatened: 'I can cut off your power!' Still there was no reply. He thundered his fists on the door again, but with no response. Dejectedly, he turned and slunk back to a stool by the workbench.

Janley moved to stand behind him. She began to massage the tight, knotted muscles in his neck. 'Then why not cut it off?' she suggested.

'I want the Examiner's advice first.'

'The Examiner!' Janley exclaimed, her voice dripping scorn.

Lesterson pulled free of her ministering hands and glared at her. 'Look, Janley, say what you like, but I'm beginning to believe he was right about the Daleks.' He shivered. 'I can feel it in my bones. If we can control them . . . Well, that'll be marvellous and they'll serve us. But if we can't . . .'

'Yes?' Janley prompted.

'Then I'll have them destroyed. They're too dangerous otherwise.' He had clearly made up his mind. 'The Examiner seems to know more about them and I need his opinion.'

He was starting to get dangerously out of her control. Janley knew that the time had come to put in the knives. 'I wouldn't bring the Examiner into it if I were you,' she advised him softly.

'I don't need your advice,' he retorted. 'You don't seem to

161

understand how serious this is. The Daleks are all right, providing we control them. The Examiner knows all about them – '

'But he doesn't know about Resno,' Janley reminded him.

'Resno!' Lesterson realized he'd completely forgotten about *that*, and about his injured assistant. So much had been happening. 'That was just a little accident.' He felt guilty about his neglect. 'How is he, anyway? I should have visited him. He should be getting better.'

'He's dead,' Janley replied coldly.

Lesterson went ashen. 'Dead?' he repeated, stunned. 'But you said . . . He was recovering, and . . .'

'You idiot,' she said. 'The Dalek *killed* him.'

It was a good job he was sitting down. He looked in serious danger of total collapse. 'But, but you *said* – '

'I lied,' she replied brutally. 'You were busy with the experiments on the Dalek and didn't need another problem.'

His haunted eyes gradually focused on her. 'You should have told me,' he said, almost in tears. 'The body . . . We have to report it.'

'Don't worry.' Janley looked down at him scornfully. 'No one will find the body.'

He seemed to understand her at last. 'You've done a terrible thing, Janley,' he reproached. 'How am I going to explain it all now?'

'You couldn't explain it *then*,' she sneered. 'The Dalek may have killed Resno, but you were to blame.'

This hit him hard. She could see the guilt and torment in his face. 'No,' he protested weakly. 'No, I wasn't . . .'

She had him hooked now. It was just a matter of playing him right. His conscience, and his fear, would make him putty in her hands. 'You took precautions, did you?' she jeered. 'You knew that the Dalek was harmless? No! You made a mistake and I covered up for you.'

'But why?' he asked. 'Why did you do that?'

Janley chose her reply carefully. 'Because the experiments on the Daleks are more important.'

'More important than human life?' he asked her, incredulously. 'No. No, I can't accept that.'

'You will,' Janley insisted. 'You must.'

162

'Must?' he echoed. 'What are you talking about – *must*?'

Janley's look of contempt seemed to have finally hit home with him. He was trembling as she sized up her next words carefully for their impact. 'You were to blame for Resno's death. I could always say that *you* murdered him. It's only your word against mine.' She let that sink in. 'The Examiner's so keen on having the Daleks destroyed. That's just the sort of ammunition he'd love. To discredit you, imprison you . . .'

Lesterson finally comprehended what she was doing. 'I'm not going to be blackmailed by you!'

Janley smiled slightly, then shrugged. 'Funny sort of black-mail,' she mused. 'I get nothing but trouble from it.' She glared at him. 'All I want you to do is to go on as you are. I'm not asking for anything. Scientific discovery can't stop now, Lesterson, just because of your queasy stomach!' She was about to continue when the door opened.

Spinning around, she saw the Doctor and Ben march into the laboratory. It was the worst possible timing; she wasn't absolutely certain yet that Lesterson was completely under her thumb. She gave Lesterson a quick glance, but it was impossible to tell whether he'd hold up or crack. Too many emotions were churning inside him to be sure of his responses.

Right now, he hid his fears behind a bluster of anger. 'I told the guard no one was to be admitted!' he stormed.

'Apparently,' the Doctor said mildly, 'he didn't think that applied to the Examiner.'

'Well, it does,' Janley said rudely.

The Doctor turned his meek gaze on to her. 'I'm over-whelmed by your courtesy,' he told her. 'Accord every access, remember?'

Ben was impatient with the Doctor's lack of bluntness. 'We're looking for Polly,' he said.

'Well, she isn't here,' Lesterson snapped. Janley saw that he looked relieved that they weren't here to expose him. 'And I haven't seen her.'

'She's been kidnapped,' Ben informed him.

'On Vulcan?' Lesterson laughed scornfully. 'Impossible. That kind of thing doesn't happen in the colony. There's no crime to speak of, except for the odd bit of bother from the rebels.'

'Well, it's happened now,' Ben said. 'We got a note telling us.'

The Doctor was standing by the workbench now. His eyes flickered away from Lesterson long enough to focus on a small handbag that lay open on the table. It was obviously Janley's. His shrewd eyes took in the usual knick-knacks, and then he saw something much more interesting. It was a small writing pad. The paper was identical to that used for the notices on the bulletin board. And also to that of the kidnap note they had received. Was it merely a coincidence? Did everyone in the colony have one of those pads? Or –

Janley had seen where the Doctor was looking. Smoothly, she reached over and shut her bag. She met the Doctor's even gaze without a flicker of emotion.

'I'm sorry,' Lesterson told Ben, and he sounded sincere. 'If what you say is true – '

'Of course it's true,' Ben snapped.

'Well, I don't know anything about it.'

The Doctor turned to stare at the scientist. 'Lesterson,' he said softly.

'Yes?'

'You haven't built any new Daleks, have you?'

'Built any?' Lesterson looked shocked, then almost amused. 'I wouldn't even know where to begin.'

'You're quite sure?' The Doctor's eyes bored into the scientist's, looking for the slightest hint of prevarication.

'Of course I'm sure! I don't have the faintest idea how to go about it!'

The Doctor nodded, satisfied that Lesterson was being truthful. 'And there were only three of them in the capsule?'

Lesterson looked confused. 'You saw for yourself that there were.'

'Then how would you explain the fact that we have just seen four of them?'

'Impossible!'

'Quite,' the Doctor agreed. 'Then there is really only one

alternative, isn't there? The Daleks must be reproducing themselves.'

Janley laughed scornfully at the suggestion. Lesterson, however, picked up the metal foil with the list of parts that the Daleks had requested. 'These things are just machines,' Janley said. 'How could they reproduce?'

'Machines?' The Doctor shook his head firmly. 'What makes you think they're just machines? The Daleks are brilliant engineers and scientists. Nothing is beyond them, given the right materials.'

Lesterson was white. 'What?' he asked.

'I said that nothing is beyond them, given the right materials.' The Doctor peererd down at Lesterson, perched on the stool like a pallid garden gnome, trembling. The sheet of flexible metal in his hands dropped to the floor. 'Are you all right?' He crossed to the thin scientist, who sat and shivered. Janley moved to intercept him, her eyes blazing.

'Leave him alone!' she snarled. 'He's just been overworking, that's all.'

The Doctor's eyes narrowed. 'He needs medical attention. A man doesn't suddenly crack like that for no reason. Ben – ' he started to run towards his companion.

'Will you go away?' Janley screeched. 'Guard! Guard!' Then she whirled around to face the Doctor. 'It's all your fault,' she told him. 'Badgering him with your questions – you've been hounding him ever since you arrived on Vulcan!'

'Don't be absurd!' the Doctor protested.

The guard tumbled into the room. Janley spun around and yelled at him: 'Bragen's orders were that *no one* was to be admitted!'

The hapless man looked confused. 'Yes, but I thought the Examiner – '

'You're not paid to think!' Janley howled. 'This man attacked Lesterson. Get him out of here. Both of them! Out, do you hear me?'

'Now look here,' the Doctor began, but he broke off as the guard stomped over to them. The man had a good six inches over even Ben, and looked as if he outweighed both of them added together. This was clearly one of those times for the better part of valour. Throwing up his hands in disgust, the Doctor allowed the hulking man to march him and Ben out of the laboratory. He could bide his time, for the moment, at any rate.

As soon as the intruders were gone, Janley gave Lesterson a quick examination. He was still on the stool, shaking uncontrollably. Obviously his nerves had cracked under the strain. After a second's thought, she crossed to the comm unit and triggered it. An unfamiliar voice answered her from the Communications Room. 'This is Janley. Tell Valmar to come over to the lab right away.' She clicked the machine off without waiting for a reply.

Taking Lesterson by the shoulders, she shook him slightly. 'Come on,' she said softly. 'Lie down for a bit. You've been doing far too much. You need rest.' Unprotesting, he allowed her to walk him into the small side room that held a day bed. It was useful when experiments had to be monitored constantly to have the small fold-out bed. Now Janley pushed him on to it. 'Put your feet up. Go on.' Lesterson nodded, and lay down.

Returning to the main lab, Janley took a clean beaker and filled it with distilled water. Then she took a small vial from her bag, similar to the one she'd used on Polly. This one she cracked into the water. There was a swirl as the escaping gas dissolved instantly. She poured the liquid into a cup and took this through to Lesterson. 'This will help,' she promised. Without a word, he took it from her and downed the drugged water. Then he lay down again and closed his eyes.

The main door opened. Janley hurried out into the lab as Valmar entered it. The guard accompanied him, obviously taking her orders seriously this time.

'It's all right,' Janley said. 'Lesterson sent for him.' The guard nodded curtly and returned outside to his post. Janley washed out the cup she was holding. 'I've had to give Lesterson a mild sleeping draught.' She set about cleaning all traces from the beaker.

'What's the matter with him?' Valmar asked.

'Overwork, I suppose.' Janley finished her work. Her tracks

were now covered. 'He suddenly broke down. Anyway, it'll give you a chance to put in the new power cable the Daleks asked for.'

'You don't miss a trick, do you?' Valmar sounded almost admiring.

Janley favoured him with a smile, then crossed to the Dalek capsule. 'We're going to lay in the cable you wanted.'

Instantly, the door slid open. Janley's soft tones had produced the response Lesterson's hammering had not. A Dalek appeared in the doorway. 'Good,' it grated.

Valmar stared at the thing somewhat uncertainly. It was the first time he'd really been close to one of the things. It gave him the creeps. He turned to Janley. 'You sure this is okay?'

'Get on with it,' she told him impatiently. Then she smiled at the Dalek. 'We help them. They help us. Isn't that correct?'

'Yes,' the Dalek agreed. 'We are your servants.'

Valmar wasn't too certain exactly who was giving the orders here. Still, he couldn't grumble, since the Daleks were supplying the weapons that he and the rebels needed.

'And don't take too long,' Janley added. 'You saw the notice, did you?'

'I saw it,' Valmar told her. He looked from Janley to the waiting Dalek. Then he crossed to where a waiting drum of cable sat. It wouldn't be too long now. The death knell of the old order was about to sound.

If only he didn't feel so disturbed when the Dalek was looking at him, all would be right with his world.

We Want No Accidents

Ben felt there was a sense of inevitability about it when the Doctor stopped off again at the bulletin board. He sighed as the Doctor pulled a battered index card and pencil from his pocket and started studying the notices.

'You've got a thing about those notes, haven't you?' he muttered. 'Look, Doctor, we're still no nearer finding Polly. What are we hanging about here for?'

'Because I can never resist a challenge, Ben' the Doctor replied, tapping one of the notes with his pencil. 'It's very ingenious, but not quite clever enough.' He chuckled, then turned to Ben. 'I've discovered a message in code. It's very simple: you just take the last letter of every word. Work it out for yourself.'

Tired of hanging about, Ben shook his head. 'Just tell me, will you?'

A little annoyed that Ben wasn't admiring his brilliance, the Doctor sighed. 'Very well. It says: "Meeting tonight at 2200 hours. Rocket Room P".' He smiled at Ben. 'It's the rebels' way of calling a meeting. I think we should attend, don't you?'

Ben finally caught on. 'Maybe get there a bit early,' he suggested.

The Doctor clapped him on the arm. 'That's the spirit. Perhaps we're closer to finding Polly than you thought.'

The Rocket Room was one of the storage areas for the supply rockets that were regularly launched back to Earth with the refined metals aboard. It was lined with cheap metal shelving and huge plastic drums for the extracted chemicals. Along one wall was a rack of spacesuits, which had clearly not seen use for quite some time. Spare parts for the rocket engines lay on the shelving, a lot of which needed dusting. There were weights and balances on another stack of shelves, and assaying equipment stacked along the floor.

It was the perfect room for the Doctor's needs: plenty of hiding places. He and Ben had taken up spots behind a stack of the plastic drums. They were in a pool of the many shadows that were cast about the room. Only three of the lights were still working. Either the room was hardly ever used, or else the colony was running short of spare lights for non-essential rooms. Either way, it was obvious why the rebels had selected it to meet in. It was out near the landing pads, away from the regular foot-traffic. The chances of being overheard here had to be virtually nil.

Unless someone knew about the meeting in advance.

'I'm getting pins and needles,' Ben grumbled. He shifted a bit to relieve his cramps and sighed. 'What time is it?'

'Five minutes after the last time you asked me. Honestly, Ben, do keep quiet, there's a good chap.' He peered out between the small gaps in the drums. Close to one of the remaining lights, what looked like the screen for a slide projector had been set up. The only difference was this was made of metal. And under another of the lights was a table with a number of chairs. The far end of the table was lost in the gloom. Behind it, barely visible, was a second door. The main entrance was opposite it. The Doctor hastily shushed Ben as the door opened.

Several people entered the room. Some of them the Doctor recognized, while others were strangers. There appeared to be six of them. One was the medical officer, Thane, and another was the tubby man Kebble. Quietly, they filed over to the table. None of them sat or spoke. It was obvious that they were waiting for other arrivals.

The door opened again and Valmar walked in. Behind him glided a Dalek, with its gun socket empty as ever. Following it came Janley, holding a bulky case. There was a low murmur of voices as Janley crossed to the table. Hauling the case on to it, she clicked its catches and let it fall open. The Doctor stiffened as he recognized what lay within.

169

It was a Dalek gun.

Valmar picked it up, and everyone could see there was a thin cable trailing from it. The cable was attached to the firing mechanism of the gun. It ended in a small box, like a TV remote control. The Dalek stopped beside Valmar, and he began to replace the gun in the housing in the Dalek casing. As he worked, Janley went to the far door and knocked softly. It opened, and a shadowy figure slipped into the room. It took its place at the head of the table. In the poor light, nothing could be seen of the stranger but a right hand that rested on the surface, unmoving.

As soon as the mysterious figure was in place, everyone moved to stand behind a chair. All eyes were on Valmar, as he finished connecting up the Dalek gun. When he was done, Janley rapped on the table to get the meeting's attention.

'We're going to demonstrate something tonight,' she announced. 'You section leaders will pass on what you see here. So far, we've been concerned only with testing the strength of the Governor with a few acts of sabotage. Now we're ready to take over.'

Kebble gestured at the Dalek. 'What is that thing? I've seen them moving about, but all we've been told is that it's a machine of some sort that Lesterson discovered inside his capsule.'

Janley nodded to her colleague. 'Valmar?'

The technician stepped forward, picking up the control pad attached to the Dalek gun-stick as he did so. 'This machine is known as a Dalek,' he informed them all. 'Lesterson removed the armaments of the Daleks, but I've rearmed this one. I've added a controlling device. We can regulate its fire-power, turning it on and off whenever we choose.'

Janley glanced at the shadowy figure at the head of the table. 'Shall we have the demonstration now?'

The hand waved agreement.

Beside the Doctor, Ben grinned. 'That's the fella we want,' he whispered. 'He must be the gaffer of this outfit.'

The Doctor nodded. Just as softly, he replied: 'Now we know why Polly was kidnapped and we were told not to interfere with the Daleks. These people think they can use the

170

Daleks to help them take over the colony.' Deep in thought, the Doctor pulled out his recorder. He was about to place it to his lips when he caught sight of Ben's look of horror. Trying to pretend he hadn't been about to play it and give them both away, the Doctor polished the end of it on one sleeve and put it away again. Ben's expression showed that he wasn't fooled for a second.

Meanwhile, Janley had crossed to the metal sheet on the stand. 'This screen is made of two-inch thick tungsten steel. You all know how hard it is. All right, Valmar.' She moved to join the group at the table.

The Dalek swivelled around to point at the screen. Valmar held the control unit. He tapped a button on the unit and tapped the Dalek on the dome. 'Fire at the screen,' he ordered.

The gun-stick spat. The air was filled with a tingle of electricity. The screen on the stand glowed, then shattered into a million shards.

The rebels were stunned by the demonstration. They all began to talk at once, a mixture of alarm and fascination. Only the figure who sat in the shadows remained still and silent.

'Quiet!' Janley glared at her comrades angrily. 'You must keep quiet! We're still vulnerable, even here.'

'You can't control a thing like that,' Kebble said. 'It'll turn on us.'

'No it won't,' Janley insisted, clearly annoyed by his lack of faith.

Kebble ignored her assurance. 'I wouldn't tell any of my group to go anywhere near it.'

It was clear that this sentiment was shared by most of the other leaders. Glaring around, Valmar stepped forward, holding up the small unit. 'I *can* control it,' he insisted.

'Prove it,' Kebble challenged. Then he shook his head. 'You daren't! I'm not talking about that thing firing at walls or bits of metal or anything.' He glanced contemptuously at the dusty remains of the sheet. 'I mean people. Have you tried testing whether you can stop it killing people? Our people?'

Valmar held out the unit. 'Look,' he said urgently, 'I can show you what I've done here. Explain how – '

'Forget it,' Kebble said flatly. 'How do you know that Dalek can tell the difference between the Governor's people and our people?'

'*I* know the difference, you fool,' Valmar snapped. 'And I control it.'

Kebble shook his head. He could see that he had the support of the others. 'We want something better than words.'

Janley was clearly worried that she was losing control of the group. She stepped forward. 'Test it on me,' she suggested. 'Will that satisfy you?' She gave Kebble an insolent stare.

All eyes were on Kebble. It was obvious to everyone that Kebble had been pushed further than he'd expected to go. If he had been angling for control of the group, he'd quite clearly lost it. He licked his lips, nervously. 'Well, yes,' he finally agreed. 'But – '

Janley ignored him and walked over to where the screen had once stood. Behind the drums, Ben grabbed the Doctor's arm. 'She's out of her mind,' he hissed.

The Doctor shook his head slightly. 'Desperate courage, Ben.'

The Dalek focused in on Janley. The gun-arm rose. Kebble leaned forward, clearly wondering whether he'd see Janley's vindication or her death. The tension in the room was incredible. Valmar's hands twitched on the control unit. Then he looked over at the person in the shadows.

'Is it all right?'

It was clear that the unseen leader was pondering the decision. The one hand visible tapped uncertainly on the table. Then it raised and gestured for Valmar to go ahead.

Valmar was shaking. He was almost certain that he controlled the Dalek fully. But now he was being asked to gamble a life on that certainty. Was he up to it? 'When I tell you to fire . . .' he said to the Dalek, stalling for time.

'I am your servant,' the Dalek informed him. Valmar nodded, uncertainly. Then he screwed up all of his courage. Tapping the disarm key on the pad, he rapped on the Dalek's dome with his free hand.

The gun-stick spat again. This time, however, there was no acrid smell, no electrical charge in the air.

Janley remained standing, a faint bead of perspiration on her brows.

Kebble, Thane and the others all breathed again. They began to crowd around Valmar, congratulating him. Valmar let the control unit slip from his nerveless fingers. He was smiling nervously, though with obvious relief.

'Get back to your places,' Janley snapped, crossing back to the table. No one questioned her right to command. They instantly leapt back to their seats. Kebble wiped his forehead.

'Are you all right?' he asked.

'Of course.' She gave him a withering look. 'I do not take needless risks.'

Valmar stepped forward. 'Well done, Janley,' he said. He was still shaking slightly.

'You haven't disarmed the Dalek,' she told him curtly. Everyone looked at the Dalek, which was studying them all in its turn. The control pad hung over the gun, rocking slightly. 'Go on,' Janley ordered him. 'Take the gun away. We want no accidents! Isn't it enough I trusted you, Valmar?'

Nodding, Valmar crossed to the Dalek. It remained still while he began disconnecting the gun from the mounting. He gave Janley a look. Even hidden as he was, the Doctor could see that Valmar was hopelessly infatuated with Janley. Only Janley seemed oblivious to the fact.

Turning to Kebble, Janley said: 'What about the girl?'

'We've got her safely locked up, never fear.'

Ben tapped the Doctor's arm. 'Hear that?'

The Doctor nodded. 'Listen,' he whispered. 'They may say where she is.'

'They'd better not harm her.' Disturbed by the thought, Ben shifted his position slightly. His foot caught one of the empty drums, and it gave out a hollow boom.

Instantly, the rebels all whirled around to stare at the drums. 'Who's there?' Janley snapped. She and the others started forward.

'They'll find us,' Ben whispered. 'You stay here. Find out where Polly is. I'll make a run for it. Distract them.'

The Doctor tried to stop him performing this foolish act,

but he wasn't quick enough. Leaping out, Ben darted for the main door of the room. Instantly, the Dalek spun about, smacking Valmar aside. The gun, still connected, whipped up to cover Ben.

'No!' Janley shouted, stepping in front of the gun. 'Kebble!'

The Dalek froze. Ben reached the door and moved to open it. With surprising speed for a man as rotund as he was, Kebble reached him. His hand snapped down in a karate chop, catching Ben at the base of his neck. Without a sound, the young sailor collapsed to the ground.

'The guards are bound to have heard that,' Janley said anxiously. 'Quickly! We must clear out of here.' She pointed to Ben. 'Take him with you,' she instructed Kebble. 'Lock him up with the girl.'

Kebble nodded. 'Right.' He and Thane picked Ben up. Valmar opened the door, looking around. As soon as he was certain they were unobserved, he gestured. The rebels filed out quietly.

The Doctor sat where he was. The Dalek remained behind, its gun still connected. So did the shadowy leader of the rebels. A mocking, familiar voice called out: 'And now – *Examiner*!'

The Dalek spun around and moved over to the drums. The gun came up.

'You might as well come out,' the leader suggested. 'We know you're in there.'

Knowing when he was beaten, the Doctor rose to his feet. He held his hands up, not at all certain it would do the slightest bit of good. He eyed the Dalek cautiously as he walked across to the table, but it was apparently content to bide its time. Taking a chance, the Doctor glanced away from it and at the man who sat in the gloom. Closer now, he was able to make out who it was.

'Bragen!'

'Of course,' Bragen said, smiling. 'Who else is fitted to be the leader of the rebels?'

The Doctor looked nervously over his shoulder. The Dalek was moving slowly back and forth. In a human, he would have called it pacing. It was impatiently waiting for a chance to get at the Doctor, that was clear. But it was equally obvious that it didn't want to upset Bragen. It must still need the humans pretty badly to resist such a clear shot at the great enemy of its people.

'And you hope to be the leader of the Daleks too, no doubt?' the Doctor said, mocking Bragen.

'I *am* the leader of the Daleks,' Bragen replied.

'You can't control even this one,' the Doctor replied. 'See if you can prevent it from killing me.' He spun about to face the Dalek. It had finally halted behind him, gun-stick at the ready.

'Stop!' Bragen ordered. 'Turn away.' The Dalek didn't move at all. The gun was still aimed, but it hadn't fired. Bragen stepped forward and tapped on the dome, as he had seen Valmar do. 'You heard me,' he insisted. 'That is an order. Go and fetch my guards.'

For a moment, the Doctor was certain he was staring at his death. The gun didn't waver. But nor did it fire. Eventually, the gun lowered and the Dalek turned away. 'I obey,' it grated. It moved off to do as it had been ordered.

The Doctor let his breath out. It had been a very close call that time. Then he raised an eyebrow. 'Did you say the guards?'

Bragen nodded. 'My guards. They will arrest you.'

The Doctor couldn't restrain a chuckle. 'You think you have it both ways, don't you, Bragen? But how will you look in front of the Governor when I explain your dual role to him?'

Smoothing a slight crease in his jacket, Bragen shook his head slightly. 'The Governor will hardly listen to an imposter,' he replied.

'An imposter?' The Doctor made a long face. 'And how do you hope to prove that?'

'My guards are about to – find the body of the real Examiner near the mercury swamps. As soon as communications with Earth are resumed, I'm sure they'll send us a description of the Examiner.'

'The one you murdered,' the Doctor said.

'The one you pretended to be,' Bragen corrected.

'Murder's a far worse crime than impersonation,' the Doctor replied hotly.

'Ah, yes.' Bragen gave a nasty smile. 'But you see, you can't prove that I'm a murderer, while I *can* prove that you're an imposter.'

The Dalek returned to the room. It was followed by two guards and Janley. She observed the Doctor without surprise.

Bragen nodded at the Doctor. 'Take this man and detain him,' he ordered the guards.

The Doctor submitted quietly. He knew that if he didn't the Dalek would not spare his life a second time. For the moment, it was prepared to wait; well, then so was he. As he passed Janley, he glanced at her. 'I don't much care for the company you keep,' he said. 'You have a poor taste in friends.' Then he marched out, flanked by the guards.

Janley's eyes lingered on the door. 'A dangerous man,' she observed.

Bragen dismissed the thought. 'He's powerless now. All we have left is the Governor.'

Janley stroked the Dalek's gun-stick thoughtfully. 'Perhaps we should have . . . dealt with the Examiner,' she said. 'Or whoever he is.' She frowned. 'Who is he really?'

'It hardly matters now,' Bragen replied. 'I will deal with him in time. And Quinn also.'

Quinn sat in the cell he had been assigned, chewing each mouthful of the food on his plate carefully. He had been given nothing to do while he was awaiting trial. His meals were the only break in the emptiness of the day, so he made them last.

Unexpectedly, there was the sound of footsteps in the corridor. Had the guards decided to amuse themselves by taking his food away now? If so, they'd find he wouldn't be quite so peaceful as they imagined.

One of the guards appeared. Then the battered-looking strange figure of the Examiner. He gave a cheery little wave. For a moment, Quinn's hopes rose. The Examiner had contacted the Earth and got him freed! Then there was a second guard. This one shoved the Examiner forward, shattering

176

Quinn's illusions. As he watched, still chewing his food carefully, the first guard took a key-pad from his pocket and held it to the lock of the adjoining cell. There was a brief, high-pitched whistle and the lock clicked.

The guard pulled the door open. 'In you go,' he told the Examiner. The man skipped lightly inside, and the guard slammed the door shut. He and his comrade then marched back down the corridor and out of sight.

'You're the last person I expected to see here,' Quinn said, taking up another forkful of whatever the food was. He still couldn't make out any flavour in it.

'Works by sound, does it?' The Examiner lived up to his title. He was peering intently at the cell's locking mechanism.

'I'm speaking to you,' Quinn said, annoyed by this odd behaviour. 'If you'd listened to me before we wouldn't be locked up here now.'

The Doctor straightened up. 'You're quite right,' he agreed, grinning like a Cheshire cat. 'I do apologize. But never fear, your imprisonment has not been wasted.'

'I don't follow you.'

The Doctor clapped his hands together happily. 'It has brought your enemy out into the open. Bragen.'

'I knew that,' Quinn snapped.

'Ah!' The Doctor's eyes twinkled. 'But did you also know that he is the leader of the rebels?'

'Bragen?' Quinn was rocked by this. 'The leader?'

'It explains a lot, doesn't it?' The Doctor seemed to be very cheerful. 'Quite a common sort of lock, really.'

'I should have realized!' Quinn said, annoyed with himself. 'Of course – who else stood to gain as much as he?'

Sitting on the floor, the Doctor began to remove items from his many pockets, quickly building a pile of appalling junk. 'Why did you ask Earth to send an Examiner here, Quinn? Couldn't you have made the Governor aware of the problem?'

Quinn shook his head. 'I tried, but he wouldn't listen. I knew the rebels were getting stronger all the time. Hensell's trouble is that he's too sure he can carry the will of the colony along by force of his personality.'

Finding half an apple, the Doctor brushed it off and started munching. 'If he finally understood the danger, could he do anything? The rebels are well organized . . .'

'Hensell's pretty popular on the whole,' Quinn replied. 'He can always call on the mine workers on the perimeter. He used to be one of the engineers there himself once.'

'So all we have to do is convince Hensell, eh?'

Quinn shook his head. He was becoming convinced that he was locked up with a maniac. 'If you'd done your job properly,' he complained, 'you wouldn't be here and I'd be out by now.'

The Doctor looked up from sorting through his junk and stared at him blankly. 'What job?'

'I told you I sent for you,' Quinn snarled. 'Why didn't you go around raising hell all over the place?'

'Because I'm not the real Examiner, Quinn, that's why.' The Doctor seemed pleased at the stunned expression on Quinn's face. 'Ben, Polly and I . . . We're just travellers, that's all. I found the real Examiner as he landed, but he was killed. I was knocked unconscious with his papers in my hand. Bragen murdered him.'

Quinn looked up, fire in his eyes. 'Everything leads back to friend Bragen, doesn't it? Just give me a chance to get my hands on him.'

'That chance may never come,' the Doctor told him, 'unless we can contact the Governor.'

Quinn grabbed the bars of his cell and shook them. 'There's just a little matter of the cell door,' he said sarcastically. 'The jail comes under Bragen's jurisdiction.'

'We'll get out,' the Doctor replied confidently. 'You must see to Hensell. I've got to get to Lesterson.'

'Lesterson?' Quinn couldn't follow that. 'What's he got to do with it?'

The Doctor stopped sorting and looked up. 'He has brought the Daleks back to life,' he said softly. 'They are far more dangerous to us than Bragen and all the rebels. I must see

178

him. He may just be working up to the full power of the Daleks.'

21

The Doctor Was Right

With a groan, Lesterson awoke from his nightmares. He couldn't recall much from them, except that they had been filled with death, despair and pain. And that somehow, it had all been his fault. He rolled over, and moaned again. His head hurt. It felt like that time he'd celebrated the finding of the capsule in the swamps and he'd had too much of Kebble's homemade brew. But he hadn't been drinking this time.

His face felt flushed, and his throat was parched. He needed water, badly. With great effort, he managed to lever himself up into a sitting position on the camp bed. The room spun wildly about him for several minutes, so he sat still, gathering the vestiges of his strength. There was some great horror lurking about just out of reach in his mind, but he couldn't quite focus on it. Well, it would come to him, probably when his head stopped hurting so much.

Eventually, he felt strong enough to stagger to his feet. The nausea and pain hammered at him again. He clutched the door-jam to avoid falling. Horrible blotches of yellow swam across his eyes. He forced himself to forget the pain for the moment. He concentrated on seeing clearly. It was a while before the world settled back to roughly normal and he could function again. He held on to the doorway and stared at the huge expanse of the laboratory that lay between him and a glass of cold, clear water.

Well, he could make it. He'd done harder things in his time. Taking a deep breath, he pushed himself through the doorway. Lurching unsteadily on his feet, he was frightened for a moment that he might fall and be unable to rise again. Then he somehow retained his balance. Slowly, drunkenly, he made his way to the workbench. Reaching it, he collapsed on to a stool. With a trembling hand, he managed to get the cup that was there and poured some water for himself. Draining it greedily, he then refilled the cup and drank it down more slowly.

It felt so good. He enjoyed the feeling as his throat finally stopped hurting. His head seemed to be clearing up a little, too. Maybe he had been overworking, after all. Hadn't Janley said something like that to him? Janley . . . That was it! She'd told someone he had been overworking. All he needed was a bit of rest and he'd be fine.

He wiped the sweat from his brow. Must be running a bit of a temperature, too. Well, he knew how to deal with that. Pulling the handkerchief from his pocket, he tipped water all over it. Then he mopped his brow. The cooling water felt wonderful on his skin. More confidently, he walked back to the other room and settled back down on the bed there. He wiped at the back of his neck with the wet cloth, then applied it to his forehead. It made him feel much better.

He heard the main door to the laboratory open. Probably Janley or Resno, come to check up on him. Well, he'd call out to them, just as soon as he got his breath back. There was the faint scent of static electricity in the air, and then it all came rushing back to him. The Daleks . . .

They had duped him! Used him, killed Resno and were somehow up to something in that damned capsule of theirs! But he'd show them: they couldn't trick him and get away with it.

He listened as the Dalek moved across to the capsule. The door to the capsule hissed open. He risked a quick look. There was a second Dalek, framed in the doorway of the artifact.

'You sent for me,' the first Dalek said to this one.

'Yes. Take up a position at the moving pavement area. Watch and report back.'

'I obey.' The Dalek spun around. Lesterson jerked back into hiding as it glided out of the laboratory again.

He was sweating now, but this time with shock. 'They communicate with one another with intelligence,' he muttered. 'They are conspiring with one another! Why didn't I realize?

181

They're clever – much cleverer than I thought.' He fastened on a thought. 'The Doctor was right, they *are* evil!'

He heard further movement from the capsule and chanced another quick look. Two more Daleks had emerged from inside the artifact and joined the one in the doorway. Together the three Daleks moved across the laboratory and exited. Lesterson clutched at the edge of the bed, his fingers digging deeply.

'But . . . one already left,' he whispered to himself. 'There *are* four! But . . .' He tried to shake the thought from his head. 'No! They can't be reproducing . . .' Much as the idea filled him with horror, he was a scientist: it was the only solution that fitted the facts.

They had duped him, promising him help, and all the while subverting the supplies he had given them to their own ends: making more Daleks.

He glanced around the frame of the door again. The laboratory was devoid of life. But the capsule entrance was still open, and the answers he sought had to be inside.

Lesterson gathered all of his strength and meagre supply of courage. The duplicity of the Daleks scared him. One had already killed Resno. They had all lied to him. What more were they capable of doing? If only he had listened to the Doctor and destroyed these monstrosities! But no, his own arrogance and scientific greed had drawn him on. And this was the end result.

He almost ran across the laboratory and into the capsule entrance. His headache still throbbed, but he refused to acknowledge it. His body, while still weak, seemed to have recovered some of its strength. But it was difficult for him to concentrate. Now he was here, what should he do? He looked around the small entrance compartment.

Facing him, the original storage area was now empty. The three Daleks that had once stood there were gone. So was the dust: the place now gleamed. The small room showed no signs of activity. To his right was the small chamber where he had hidden the Dalek he had first reactivated. The doorway was now open, but instead of a tiny compartment barely large enough to hold a single Dalek it now led to a long, low tunnel. Nervously, Lesterson bent over and moved into this passageway. About four feet inside it, he could barely make out the edges of a huge shutter that had once closed off this end of the compartment.

He made his way down the passageway. There were low-level lights set in the walls, barely strong enough for him to see his way. Probably the Dalek eyes could see well into the infrared, so this was undoubtedly a flood-lit passage as far as they were concerned. The pathway dipped downwards at about a ten-degree angle for some distance before straightening out again. Lesterson estimated that he must have travelled some fifty feet already.

The capsule hadn't appeared to be that long from the outside. As he had suspected, the small portion that they had uncovered from the swamp was merely the tip of the iceberg – like the conning tower of a submarine. How far down into the solid rock of Vulcan did this artifact extend?

And what had the Daleks been hiding within it?

Finally, the tunnel seemed to be coming to an end. Brighter lights were apparent at the exit area. Cautiously, Lesterson edged his way out of the tunnel and into this light.

He was on some sort of a catwalk, he guessed. It ran about the wall of an immense chamber, easily a hundred feet across and about fifty feet high. To his right, the metal floor sloped down, offering the Daleks access to the floor below. There was a foot-high lip to the catwalk, presumably to prevent Daleks going over the edge. Lesterson fell to the floor and crawled to the edge before peering down at the room below. What he saw made him shake with horror.

Directly below him was some kind of computer control station. There were lights flashing, dials registering and noises issuing from the bank of machinery. One Dalek stood before it, apparently on monitor duty. Another Dalek was adjusting a set of controls several feet away from the first.

Five Daleks ... and six ...

How *many* of them were there now?

At the far end of the room from these two Daleks there was a large portal. From this doorway ran a long, metallic conveyor belt. It ended about ten feet from the monitoring station in some kind of platform. A ramp led from the platform to the floor. A second archway to the left of the first had what looked like some sort of crane system running from it towards the conveyor belt. Set at intervals above both the belt and the crane were spider-like machines, with varied nozzles and tool attachments. Some of these were connected to huge vats in the ceiling of the room.

The rest of the left-hand side of the room was taken up with what looked like a cross between a huge cauldron and a swimming pool. Steaming liquid bubbled within it, obscuring what it might contain. It stood about three feet from the floor, and appeared to continue into another room beyond the wall.

As Lesterson watched, mesmerized, there was a whine of machinery starting up. Several hidden motors began to operate, adding their noises to the din. There was a rattle as the crane system began to come to life.

A shadow passed through the doorway of the conveyor belt, emerging into the light of the room. It was the lower half of a Dalek casing. One of the spider-machines descended, extruding probes and tools into this mechanism. There were several sparks and sounds as the spider-thing performed some final operation before withdrawing. A second device then shot jets of some kind of liquid over the casing. A third moved in to add the contents of further nozzles.

Glistening, the Dalek base moved towards the intersection with the crane mechanisms. Lesterson stared in shock as the top half of a Dalek casing came through the other archway, born along by the crane, until it was positioned directly above the lower half.

It was a Dalek assembly line! The Daleks weren't merely reproducing themselves – they were *mass*-producing themselves! It was incredible that these robot-things could act like this.

The Dalek that had set the mechanism into motion now moved towards the seething pool. It paused beside it to slip its sucker-pad on to what looked like a large, metal fishing net. Then it glided alongside the liquid before lowering the net out of sight into the steaming waters. After a moment, the net was raised.

Lesterson saw what it contained and wanted to be sick.

The thing was a writhing mass of tentacles, a bilious green in colour. Two of these limbs ended in bird-like claws that flexed and clicked. Some kind of slime enveloped the sickening bundle. It was pulsing slowly but regularly. Lesterson realized instantly that this, this whatever-it-was, was *alive*.

The Dalek spun around and moved to the waiting Dalek casing. Carefully, it deposited the green mess within the base. The thing writhed about a moment, as if making itself comfortable. The two sets of claws clutched at parts of the mechanism. The tentacles writhed, slotting into prepared spaces. As Lesterson held his breath, he saw several needle-like probes emerge from the interior of the Dalek base and inject into the blob.

Feeding tubes? Computer linkages?

Whatever they were, one horrible truth was becoming quite apparent.

With a whine, the crane lowered the top half of the casing. There were several loud clicks as bolts clamped the two parts of the shell together.

The Daleks weren't robots, after all. They were some kind of cybernetic being. The robotic structure was merely some kind of shell, housing that hideous creature. Some form of spacesuit or body armour, or both. An electronic womb for the being that was the real Dalek.

The two lights on this new casing lit up. The three limbs – this machine, like the other two below, still possessed a gun-stick – moved. The creature within was beginning to learn how to operate the controls.

It was learning how to be a Dalek.

The conveyor belt started up once more. A final spider-like mechanism hovered over the completed metal body, delivering a final spray. Then the casing came to the end of the belt. Under its own power, it moved on to the platform, then turned to face the two waiting Daleks below.

They both looked at this new creature. 'Welcome to the new race of Daleks,' they intoned together. The new Dalek moved down the ramp and joined them on the floor of the manufacturing plant. Three eyes swivelled to look at the archway at the far end of the room.

The base half of another casing appeared. The Dalek with

185

the net returned to the seething cauldron. The crane began to move again, bringing in a fresh upper half of a Dalek shell.

Lesterson fell back into the tunnel with a faint whimper.

They weren't manufacturing more Daleks, they were *breeding* them! The Daleks were alive, aware, intelligent – and malevolent. They had lied to, killed and manipulated the humans to produce this Dalek factory.

Lesterson closed his eyes. He felt like screaming.

What had he done? What had he done?

22

I'm Going to Wipe Out the Daleks

Shaking with terror, Lesterson stumbled back down the tunnel. He had to get away from the Daleks, he *had* to! They were evil! He had to stop them. He had to warn the colony. He had to get away.

He staggered out of the far end of the tunnel, back into his laboratory. Only a few hours ago the room had seemed to him to be the best and most exciting place in the universe. He had been happily experimenting away, doing the research that he had always loved so much. Now the lab reminded him only of how stupid, how gullible he had been. All about were scattered mechanisms and notes that he had compiled on the Daleks. Sheaths of their metallic paper lay about, blueprints of machines that they had claimed they would build. What a fool he'd been to believe them! Angrily, he swept the prints to the floor.

He looked back at the capsule. He had to prevent the new Daleks from getting out! He couldn't use the Dalek locking device on the capsule. Even if it worked, the Daleks could just unlock it again. Besides, he rather thought that the Examiner still had it. No, he wanted something that the Daleks couldn't use their science on. His eyes flickered about the laboratory, finally coming to rest on a large cabinet that he stored his supplies in. It was about the size of the door – perfect!

Lesterson rushed across to the cabinet. It was heavy and he was still weak from his earlier collapse. But determination gave him tenacity. Sweating, cursing and constantly expecting to see Daleks milling about him, he managed to manhandle the cabinet across the room and in front of the open hatchway. Exhausted, he leaned against it. The Daleks had such small suckers for hands that they'd never be able to move this.

The door to the outside corridor opened. Lesterson almost had a heart attack, expecting to see one of the free Daleks gliding in. He breathed a deep sigh of relief when Janley entered the room. She stared at him in amazement.

'What is it?' she asked, frowning. 'What's the matter with you?'

Lesterson tried to catch his thoughts, to put them into some coherent whole. It was important that she listen and understand him. He had to sound rational.

'Are you ill?' she asked anxiously. 'You've been working too hard. You really must rest.' She crossed the room and tried to take hold of his arm.

He shook her free, terrified she'd put him to sleep again. He couldn't rest now, not with this danger hanging over the whole colony. 'They're in there,' he babbled, gesturing over his shoulder at the capsule. 'Making themselves . . . Duplicating . . .' His voice trailed off as a sudden thought came to him. They still needed power for all of this, and there was just the one source: the generator he'd so foolishly made available to them. He staggered across the room, brushing Janley to one side. 'I started this,' he told her, racked with guilt.

'What are you talking about?' It was clear from her expression that she still had no idea of the damage he'd done.

'Opening the capsule,' he started to explain. 'It's my fault.' He turned down the output controls to zero, and started to disconnect the cables. Janley grabbed his arm, trying to drag him away from the controls. With one hand, he gave her a hefty push that sent her flying. 'Don't try and stop me!' he warned her. Then he turned back to his work, tearing the cables free. The whine of the generator gradually slowed down to nothing and he finally gave a shaky smile.

Janley picked herself up from the floor. Her eyes darted from the machine to Lesterson and then to the loose ends of the cables that lay like dead snakes on the floor. 'What happened?' she asked. 'What have you done?'

'They forgot that *I* control them,' Lesterson ranted, his eyes wild. '*I* gave them life back again, and now I've taken it away.

They thought they were clever, but I've beaten them. I've stopped their plans. They're finished now.'

Janley realized what he was doing. 'The Daleks . . .' she breathed, seeing her own plans and ambitions being destroyed too.

'Evil,' he told her fanatically. 'Horrible! I know what I'm going to do.' His mind raced feverishly. 'Laser torches! I'm going to have them melted down. Melt the Daleks away to pools of metal . . .' His voice trailed away into incoherence.

This was too much for Janley to bear. 'No you won't, Lesterson,' she said firmly. 'You're sick. You don't know what you're saying.' She backed away from him as he crossed the lab towards her.

'Do you think I care what you can do?' he scoffed. 'Go on, tell everybody I was responsible for the death of Resno. I don't care. I'll take full blame. But I'm going to wipe out every last Dalek . . .' He reached for a long metal rod and turned to face her, holding it firmly in both hands.

Janley took a single look and fled, clearly terrified he was going to use it on her head.

'Go on!' he screamed down the corridor after her. 'Go and tell them all about Resno! I don't care.' He had a mission now, one that was too important to worry about petty details like the death of one human being. 'I'm still going to destroy the Daleks.' Crossing to the comm unit, he picked up the handset. 'Hello? Get me the Examiner – now!'

'I'm sorry, Lesterson,' came the reply. It was that uppity tech, Valmar. 'The Examiner is in prison. Bragen's given orders that – '

'Prison?' Lesterson faltered, confused. 'Who put him there? Why?' Before Valmar could reply, the scientist burst out: 'But I've got to talk to him! I've *got* to! Don't you understand me?'

'I'm sorry.' Valmar clicked off the connection.

Lesterson stared at the dead unit in his hand, confused. He knew that the Examiner would have worked with him on this. *He* had wanted the Daleks destroyed from the start. If only Lesterson had listened. Now it looked like it might be too late for that. 'The Governor,' he finally decided. 'Got to tell him. Melt them down, that's what we'll do.' He was dangerously close to the precipice of madness.

There was a scraping sound from behind him. Lesterson whirled around. The heavy cabinet was moving aside from the capsule entrance. Lesterson bit his knuckles, watching as a single Dalek effortlessly pushed the huge cabinet out of the way. Then its eye-stick swung to cover him.

'How did you get here?' Lesterson whimpered. 'I cut off your power!'

The Dalek glided towards him. It was one of the disarmed ones. How many of them were there? 'We can store power,' it informed him. 'Soon we will have our own supply.'

'Your own power?' Lesterson stammered.

'Why was the capsule door closed?' the Dalek demanded. It was almost up to Lesterson now.

With a delirious cry, the scientist spun around and fled the laboratory. The Dalek stopped still, its eye trained on the doorway. Behind it, another Dalek appeared in the doorway to the capsule. The first Dalek swivelled its dome about to look back.

'Seal off the capsule's secret entrance,' it ordered.

'I obey.' It spun around, ready to implement the order.

The first Dalek moved to the door, examining the corridor. There were no signs of humans. 'Wait,' it commanded. The second Dalek froze in place. 'No more than three Daleks are to be seen together at any time.'

'I obey.'

'Continue,' the first Dalek said. The second moved back to close off the entrance to the manufacturing plant. The first Dalek moved into the corridor outside the laboratory. There was no sign of Lesterson. The Dalek, satisfied, returned to the laboratory. It moved to the generator, studying the connections that Lesterson had broken.

'We are not yet ready to teach these human beings the law of the Daleks,' it said to itself. But soon, very soon, they would be.

Lesterson ran down the corridor, weaving erratically to avoid startled colonists. He ignored them, concentrating on the single thought in his mind: he had to contact the Examiner. *He* would know what to do about the Daleks. He would be able to save Vulcan from the plague that Lesterson had unleashed. In the back of his mind he knew that there was a problem with his solution, but he couldn't quite grasp it. Wiping his sweating brows with his sleeve, he stumbled onward, searching.

Finally, he saw one of Bragen's guards. The bulky man was off to do whatever they did when there was no real need for them. Lesterson cried out incoherently, and the guard turned around. The scientist grabbed his sleeve, partly to stop the man from leaving, partly for support. His legs were shaking badly.

'You can help me!' Lesterson said in a quavering voice.

The guard sniffed at Lesterson's face, but there was no reek of alcohol. 'What's the matter?' he asked brusquely, trying to shake loose the bony fist clutching his sleeve.

'Where's the Examiner?' Lesterson demanded, his eyes flickering all around the corridor, as if he expected the man to pop out any second and yell *Boo*.

'The Examiner's in prison,' the guard replied. He finally managed to pry Lesterson's fingers from his uniform.

That was the fallacy in his solution. Wearily, Lesterson fell back against the wall. 'That's right,' he muttered to himself. 'I forgot.'

The thuggish guard peered at him suspiciously. 'What's the matter with you?' he demanded. While there was no smell of alcohol, the thin scientist was exhibiting all the earmarks of having taken several measures too many. 'Why were you running?' He started to reach for the possible drunk.

Lesterson's fuzzy brain managed to realize that the guard might be arresting him next. Maybe the Daleks had convinced Bragen that he was a source of trouble. They seemed able to lie as easily as they thought. Lesterson couldn't risk being locked up, shut away from everyone. Howling wildly, he slapped down the guard's hand and then turned and ran back down the corridor.

Suspicion hardened into certainty in the guard's mind. Lesterson was either drunk or out of his mind. 'Hey!' he yelled.

'Stop!' When Lesterson continued running, the guard took off after him. There was no telling what the fool would do if he weren't subdued.

Polly had recovered from her drug-induced sleep only an hour or so before. She was vaguely aware that some time must have passed, but it was impossible for her to tell how long it might have been. She was tied and gagged. The ropes on her wrists were chafing her skin. Her feet were also tied, and there was a cramp in her left calf muscle. Her head was still swimming from the effects of whatever she'd been given to knock her out. All she could remember was that Janley had been behind it. Why, she had no idea.

The pain of the cramp had made her cry out wordlessly. Polly hadn't expected anyone to hear her, but a moment later Thane came through the doorway. Polly had managed to struggle into a sitting position, and realized she was on a bed. Obviously she was being held in one of Thane's wards.

The medic had an expression on her face that defied reading. Anger, irritation, helplessness, mixed with other feelings that seemed to be vying for control of the middle-aged woman. She came across to the bed, her eyes refusing to meet Polly's.

'Awake again?' she asked. She quickly looked Polly over and saw why the girl had cried out. With practised hands, Thane massaged the knotted muscle in Polly's leg. After a moment, it loosened and the pain went away.

Polly wished she could ask questions, to discover what was happening. But she suspected that Thane wouldn't have told her. It was quite clear that the medic was uncomfortble with her position as temporary jailer, and was too embarrassed to meet Polly's accusing gaze.

'I'd better let Janley know you're awake,' Thane said. 'She can decide what to do with you.' She ignored Polly's gurgles and fled into her office next door.

Settling back on the bed, Polly tried to work out what was happening. Janley was obviously one of the rebels. Maybe she'd been worried by Polly's questions, afraid that the Examiner was on their trail. Were the Doctor and Ben also prisoners of the rebels, held somewhere else? Had the rebels started their attempt to take over the colony? No, that didn't make sense; she'd have been in one of Bragen's cells in that case, not here. They were trying to keep her hidden, that much was obvious.

She gave up thinking about it. The old Doctor had always said it was foolish to try and think things out without the facts. And she had precious few to go on. Instead, she tried to loosen her bonds. It didn't take long to realize she wasn't going to merely wriggle out of them. They were tied very professionally. What she needed was some way to cut through them. Maybe Thane had a scalpel lying around somewhere. She had to wriggle a lot, but eventually Polly managed to get into a sitting position on the bed.

The room was devoid of anything in the line of furniture save for a second bed and a small table between them. IMC obviously didn't aim to make staying in the sick bay a pleasant experience. It might encourage malingering.

Through the open doorway, Polly could see Thane. The medic had her back towards the small room, clearly unable to bring herself to stare her prisoner in the face. That raised Polly's hopes. If she were quiet, maybe there would be some way out of this whole mess . . . Her hopes were instantly dashed as the outer door opened. Janley and a portly man entered.

Thane whipped to her feet instantly. 'Janley, Kebble,' she said, with obvious relief.

'We'll take her now,' Janley said curtly. 'I've thought of a better place to hide her.' She nodded to Kebble and the two of them came through to Polly's bed. Kebble grabbed hold of her, hauling her to her feet. 'Untie her feet,' Janley instructed him. 'She may as well walk.'

Kebble did as he was instructed, and Polly sighed with relief. It felt good to be able to flex her toes again without cutting off the circulation in them.

'All right,' Janley said roughly. She grabbed one of Polly's arms while Kebble took the other. 'Come on.'

Thane peered around the outer door of her office. 'There's no one in sight,' she reported.

'Good. Wait here for your instructions.' Janley dragged Polly out into the corridor. 'You keep up with us. And heaven help you if you give me any trouble, understand?' Polly nodded. 'Good.'

They went quickly down the corridor. Polly recognized the route they were taking, and wasn't surprised to see that they arrived at Lesterson's laboratory. What did surprise her was that there was one of Bragen's security men standing on guard outside it. Even more puzzling was the fact that he didn't seem at all bothered that Janley was holding Polly captive. He must be another of the rebels, Polly assumed. He opened the door for Janley, and then closed it again behind them.

Polly looked around the lab in wonder. How long had she been unconscious? The whole place was very different now. The single wire from the generator to the Dalek capsule seemed to have been breeding; there were about thirty lines snaking across the floor. Equipment was scattered about the room on palettes, and the workbenches were lined with electronic parts.

More ominously, two Daleks were loading these into the capsule.

Janley crossed to the closest one. Its eye-stick swivelled to look at her. 'Did Lesterson come back?' she demanded.

'No,' the Dalek replied. The eye-stick moved to stare at Polly. 'Why is this human restricted?' it asked.

'She is against the Daleks,' Janley told it. Turning back to Polly, she removed the gag from the girl's mouth. 'Not afraid, are you? Nothing will happen to you if you're smart and behave.'

Kebble untied Polly's wrists. As she massaged the chafed skin, he fetched her a glass of water from the bench. 'Here,' he said gently, 'you'll need this.' Polly accepted the glass gratefully, and quickly downed the cool, refreshing water. Kebble took the glass back and refilled it. 'Don't be frightened,' he told her as she sipped at this drink.

'Of the Daleks?' Polly asked, eyeing the one still watching her. 'Of course I am, and so should you be.'

Janley laughed with scorn. 'The Daleks are going to help us,' she said.

194

'Us being the rebels, I suppose?' While they were being talkative, Polly intended to milk them for whatever information she could get. Every little bit would help her.

Janley shrugged. 'If you like to call us that.'

Polly shook her head. 'So you're getting ready to take over, is that it?'

'With the Daleks' help,' Kebble said eagerly. 'We're almost ready to make our move.'

'And when you've won,' Polly replied, 'the Daleks just go back to being servants again? You're bigger fools than I thought.'

'We are your servants,' the Dalek insisted, obviously trying to reassure Janley and Kebble.

'When it suits you,' Polly snapped. She watched the faces of her fellow humans for any sign of a reaction to her words. Kebble looked a trifle uncertain, but Janley's face possessed the certainty of fanaticism.

'You'll see,' she promised Polly.

'What will you do with the girl?' the Dalek asked. 'You do not aim to harm her?'

'Of course not,' Kebble replied. 'We just need to keep her out of the way for a while.'

'There is space within our capsule,' the Dalek suggested. 'She could be detained there without risk of discovery.'

Janley smiled. 'I was hoping you'd say that.'

'In,' Kebble told Polly, giving her a gentle push in the direction of the capsule. To Janley, he said: 'You want me to stay with her?'

'Yes. You may have to help Valmar. He'll be along soon to finish off the work on the new power cable for the Daleks.'

The Dalek eye-stick moved back to survey her again. 'When will the work be completed?' It ignored Kebble and Polly as they entered the capsule. The important thing to it was clearly the power supply the Daleks needed.

Janley didn't answer directly. 'What is this cable you Daleks are laying anyway?'

The Dalek evaluated its reply. It would not hurt to be truthful with this human: she believed that they were helping her. 'Daleks operate on static electricity,' it explained.

'Static?' The scientist in Janley was intrigued. 'Is that posible?'

'Yes. To create the needed static charge, the Daleks need a completed cable circuit.'

'I see,' Janley said, intrigued. 'You are converting the electricity we supply you with into a form that you can use.'

'That is correct,' the Dalek answered. 'When will the human being complete the work?'

'He'll be here shortly,' Janley told it. 'It's much easier now. There is no one to interfere with our plans.'

The Dalek hesitated very briefly. 'No,' it agreed. 'We proceed as we anticipated. Soon we shall have the power we require.' Then it focused on Janley again. 'Then we can help you to take control of the other humans.'

'Yes,' Janley agreed, a smile playing on her lips. 'Then *I* shall have the power that *I* require.' She ran her hand along the dome of the Dalek. 'This is such an excellent arrangement for us both.'

The Dalek returned to its work. 'Yes,' it grated. 'Soon the need for secrecy in our planning will be over.' As it had expected, Janley assumed that it was referring to both the Daleks and the rebels – and not simply to the Daleks.

23

I Can't Stop Them

The Doctor had eventually discovered what he was looking for: a small glass stirring rod. Naturally, it was in the last pocket he had tried. Now he was busily stuffing everything back into his pockets that he had earlier removed. Quinn gave a baffled sigh of irritation.

'What *are* you doing?' he demanded. He was finding the Examiner's behaviour to be more and more peculiar.

'Working on an escape,' the Doctor replied. He picked up a small square of glass he'd found in another pocket and started to tap it with the glass rod. It emitted a series of chimes.

'Do you have to do that?' Quinn asked, annoyed.

'I wonder how they're converting the power,' the Doctor mused. He struck the glass several more times.

'What are you talking about now?' Quinn wished the strange little man could keep his mind centred on a single subject at a time. These dislocations in the conversation were beginning to be quite irritating.

'The Daleks are powered by static electricity,' the Doctor explained, looking about the small cell with an absorbed expression on his face. 'To them it's like the blood in your veins, a constant life-stream.'

'That's nonsense,' Quinn said firmly. He had a background in engineering. 'Static isn't workable.'

'It is to the Daleks,' the Doctor assured him. 'Their minds and their science don't operate along the same lines as a human's. They've conquered static, just as they've conquered anti-magnetics.'

'Anti-magnetics?' Quinn shook his head. 'I can't take any more of this nonsense. You're not making any sense.'

'I just can't seem to hit the right note,' the Doctor complained, tapping the glass again. Then his eyes lit up. 'Aha!' He jumped to his feet and dashed over to the small table his cell was provided with. On it was a tall drinking glass and a pitcher that was about a third full of water. The Doctor emptied the pitcher into the glass, which was now just over half full. Using his rod, he tapped the glass. A clear note rang out. Thoughtfully, the Doctor took a sip, then hit the glass again. Another note sounded, slightly lower in pitch.

Quinn was watching his performance with an incredulous expression. 'Of all the silly things!' he said.

The Doctor smiled at him. 'Do you have any water?' he asked.

Having finished off his supply with his meal, Quinn shook his head. 'No, I don't.'

'Pity.' The Doctor chewed his lip. 'Do you think the guard will get us some?'

'How should I know?' Quinn sighed. How could he ever have imagined that this idiot could have helped him with anything? Then he glanced into the waiting area outside the cells. Voices were arguing out there, and getting louder.

'You can't go in there!' the unseen guard said firmly.

'It's important, desperately important!' That was Lesterson's voice. What was *he* doing here?

'Bragen gave orders,' the guard responded.

'Get out of my way!' There was a muffled thud and the guard cried out. Both the Doctor and Quinn were watching as Lesterson ran into the room outside the cells.

He looked terrible: his hair was a mess, and there was a wild look to his eyes. A nervous tic made his mouth twitch, and both of his hands were shaking. 'Examiner!' he cried. 'The Daleks!'

'What about them?' the Doctor asked gently.

'They're duplicating themselves!' Lesterson glanced over his shoulder. The guard he'd pushed came through the doorway, along with the security man he'd fled from earlier. Both men grbbed his arms. 'I've seen them!' the scientist yelled. 'They've got their own power now. I can't stop them!'

The guards struggled with the writhing man. A third guard

arrived, clearly the duty officer. Both men looked at him for instructions.

The officer considered: Lesterson was an important man in the colony, and might get them into trouble. On the other hand, he was clearly not being rational right now.

'Take him to Bragen,' the officer decided. Let *him* handle this one. The two guards dragged the kicking and screaming scientist out. The officer glanced at the two prisoners, making certain that their cells had not been tampered with in any way. He was about to leave again when the Doctor gave him a winning smile.

'I say,' he asked politely. 'Do you think we might have a little more water? Please?'

That was more like it; showing the proper respect. The officer nodded curtly and left.

Quinn stared at the Doctor in disbelief. 'Is that all you can say? Lesterson fights his way down here to try and speak to you and all you can do is ask for more water?' He threw himself on to his bed, disgusted.

'But I need more water,' the Doctor said.

The officer returned a moment later with a fresh decanter, filled almost to the brim. He took the electronic key from his pocket. 'Get away from the door and stand against the far wall,' he ordered. He wasn't going to risk being jumped when he entered the cell, even if the Examiner didn't look the violent type. Neither had Lesterson, and look what he'd just pulled! But the Examiner simply nodded and jumped back as ordered. The guard triggered the key, which sent the musical note that operated the lock. He slid the door slightly ajar and put the decanter just inside on the floor. Then he slammed the door closed and left.

Pulling his recorder from his pocket, the Doctor played the highest note he could. Just a little bit shy of the right one. He shook his head, slipping the instrument back into his pocket. Taking the water, he went back to his original line of thought and filled the glass. Then he struck it with the glass rod.

The musical note brought illumination to Quinn. He finally realized what the Doctor was up to: attempting to duplicate the sound that would open their locks. He jumped to his feet

199

and crossed to the partition between their cells. 'Sorry about my earlier outburst,' he murmured.

The Doctor held up a hand to silence him. Then he rubbed a finger around the rim of the glass, adding a few more drops of water. Carefully, he tapped it again. 'Nearly there,' he said softly.

Bragen was working on the papers again, seated at Hensell's desk. He liked to work there. The desk was a symbol of power, and Bragen knew that it would soon be his – as it should be. Like the uniform he wore, the desk spoke of wealth and power. It let everyone know who was in control. Absorbed in his reflections, Bragen didn't even pay attention to the Dalek in the room with him. It was laying some kind of cable around the perimeter of the office from a reel it held in its single arm.

There was a sharp knock on the door at the far end of the office. 'Come!' Bragen called. This had better be important, or he'd have to discipline those idiotic guards of his. How could he work with these constant interruptions?

He wasn't expecting to see Lesterson being dragged in by two of his men. Nor could he have anticipated the gash across the scientist's forehead that dripped blood on to the beautiful clean carpet. 'What's this?' he demanded. His men did have a tendency to be a bit rough with their charges, but even these morons should have known better than to beat up the colony's foremost scientist.

'He tried to break in and talk to the Examiner,' the first guard explained.

'Is that any reason to do *this* to him?' Bragen demanded, coming out from behind his desk.

'He fell down when we apprehended him,' the guard said feebly.

Bragen shot the man a filthy look. 'Don't try that one on me,' he warned the man. 'If Lesterson decides to press charges against you, I'll throw the book at you.' Putting on his most sincere smile, Bragen bent down to the scientist, who was staring across the office. 'Lesterson, how do you feel?'

Lesterson gave a shudder, then turned to Bragen. 'What's the Dalek doing?'

The question threw Bragen for a moment. He'd expected anger, resentment, even threats. 'I thought you knew,' he replied. He shrugged. 'Something to do with the new emergency power supply.'

The Dalek continued laying the cable, apparently oblivious to Lesterson's presence. None of the humans could know that it had amplified its audio receptors and was listening to every word spoken by them.

Lesterson shook his head. 'It's a trick!' he told Bragen, pulling free of the guards. At Bragen's nod, they released their hold on the man. Lesterson almost fell over before he managed to stand more or less upright, wavering slightly. 'I didn't ask for it.'

Bragen frowned. 'I've had reports from your department,' he replied. 'Requisitions, specifications and so forth.' He waved at the stack of papers on the desk. 'I'm sure you must know about them.'

'I know nothing.' Lesterson ignored him and stumbled unsteadily across the room to the Dalek. 'What are you doing?' he screamed.

The Dalek turned its eye-stick toward him. 'Laying the new emergency power supply as you ordered, master,' it intoned.

'Liar!' he yelled.

Disturbed by this exchange, Bragen stepped forward. 'I've been receiving reports of your erratic behaviour, Lesterson,' he said gently. 'But I hadn't believed them before now.'

'I can explain everything,' Lesterson replied. 'If you get rid of that!' He pointed a quivering finger at the Dalek.

Unable to understand Lesterson's switch in attitude towards the Dalek, Bragen decided to humour the man. 'Finish now,' he instructed the Dalek.

It let the cable fall to the floor. 'I am your servant,' it acknowledged. Spinning around, it glided from the room. Beyond the door, though, it paused and listened.

Lesterson shuddered, but managed to pull his tattered wits together briefly. 'Where's the Governor?'

'At the perimeter,' Bragen answered. 'Talking with the miners. Why? I have full authority in his ab — '

'Call him!' Lesterson snapped. 'Get him back here as

quickly as possible. We're all in terrible danger! The Examiner was right. Right all the time!'

Bragen mused over this demand. He really needed a little more time before Hensell returned for his plans to mature. He couldn't afford to do as Lesterson suggested, but he needed a plausible excuse for refusing. As he pondered his response, Janley walked into the office.

Lesterson jumped, the tic in his cheek pulsing faster. 'Don't let her interfere, Bragen!' he begged. 'She's in league with them – the Daleks!'

Janley gave him a pitying smile. 'That's not the way to talk, Lesterson,' she said kindly. 'Just take everything calmly. You're not well, that's all it is.'

'I'm perfectly fine,' Lesterson said. At Bragen's direction, one of the guards slid a chair behind Lesterson and eased the scientist into it.

'Now please, Lesterson,' Janley said, as if she were talking to a child. 'You really ought to be in the hospital. Thane's been expecting you. You promised you'd report in to her.'

'I promised nothing of the kind!' Lesterson said indignantly.

'Surely you remember?' Janley coaxed. Bragen had to admire her technique; she was really very convincing. 'Well, never mind.' She gave Lesterson a rather pitying smile. 'I understand.'

'Such a pity,' Bragen sighed. 'Still, it's probably only temporary.'

Lesterson finally caught on. 'You're trying to say I'm mad!' he exclaimed.

'No, of course not,' Janley said gently.

'Not mad,' Bragen agreed, just as insincerely. 'Of course not, my dear fellow.'

'I tell you, I saw those Daleks!' Lesterson said, jumping to his feet again. 'They were reproducing! I saw it. I swear to you!' He looked from Janley to Bragen and saw that neither of them was really listening to a word he was saying. 'Why don't you believe me? I saw them!'

'What is he going on about?' Bragen asked Janley.

She shrugged. 'He suddenly started saying things like this in the lab,' she apologized. 'Not long after he collapsed. I'm sorry, Bragen, but I really think his mind must have snapped.'

'No!' Lesterson screamed. 'No! No!' He started to lunge at Janley, whimpering. The guards grabbed him, in firm but gentle grips.

Bragen shook his head sadly. 'I'm sorry to see you like this, Lesterson,' he murmured. 'Believe me, this is all for your own good.' To the guards, he added: 'Take him away. See that he's kept under restraint. But be gentle with him. He's sick, the poor fellow.'

As Lesterson was dragged, kicking and protesting from the room, the last thing Bragen heard was his voice, screaming: *'Will nobody listen to me?'*

When they were alone, Bragen returned to his desk. He made a note to have the cleaners be certain to remove all traces of Lesterson's blood from the carpet. It wouldn't do to start his new role as Governor with blood on the floor. Then he looked at Janley. 'All right, what *was* he going on about?'

Janley shook her head. 'Search me. Like I said, he suddenly started ranting about the Daleks breeding. He seems to think they're not robots anymore. Perhaps he really has had a breakdown.'

'It's possible. These scientific types tend to overdo it, don't they?' Bragen mused for a moment. 'There isn't any possibility he's right, is there? That the Daleks might be dangerous? I need them on our side for the takeover of the colony.'

'There's no need to worry,' Janley assured him. She noted with a spark of anger that Bragen had used the first person singular and not the plural. Was he trying to edge her out? It would be very foolish of him to even think it. 'Valmar can control the Daleks,' she said. 'And I can control Valmar.'

'Good.' Bragen tapped the edge of the desk with his finger-tips. 'This isn't the time to alter our plans.'

'There's no need for that,' Janley promised him. 'Everything will go just as it's supposed to. In just a matter of hours, you and I will be in charge of the colony.'

Inside the Dalek capsule, Polly was astonished how things had changed. There were a number of rooms opened up from the entrance that had certainly not been visible the night she, Ben and the Doctor had first entered the artifact. She wondered how many more secrets this thing held. The Daleks were showing only what they wished the humans to know about.

Valmar and Kebble were with her in the room, working on some piece of Dalek technology. It was a large box, about four feet cubed, with a power cable connection at one end. There was no obvious outlet for the power. So that they wouldn't have to constantly watch her while they worked, Kebble had retied her hands. The knots weren't as tight this time – he wasn't as callous as Janley – and Polly was beginning to believe she might be able to slip them off if she had the time to work on it.

'Pass me that small screwdriver,' Valmar ordered her.

'I can't,' Polly snapped. 'My hands are tied.' She held them up to prove her point. 'Anyway, I wouldn't even if I could.'

Valmar gave her a rueful smile and grabbed the tool himself. Kebble was busy hauling in power cables to connect to the other side of the box. A single unarmed Dalek was helping to feed the wires to Kebble. Finally the Dalek turned and left. Polly saw it exit the capsule.

'More?' Valmar asked, irritated, as he saw the cables. 'I can't handle any more.'

'This is the lot,' Kebble assured him. He was as weary as Valmar.

'Listen,' Polly said softly. 'The Dalek's gone now.'

Kebble gave her a sharp look. 'That doesn't mean you can start talking.'

'Oh, leave her alone, Kebble,' Valmar said. He had always found the tubby man too intense. Besides, in a funny kind of way, he rather liked Polly. A bit brash, maybe, but she had spirit. 'She isn't doing any harm.'

Kebble glowered at Polly, but held his peace.

'You think you're very tough, don't you?' Polly said to him. 'Pushing me around like this. I'd like to see you come up against a real man.'

Valmar sniggered. Kebble gave her a filthy look. 'Like who?'

'Like Ben, for one.' Polly was certain that he and the Doctor were out looking for her by now. It was only a matter of time before they found her.

Kebble laughed. 'Don't you worry about him,' he told her, chuckling. 'We've already got him safely stowed away.'

Polly's confidence drained. 'You've got Ben?'

'Right.' Kebble winked at her. 'He's just sleeping off a slight, fall.'

'Oh, leave the girl alone,' Valmar snapped. He had no patience for the games Kebble was playing. 'It's all right,' he told her. 'Ben won't be harmed either. He's just being kept out of things for the moment.'

Despite the fact he was one of her captors, Polly couldn't help liking the handsome young man. 'Your name's Valmar, isn't it?'

'That's me,' he agreed. He spliced in another wire, then began to tighten the connectors. Soon be done.

'You want the Daleks to help you fight the Governor,' Polly said. 'But don't you see? Once you begin fighting, they'll turn on you too.'

'What?' Kebble laughed at this suggestion. 'Three animated pepper pots?'

Valmar looked thoughtful. 'One of them did kill Resno,' he said slowly. 'And you saw what that Dalek did to the sheet of two-inch steel.'

'Believe me,' Polly told him, pressing home her advantage, 'that's just the beginning.'

'Don't listen to her!' Kebble warned. 'She's just feeding you the Examiner's line.'

Polly could see that there was some doubt in Valmar's eyes. He was starting to see that what Polly was saying wasn't all idle chatter. But the mention of the Examiner's name made his expression harden again. She realized that Valmar wasn't about to trust anyone he thought was connected to the powers that be. She decided to try a little honesty on him. 'He isn't really the Examiner,' she said. That made both of them stare at her. 'We're just travellers, you see. We landed here on Vulcan by accident.'

'Some accident!' Kebble scoffed. 'Where were you heading, then? There's nothing else around here for a dozen parsecs!'

'Our ship isn't very reliable,' Polly said feebly. 'It sort of meanders around. The Doctor, the man you've been calling the Examiner, is the only one who knows how it works. And he's not really been himself lately.' That's an understatement, she thought. ' Anyway, when we landed, the Doctor found the real Examiner. He'd been murdered when he arrived.'

Kebble laughed rudely. 'Fairy stories,' he jeered.

With a wave of his hand, Valmar cut him off. The girl's story had a ring of truth to it. 'This Doctor of yours,' he said. 'He knows something about the Daleks?'

'Yes,' Polly replied. 'He's talked about them in the past, about how evil and dangerous they were. He's come up against them a number of times, I think. Anyway, he's trying to warn everyone about them. That's the only reason we stayed here.'

A shadow suddenly fell across them. Polly jumped as a Dalek slid into the room. Did it know what she had been saying? Had it overheard her?

'When will the work be completed?' the Dalek demanded.

Valmar looked at it with fresh eyes. There was something definitely unwholesome about it, now he considered the matter. Was he doing the right thing, trusting them like this? 'I don't know,' he lied, playing for time. He had to get things straight in his own mind first. 'I'll need another junction box like this one.' He gestured to the Dalek device he was wiring up. The Dalek stared at him. Did it believe his excuse?

'I will organize one,' the Dalek said. It left the capsule again. Valmar gave Polly a weak grin.

She didn't return it. 'You've all underestimated these Daleks,' she warned him.

'Better brains than us, I suppose?' Kebble said, humouring her.

'I only know what the Doctor has told me,' Polly answered. 'He says that they are capable of exterminating whole nations.'

Valmar considered this. 'Perhaps,' he agreed. 'But what would they want to kill us for? Once we're in charge, they'll have nothing to worry about. We're friendly with these Daleks.'

'Don't you understand yet?' Polly asked. 'Humans can't be friends with the Daleks. They don't have friends.'

Valmar snorted. 'I don't see why not. Everyone has friends.'

'Not the Daleks. It's a hatred they have, "a dislike of the unlike", that's what the Doctor called it. They think they're the superior beings in the universe, and that all others should be either slaves or dead.'

'Cultural xenophobia?' Valmar shrugged. 'The girl might have something there, you know, Kebble. It is possible . . .'

'Our plans call for using the Daleks,' Kebble replied. 'Do you want to tell Janley you think they can't be trusted? I wouldn't want to try it!'

'Janley!' Polly spat. 'She'll betray the lot of you if she gets a chance.'

Valmar's eyes suddenly lost every trace of sympathy for her. He turned his back. Before Polly could ask what was wrong, the Dalek reappeared in the doorway.

'The junction box is outside when you require it,' it told Valmar.

'Thank you.' He concentrated on his work as the Dalek glided away.

Kebble had seen Polly's hurt expression. He gave her a self-satisfied smile. 'You know what your trouble is?' he told her. 'You talk too much. Just when you're ahead, you have to go and insult Janley.' Seeing that Polly still didn't follow, he explained: 'Didn't you know? Valmar's soft on Janley.'

Polly stared at Valmar's back, feeling such a fool. How could she have missed the tell-tale signs? If she'd been thinking, she'd never have said anything. It was all too obvious that her big mouth had lost her the only potential ally that any of them had found among the rebels.

Now what was she going to do?

24

The People Will Do Exactly as They Are Told

Governor Hensell was feeling tired and irritable. He stepped off the moving pavement at the Hub, rubbing his weary eyes. The drive back from the perimeter had been exhausting and he had only parked the vehicle a few minutes before. He was in dire need of a shower and a good night's sleep. If he *could* sleep with the knowledge that the miners were not being reasonable in their demands.

He wasn't looking forward to having to report back to IMC that the mine workers had rejected the new production schedules with barely a thought. That would stick in their craws like a chicken bone. And when he had to admit that there was even talk of unionizing, well, he knew how popular *that* notion was with the Board. He'd be lucky if they didn't want his immediate resignation.

The one good sign – and it showed how tired and desperate for some cheer he was that he thought it so – was that until the comm link with Earth was restored he simply couldn't report any of this back. Maybe after a good night's rest he could think of some fresh tack to take in negotiations. Right now, he was wiped completely clean of ideas.

As he walked down the corridor towards his office, he stopped dead in his tracks. One of Lesterson's Daleks was working in the corridor. Instead of a sucker attachment on the one arm it possessed, there was some sort of cable-laying drum. As the Dalek moved ahead, it was leaving a twisted mass of wires down the side of the corridor.

What the blazes was going on? He hadn't given permission for the Daleks to be out of the laboratory, let alone doing this kind of thing. He stared around and saw one of Bragen's guards marching down the corridor. He was wearing a riot helmet with the visor up and cradling a machine gun in his arms.

'What are all these cables lying about?' Hensell demanded angrily as the guard drew closer.

The man gave him a sharp stare. 'New emergency power supply,' the man said. He sounded bored.

'Oh?' Hensell asked. 'And whose idea was that?'

The guard looked at him insolently. 'What do you want to know for?'

'What do I . . . ?' Hensell couldn't believe what he was hearing. 'Don't you know who I am? I am the Governor!'

That made the man jump. He instantly straightened at attention. 'Sorry, sir.'

Hensell was slightly mollified. 'Where are you from?'

'The interior, sir.'

The maze of the processing works. Hensell hadn't been there in a long time. He hated the noisy machinery and the stench. And since they didn't have video yet, or their own newspaper, it was understandable that the man hadn't recognized Hensell. But it didn't explain one other thing that irked Hensell. 'And just why are you carrying a machine gun?'

'I'm a squad leader in Bragen's Guard, sir,' the man replied smartly.

'I see,' Hensell said tightly. '*Bragen's* Guard, eh?' It became instantly obvious that Bragen had made maximum use of every opportunity he had managed to pry out of the Deputy Governorship. It was high time the man was taken down a peg or two. 'Right, carry on!'

The guard saluted crisply, then hurried away, clearly glad to be let off so lightly. Hensell marched off towards his office, determined that Bragen would not get off quite so easily.

The Doctor tootled idly on his recorder, waiting. Their jailer came around every hour on the hour to check on the two prisoners; presumably to make certain that they hadn't killed themselves to evade justice, or something. It was about time for him to come along . . .

There was the sound of footsteps outside. In a flash, the Doctor was on his feet, the recorder slipped into an inside pocket. He picked up the full glass of water and sipped at it. Quinn lay on his bunk, apparently asleep. The guard glared frostily at the Doctor, then moved closer to the cells to check that Quinn was still alive.

Now! The Doctor spun around, throwing the water full into the face of the startled guard. As he gave a wordless yell, Quinn was on his feet. Reaching through the bars, he whipped his arms about the man's throat and jerked. The guard went limp.

The Doctor pushed open his cell door and hurried around to the guard. He unclipped the sound key from the man's belt and handed it up to Quinn. Quinn let the guard slump to the floor and hit the key-pad. On the tone, his door sprang open. Grabbing the guard by the collar, he pulled the man into the Doctor's cell. He was about to lock the door again when the Doctor shook his head.

'Just a moment!' He popped into the cell and picked up the jug of water and the glass. 'We don't want him copying our escape, do we?' The Doctor looked back at the guard. 'Though he looks to be tone deaf to me.'

'Will you come on?' Quinn grumbled. He slammed the door shut on their one-time jailer, and then led the Doctor cautiously out into the outer processing area. The other two guards were still missing, presumably still dealing with Lesterson. 'Right. Let's go!'

By the time that he reached his office, Hensell's plans had changed slightly. He had seen several other guards on the trip, all of them armed and ready for trouble. It was just barely possible that there might be some perfectly reasonable explanation for Bragen's outrageous conduct. Hensell would give him every opportunity to explain what it could possibly be – and then fire the man.

At the doorway to his office, Hensell saw a Dalek waiting. It was apparently on standby duty of some sort. He shivered as the eye-stick followed his movements, but he didn't speak. Nor did the Dalek.

The final insult came as Hensell entered his office. Bragen was seated at *his* desk. There was a pile of papers atop it, that the Deputy Governor was working his way down. He didn't even bother to look up as Hensell crossed the long stretch of floor.

'These trips grow more and more demanding,' Hensell said, more to let Bragen know he'd better acknowledge Hensell's arrival than out of a desire to make conversation.

'I didn't expect you, Governor,' Bragen replied, jotting a note on the sheet he was working on. He still didn't look up.

'That's obvious. I had quite enough with those miners.' When Bragen didn't reply, Hensell snapped: 'Well? What's been happening here?'

'One moment.' Bragen scrawled his signature across the bottom of the sheet.

Hensell went white with rage. 'I asked you a question, man!'

'And I heard you,' Bragen said, insolently.

'Your work can wait,' Hensell snarled. 'You can show it to me in the morning, after I'm rested. Right now, I've a few questions that I want answered. I want to know what's happening with the Examiner, first of all.'

Bragen finally looked up. He didn't appear to be in the slightest bit worried. 'The Examiner is at present in prison.'

'In prison?' Hensell had a growing sense of unreality. What had Bragen been up to while he was gone? Was the man insane? 'That's a bit dangerous, isn't it? Who put him there?'

'I did.'

'*You* did?' Hensell shook his head in bewilderment. 'For heaven's sake, man, why?'

'Because he's an imposter, Governor. Quite possibly a murderer as well. My men found the body of the real Examiner in the mercury swamps.'

Shaking his head in disbelief, Hensell said: 'I hope you're sure of your facts.'

'Quite sure,' Bragen said coolly.

'This could have far-reaching consequences,' Hensell pointed out. He didn't have to remind Bragen, surely, of the political clout and vast authority that an Examiner commanded? If Bragen had arrested the man by mistake, both of them could lose their positions, and never work again. If they weren't sent to prison for interfering with the Examiner's work.

'As far as I am concerned,' Bragen informed him, 'the matter is closed. Now, if there's nothing further, I do have a great deal of work to do.' He gestured at the stack of papers on Hensell's desk.

'Nothing further?' Hensell howled, outraged. 'Who the devil do you think you're talking to? This has gone on long enough. And stand up when I'm talking to you!'

'I prefer to remain seated.' Bragen eyed the Governor coldly.

'Do you?' Hensell turned to look back at the door. 'We shall see about that. Guards!'

Two of Bragen's armed men entered the room and saluted smartly. That was more like it. Hensell pointed at Bragen. 'Take this man out of my office.'

Neither man moved a muscle. Bragen gave a faint smile as Hensell's voice rose in pitch and volume. 'Did you hear me? That is an order!' Still the men didn't act.

'My dear Hensell,' Bragen said with a kindly smile, 'you forget. They are not *your* guards, they are *mine*.'

'I am the Governor!' Hensell snapped.

'No.' Bragen gave a slight shake of his head. 'Not now. I am.' He settled back in his chair and steepled his fingers. He watched Hensell over the top of them.

The situation seemed finally to have sunk in. 'I see.' Hensell was calmer, his temper on a tight rein. 'Your guards. Yes, Quinn warned me about your guards, but we all took them much too lightly. Well, we'll soon change that.' He turned to leave the office, but at Bragen's gesture the two guards blocked his way. Hensell lost his tenuous control over his temper and swung back to face Bragen. 'You imbecile!' he snarled. 'How long do you think your handful of guards can last when the people hear that I am being held a prisoner in my own capital?'

'The people will do exactly as they are told, Hensell,' Bragen answered. He pressed a recessed button in the desk, then stood up. He carefully straightened his pompous jacket and then looked at Hensell. 'It will, of course, be easier for them if you cooperate fully with us.' He gestured for the

Governor – *ex*-Governor – to take the seat. Behind Hensell, the Dalek that had been waiting outside entered. 'Wait there,' Bragen told the Dalek. To the guards, he said: 'Dismissed.' They saluted briskly and left.

Feeling a little more secure now that the guards were gone, Hensell took the chair and sat down. 'So?' he purred. 'You want my cooperation, do you?'

'It would reduce bloodshed,' Bragen said practically. 'I might even let you keep the title of Governor.'

'Might you now?' Hensell asked, cheerily. Then his face darkened. 'I'll tell you what you *will* do. You'll order all of your guards to disarm, and then you'll place yourself under arrest immediately!'

Bragen looked vaguely disappointed. 'You reject my offer?' he asked with a sigh. 'I thought it a generous one, considering the circumstances.'

'What circumstances?' It was becoming more and more obvious that Bragen was demented. There was no other possible explanation for his behaviour. The man was completely raving. Hensell tried to imagine how he could get help to overcome Bragen. Quinn was undoubtedly still in jail; and so, apparently, was the Examiner. Bragen's tale about him being a criminal was clearly another of his insane lies. So who did that leave him to call on for help? His fingers strayed slowly towards the comm unit.

Bragen picked up a bundle from the side table. 'Take a look at this,' he invited. He unwrapped the cloth to reveal a long cylinder with a universal joint at one end.

Hensell had never seen anything quite like it before. 'What is it?' he asked.

'The reason the colony is now mine,' Bragen told him. Holding it firmly, he crossed to the waiting Dalek. Placing it into the empty socket beside the arm, Bragen pushed hard. There was a snap as metallic connections locked. The stubby arm whirred softly, then began to change its orientation as the Dalek took control of it.

Suddenly worried, Hensell stood up. 'Is it a weapon of some kind? I demand to know what it does!'

213

'Then I'll arrange a demonstration for you,' Bragen replied. 'Do you still refuse my offer?'

The Governor stood straight and tall. 'I will not be intimidated!'

Bragen sighed. What a theatrical gesture! 'No, of course not. In character to the last, Hensell.' To the Dalek, he said: 'Kill him!'

The Dalek's gun-stick rose, centred and fired. Hensell screamed as the deadly rays tore into his body, ravaging every last cell, exploding them from the inside out. Then he collapsed to the floor, his corpse smouldering slightly.

Immediately, Bragen reached down and gripped the Dalek's gun. It was still slightly warm. The Dalek released the connections and Bragen withdrew the weapon from its mount in a fluid movement. Then he placed it back in the cloth.

The Dalek's eye-stick stared at him. 'Why do human beings kill human beings?' it asked.

Philosophy from a tin can? Bragen grunted. 'Get on with your work!'

'Yes, master,' the Dalek acknowledged. 'I obey!'

'Yes,' Bragen said, with almost hypnotic intensity. 'Obey me! I will have complete and instant obedience from now on from everyone.' His eyes burned with a fanatic intensity.

The Dalek spun about and rolled silently away.

Quinn wasn't completely convinced, but he allowed the Doctor to have his way. Their first stop after the jail break was Lesterson's laboratory. When he saw the scale of the changes that had been made there, he had no further doubts about the Doctor's instincts. Power cables led from the main generator into the capsule. A quick glance showed him that someone had diverted almost half of the colony's power supply into the capsule.

Who would have authorized it?

And what were the Daleks doing with that amount of raw energy?

A stack of empty pallets in the far corner of the room suggested that literally thousands of credits worth of spare parts had been taken into the capsule. More materials were stacked about the room.

'How could they fit all of this into such a small capsule?' he whispered. There was no telling if they were in danger of discovery. 'And what are they doing there?'

'The capsule may not be so small,' the Doctor replied gravely. 'You don't know how far down it goes. Besides, the Daleks have also mastered dimensional manipulation.' Seeing Quinn's blank look, the Doctor explained: 'It could be larger on the inside than on the out.' Certainly the Dalek time machines he'd encountered in the past had had this ability. 'As to what they are doing in there; well, that capsule is like a Dalek seed. It falls to the surface of some useful world and takes root. Like a seed, all it needs is a power source and raw materials. Vulcan is very rich in raw materials, isn't it?'

'And the power they're getting from *us*,' Quinn said bitterly. 'But what's it used for?'

'You heard Lesterson,' the Doctor told him. 'The Daleks are reproducing. Who knows how many there are of them by now?' His ears suddenly caught a noise from inside the capsule. A Dalek glided out of the capsule. It was one of the unarmed ones, which meant that they were still keeping up their pretence of slavery to the humans. The Doctor pushed Quinn down behind a stack of boxes and crouched down beside him.

Valmar followed one of the Daleks out of the capsule, checking the connections on the latest cable as he did so.

'I'll just have to check out the completed circuit now,' he informed the Dalek. 'Otherwise, it looks like it's exactly as you asked for it to be.'

'Very well,' the Dalek agreed.

Still troubled by what Polly had said, Valmar stared at the machine thoughtfully. 'Why can't you carry on with the power you're drawing from the colony? Why go to all this trouble?'

'Until now,' the Dalek answered, 'we have had to recharge from the colony supply. With static power in place, the Daleks will be twice as . . . useful.'

Valmar wondered if he had imagined that slight pause

between the final words. Could he believe the Daleks? Or was this all some Machiavellian plot of theirs? If only he had the time to do a few experiments and check on the data he'd been fed. But time was one thing that he seemed to be constantly short of. Another was his implicit belief that what he was doing was right. He made a useless rebel, really. If it hadn't been for Hensell's attitude and the injustice of the Company, he'd never have considered joining the rebels.

And, to be honest, if it hadn't been for his foolish attraction to Janley. She'd never given him the slightest encouragement, after all. But he lived in constant hope that one day she would do.

As if in answer to his thoughts, Janley herself rushed through the doorway, skidding to a halt.

'Valmar!' she snapped, her face flushed and her hair in uncharacteristic disarray. 'Quick, come on!'

'What's the matter?' he asked, rushing to join her.

'The Governor's back,' she told him. 'We're not yet ready! Come on!'

Valmar glanced back at the capsule. 'What about the girl?'

'Leave her,' Janley said. 'The Daleks will take care of her.'

The unarmed Dalek moved to join them. 'I will follow you,' it informed Janley.

Suspiciously, Valmar glared at it. 'What for?'

'I am your servant.'

There wasn't time to argue. Janley grabbed Valmar's arm, hurrying him out into the corridor. The Dalek glided after them.

A moment after the Dalek left the room, the Doctor popped out of his hiding place. He stared at the mass of cables in concern. 'An electrical circuit of their own,' he said, his voice strained with fear. 'They're supplying their own static electricity to the colony. I wonder how much longer we've got?'

'Till what?' Quinn asked.

'When the circuit is in operation, the Daleks will be able to move freely about the colony,' the Doctor told him. 'And that will be the death warrant for every human being here!' Then he turned, ignoring Quinn, and started into the capsule.

*

Kebble waited near the door of the capsule, a slight smile on his face. He'd overheard two people he recognized as Quinn and the Doctor talking outside the capsule as they approached. He picked up a heavy wrench and tapped his palm with it.

It would make a lovely dent in someone's skull . . .

Polly threw herself across the small compartment. Her hands were tied, but not her legs. And she hadn't been gagged again. 'Doctor!' she screamed. 'Look out!' As Kebble half turned, Polly hit him with all of the force she could muster.

Kebble slammed her back against the metal wall of the capsule, winding her. But Polly's warning had alerted his would-be victims, who were entering the capsule. Quinn pushed past the Doctor and leaped on to Kebble. Glad of a target he could finally take some of his frustrations and anger out on, Quinn pummelled the heavier man with blows to the head and stomach. Huffing with pain, Kebble allowed his guard to drop. With a cry of pent-up anger, Quinn linked both his hands and brought them down in a single, vicious chop to Kebble's neck. Kebble fell like a brick.

Polly staggered to her feet and rushed down to the Doctor. 'Are you all right?' she asked anxiously.

The Doctor nodded and smiled as he undid the ropes about her wrists. 'Quick thinking, Polly,' he complimented her. 'Now, who was that man who left with the Daleks?'

'Valmar,' she told him as she massaged the circulation back into her fingers. 'He's been working with the Daleks.'

'On their static power supply,' the Doctor said, nodding. 'Yes, we heard that bit.'

Polly grabbed him with both hands. 'Doctor, they've got Ben!'

'Yes. He ran away from them when we . . .' Shaking his head, he pulled free of her. 'It's a long story, but I wouldn't be too worried about him. I think that boy can look after himself.' He pointed to the power lines. 'Right now, we have to disable the Daleks.'

There was a sound from the far wall. A door was slowly rising, revealing a Dalek waiting behind it. As soon as it reached the mid-section height, all three of them could see that this Dalek was complete with its gun-stick.

The Doctor snatched up the wrench Kebble had been intending to use. 'Run,' he said grimly.

Quinn eyed the futile weapon. 'That won't stop a Dalek,' he argued.

'Maybe, maybe not,' the Doctor replied. 'Go on – run!'

'But what about – ' Quinn began.

The Doctor gave him and Polly a hearty shove. '*Go on!*'

Quinn grabbed Polly's hand and dragged her from the capsule and into Lesterson's laboratory. They fled through the open doors, the Doctor hot on their heels. Inside the capsule, the door was finally fully open. The armed Dalek glided out, followed by a second. The Doctor paused to close the laboratory doors. Both had a large semicircular handle. He jammed the heavy wrench through the handles, blocking off the door.

On the other side of the doors, the first Dalek stopped. It pushed at the doors to no avail.

'Have they escaped?' the second Dalek asked.

'Yes,' it responded. 'Return to the capsule and report this.'

The second Dalek whirled about. 'I obey.'

The first Dalek slammed into the doors again. They shook, but refused to give. Raising its gun-stick, the Dalek focused the power on a tight beam. Then it began continuous fire. A thin trickle of molten metal ran down the door as it began to cut out the lock.

'Welcome to the new race of the Daleks!'

The latest Dalek off the assembly line moved to join the others in the plant. Behind it, another rolled into place for final cleaning before moving along.

The Dalek at the master panel surveyed the read-outs with satisfaction. A Dalek was being completed every one minute on the human scale of counting. There were now several hundred Daleks spread throughout the capsule.

The latest Dalek glided to join it at the panel. 'Why are we waiting here?' it asked. Its internal computers provided it with the basic information it needed for its tasks, but this specific reason was not in its programming.

'The humans are locked in a power struggle,' the first Dalek answered. 'Shortly, they will begin to fight among themselves.'

'Then we will strike!' The new Dalek understood the logic now.

'Yes. And we will exterminate all humans!'

The mass of Daleks in the room all took up this single thought:

'*EXTERMINATE!*'

25

Every One Must Be Killed

The Doctor stared down in despair at the Dalek gun-stick on Hensell's desk. The killing had finally begun in earnest.

On the floor, Quinn looked up bleakly from the Governor's body. 'The one man who might have saved us,' he said softly. Polly placed a comforting hand on his shoulder, and he managed a wan smile.

'Don't worry,' the Doctor said, with more conviction than he felt. 'The people will follow you, too.' But he knew how often humans milled about in disorder once their leaders were dead. It might take a while for Quinn to gain control, and he doubted that Bragen would simply stand by and allow power to trickle from his greedy grasp.

'Maybe.' Quinn stood up with a sigh. 'But there wasn't any maybe about Hensell. He was old-fashioned and even single-minded, but he did some wonderful work for this colony. The people may have argued sometimes, but they were willing to trust him.' He shook his head. 'Events turned out against him. But why? *Why* was he killed?'

'I can answer that.'

The Doctor, Quinn and Polly spun around. Bragen and two of his armed guards stood in the doorway. The machine guns were trained on them.

'The Governor wanted to have the Daleks destroyed,' Bragen said smoothly. 'So one of them killed him. As a result, I've been forced to declare martial law. You will be returned to prison, properly guarded this time.' He nodded to his men.

'Martial law!' the Doctor said scornfully. 'What good do you think that'll do against the Daleks?'

'The Daleks will do as I tell them,' Bragen replied.

'We'll see about that, shall we?' the Doctor asked, defiantly.

The two guards stood by. 'Take them away,' Bragen said. As the prisoners were marched out, Bragen walked to the window. Dawn was breaking over the surface of Vulcan. The sun, a bloated, blood-red ball, was creeping up over the horizon.

'The dawn of a new day,' Bragen mused. 'A day that will end in a new order for this world – *my* order!'

The Doctor's mind was ticking over frantically as they were marched back towards the cells. His escape trick wouldn't work twice. It was imperative that he remain free, so they had to escape before they were imprisoned. The Daleks were almost ready to strike, now. But what could he do against two men with machine guns?

He came to a sudden halt. The corridor ahead of them was blocked by a single unmoving Dalek.

'Move,' one of the guards ordered, his weapon digging into the Doctor's back.

'The Dalek,' the Doctor replied, in horror.

Polly stared at it. 'What about it?'

'Can't you see?' the Doctor asked her, his face ashen. 'It's armed!'

Polly's face drained of all colour. The Dalek had its gun-stick almost casually pointing to one side of them, but she was under no illusion that it would not be able to train on them all and fire if the Dalek wished it.

The guards seemed unconcerned. 'Keep moving,' the first one insisted, giving Polly a jab with the barrel of his gun. The three prisoners did as they were told.

The gun-stick moved fractionally. It was now centred on the five humans. 'This area is restricted,' the Dalek grated.

'On whose authority?' Quinn demanded, forgetting for a moment that he had none of his own.

The guard slammed the butt of his gun roughly into Quinn's shoulder. 'Silence!' he ordered.

The Dalek's eye-stick moved across the group until it stared at the Doctor. The gun-stick seemed to hesitate a moment. Then the Dalek said: 'Repeat: this area is restricted.'

'Now who's giving the orders?' the Doctor asked softly.

A second Dalek moved into place at an intersection. 'Obey, or you will be exterminated,' it insisted.

'Now what do we do, Doctor?' Polly asked.

'I think we'd better return the way we came, don't you?' The Doctor turned his back carefully and stared at the guards. 'If you can't take us to the cells,' he suggested, 'perhaps we should return to Bragen for further instructions, eh?' Without waiting to see what they would do, he pushed past them and started back down the corridor. Polly and Quinn fell in behind him.

The two guards looked at one another uncertainly. They had lost control of this situation completely. Not wishing to lose their prisoners, they hurried after them back the way they had come.

The two Daleks looked at one another. 'They will all be exterminated,' the second one stated.

The revolution was simpler than anyone had expected. Together, the rebels and Bragen's guards simply moved in on the central areas and took control. Since none of the regular colonists had weapons, the guns of the rebels and the assault rifles of the guards tended to discourage protest. The few who did try and resist were shot down without mercy.

The Hub was taken in minutes and then secured. The rocket pads followed, and then the mine areas. The rebels had won over many of the miners to their side, with promises of fairer work quotas and better conditions. With the perimeter and the interior both secured the vast majority of the colonists accepted the new order.

Without someone to rally behind, the average person wasn't inclined to go up against the guns of the new regime. Neither Hensell nor Quinn had been heard from, and Bragen – the next in line – was the one orchestrating the takeover. No one else really had the authority or charisma to organize resistance.

'It's over,' Janley said with considerable satisfaction as the reports flooded back to her and Bragen. 'We've won! I'll pass along the word to Valmar, Kebble and the rest.'

'Wait!' Bragen held up his hand. Puzzled, Janley stared at him. 'The revolution is not over yet.'

'What more is there to do?' Janley couldn't understand him. 'Hensell is dead and you're now firmly entrenched as Governor.' She shrugged. 'The battle's over.'

'Not quite.' Bragen studied her across his desk, which was now cleared of all paperwork. 'You mentioned Valmar and that rabble. Now they must be dealt with.'

It was obvious what he meant. Janley stared at him in shock. 'But those are your own men. They fought for you.'

'Of course,' he agreed.

'Then . . .' She shook her head. 'I don't understand.'

Bragen realized that he was going to have to spell it out for her. She wanted power almost as badly as he did, but she didn't seem to understand the full ramifications of her lusts. 'Do you think I can ever be secure in this chair with that rabble on the loose? They revolted against Hensell today, tomorrow it will be my turn! One taste of power will not be enough. They will make demands, try to seize more and more. And I will not give it up.' He stood up and moved from behind his desk to join her. He could see the uncertainty in her eyes. 'Let them revolt! Tell them that the guards have seized control. Urge them to attack. Then we will crush them utterly!'

Janley was struggling with herself. The rebels had trusted her to help them. They were good people, on the whole. To betray them as Bragen asked her was almost too much to contemplate. Except . . . 'You said "we",' she whispered.

'Yes.' Bragen gently stroked her cheek. 'We've come a long way, you and I. Are you going to fail me now? We can share this power together.'

Janley still resisted slightly, but her will was failing. Bragen was offering her what she had always desired – power. It was worth trading in the lives of a few miserable fanatics like Valmar. Thane and the rest, surely?

Outside the doorway, Valmar hesitated. He had been on his way to report total success when he had heard Janley and Bragen talk. At first he had hesitated because he did not want

223

to disturb them. Now he listened carefully to what they were planning.

A moment before, he had been exuberant and happier than he had ever been. Now his heart was shrivelling within him. What a fool he had been! Trusting and even loving Janley.

Janley's conscience was still kicking a little. 'Couldn't you just arrest them?' she asked. Her voice was quite faint. She was intoxicated with her dreams.

'No,' Bragen told her. 'Alive, they will be a focus for rebellion once again. Every one must be killed!'

Giddily, Janley murmured: 'Must they all be slaughtered?' Her conscience was in its death-throes.

'All of them,' Bragen confirmed. His eyes glittered as he stroked her hair. 'Well? Are you still with me?' She seemed ready to agree. But, just in case ... His hand reached down to the pistol he wore in his belt. Quietly, he slipped the safety catch off. If she refused him, he didn't dare let her leave this room to warn the others.

Janley finally nodded. 'I suppose so,' she agreed.

Bragen drew his pistol and dropped it on to the desk behind him. 'Then do as I say.' He caught the horrified look she threw at the gun and smiled coldly. 'I'm so glad you agreed with me.'

Janley stared at the pistol with real fear. He would have killed me, she thought. After everything ... He would have killed me!

Outside the room, nursing his bitterness over their betrayal, Valmar hurried away.

The guards leading the Doctor, Polly and Quinn had reasserted themselves. One marched ahead of them, ready to speak with Bragen when they arrived. The second was behind Quinn, watching the prisoners.

Everywhere there were signs of the change of power. Bragen's guards hurried about, along with armed colonists – obviously part of the rebel forces. There were pools of blood on some of the floors, but no signs of bodies. Once in a while there was the subdued sound of gunfire.

Each time, Quinn's face twisted with his own pain. He really cared about the people, that much was obvious.

A Dalek glided out of the cross-corridor just ahead of the Doctor. For a moment, it was between the prisoners and the leading guard. The Doctor was prepared for action, even though he was astonished that a Dalek should provide his opportunity. He whipped his recorder from his inside pocket and jabbed with it at the rear guard's face. 'Now!' he yelled.

The guard threw up his hands instinctively to shield his eyes. Quinn pirouetted and put every ounce of his anger and disgust into the blow that slammed into the guard's stomach. The guard collapsed.

The leading guard spun around at the sounds of struggle. The Dalek's dome swivelled also. It was one of the unarmed Daleks, so it had no weapon to use. For a moment, it hesitated, blocking the guard for reacting with his own machine gun.

'Run!' the Doctor yelled. Arms and legs windmilling, he followed his own advice. Quinn snatched up the unconscious guard's weapon as he and Polly followed their leader.

Valmar pushed Ben back into the rooms the Doctor and his companions had shared. 'Quiet!' he snapped as Ben opened his mouth. He glanced down the empty corridor.

Ben was at a loss to work out what was happening. Valmar had fetched Ben from the storage room he'd been tied up in only to bring him back here. Ben had more than half-expected a bullet in his back at any point on their journey. But Valmar had been careful to hide from any guards they had passed, demanding silence all along. Now Ben wanted some answers. 'What have you brought me here for?' he demanded. 'And just whose side are you on, anyway?'

'The winning side, I thought,' Valmar said bitterly.

'So what changed your mind?'

'Bragen.' Valmar shook his head. 'The colony's suddenly become too small for him to share. He wants all of us rebels out of the way now.'

It was starting to make sense to Ben. 'Yeah,' he said sympathetically. 'It often happens like that, mate, when you follow blokes like him. The promises in the ear, the bullet in the guts.'

Valmar turned to face him. 'Look,' he said, feverishly, 'I'm going to try and get your friends free if I can. You wait here for them, okay?' He didn't wait for an answer. He ran from the room and down the corridor.

Ben stared after him. Now what? Could he trust the bloke? Well, Valmar *had* set him free. And his story made sense. Chafing at the thought of letting someone else do all the action, Ben decided he'd give the man fifteen minutes. Then he'd be off to do what he could on his own.

The comm unit on Bragen's desk beeped for his attention. Bragen slapped the switch, and the screen showed one of his squad leaders. 'Report,' Bragen ordered.

'The rebels are gathering,' the man said, glancing back over his shoulder. We have them all under observation.'

'Excellent. Don't let them concentrate into large groups. Let them think they're unobserved, then hit them before they can link together and organize. They should be ready to make their move any time now.'

'Right,' the squad leader acknowledged. He cut the link.

Bragen stared blankly at the shimmering surface of his desk for a moment. The final hand in this game was about to be played out. He held all of the aces, and the rebels were left with nothing. All that was left was to set the stage for the final executions.

He hit the signal for general transmission over the comm unit. Every unit throughout the colony would carry his words. 'People of Vulcan, this is your new Governor talking to you,' he began.

At the sound of Bragen's voice, Thane glanced up at the comm unit close to her head. She hated the bulk of the weapon she carried, and disliked what she, as a doctor, knew it would do to people. But sometimes you had to act on what you knew was right. They had replaced Hensell's corrupt administration, but they could never leave it in the hands of Bragen. He would be a worse tyrant than Hensell could even have dreamed of becoming.

One of her men ducked into cover beside her. 'Five minutes,' he whispered. Thane nodded.

Above their heads, Bragen's voice droned on: 'I have to announce that Governor Hensell has been murdered by the rebels. I have taken control temporarily until order is restored.'

In one of the rest rooms, Lesterson listened with half an ear to Bragen's droning. His other ear was pressed against the door. The guards had thrown him in here when the fighting had begun and locked him in. He had worked carefully on picking the lock, all the while hearing gun-shots and screams. It had fallen silent outside now, and he eased the door open a crack. The corridor was clear, save for one mangled body stretched out on the floor in a pool of blood. Lesterson whimpered slightly as he staggered through the doorway and headed back to his laboratory.

All around him, Bragen's detestable voice carried on: 'People living in the perimeter and interior should remain calm. We know who the murderers are.'

A squad of four Daleks trundled down the corridor by the sick bay. All of them were armed. They ignored everything that Bragen was saying. It could not possibly be of any interest to them.

'I shall keep you informed of events as soon as I can,' Bragen finished. 'So listen for the signal again on your comm units. That is all.' He switched off the transmitter and sat back in his chair with a smile. There! The people were reassured. They knew that Bragen's firm but benevolent hand was protecting them. All was well with the world.

Ben stood behind the door as it burst open. In his upraised hand he held a table lamp ready to brain whoever was breaking in.

'Ah, there you are,' the Doctor said, cheerfully plucking the lamp from Ben's numb fingers. 'I knew you'd be all right.'

'Ben!' Polly ran in and gave him a huge hug.

227

'Pol!' He liked this bit, at least. 'Are you okay?'

'I am now.' She pulled free of his grip.

Reluctantly, he let her go. Glancing at the Doctor, he said: 'Valmar found you, did he?'

'No,' Polly replied, puzzled.

Quinn was standing guard in the doorway, the machine gun in his arms at the ready. 'What's this about Valmar?' he demanded.

'Seems Bragen's gone power mad,' Ben explained. 'He's inciting the rebels to revolt so he can have them all finished off.'

'Imbeciles!' the Doctor muttered. 'The Daleks don't care who they fight. They'll exterminate every single human being on this planet. Bragen's simply playing into their hands by killing the rebels off.' He made up his mind and tapped Quinn on the shoulder. 'Stay here,' he ordered. 'Keep them with you.' He shot off down the corridor.

'Hey!' Ben yelled. 'Wait for me!' He tried to leave, but Quinn pushed him back.

'The Doctor seems to know what he's doing,' he told Ben. 'So do as he asks, and stay here. Okay?'

Ben wasn't as certain as Quinn about the Doctor's mental state. Aside from the confusion from his bout of renewal, the situation they were in was enough to send anybody cuckoo. But since Quinn had their only weapon and also, apparently, the will to use it, this probably wasn't the best time to question his orders. Ben settled back to wait.

The Daleks all stood still for a moment throughout the colony. Their inbuilt computers registered a transmission from the capsule.

'*Exterminate all humans!*'

'Orders received,' each Dalek sent back. 'Commencing extermination.'

With their guns set on full intensity, the hundreds of Daleks now on the loose in the corridors moved off again to locate their victims.

The Doctor ran headlong down the corridor towards Lesterson's laboratory. That was the heart of the Dalek power, and his only chance of stopping them. It was imperative that he act now, or the colony was doomed.

Skidding around a corner, his arms flailing as he tried to keep his balance, he almost collided with a band of the rebels. At their head was Kebble. He still had a sore neck thanks to the Doctor, and obviously intended to settle the score.

'Just a moment, Examiner,' he snapped.

The Doctor spun about, but one of the three rebels with Kebble had slipped behind him, his weapon upraised. 'Hold it!' the man snapped.

Turning back, the Doctor's eyes widened in horror. 'Get down, all of you!' he yelled, flinging himself on to Kebble.

The startled rebel collapsed under the Doctor's weight. The attack saved his life. The Dalek that had just rounded the corner fired. One of the rebels screamed out in death agony as the Dalek's ray hit him. The Dalek spun about to fire on the remaining two rebels. As it did so, the Doctor hauled Kebble to his feet.

'Run like the wind!' he yelled, and dashed off down the corridor.

The Dalek fired again. The two rebels screamed. One had managed to bring his gun up. In his death agony, his finger tightened on the trigger. Bullets whined off the Dalek's casing, doing little more than gashing the finish. As the two men collapsed, the Dalek pushed them unfeelingly aside and set off in pursuit of the two remaining targets.

26

You Have to Admire Them

In Lesterson's laboratory, Valmar sighed and put down his tools. The three Daleks he had rearmed stared impassively back at him. Each of them had one of Valmar's control boxes wired into their weapons. The rebel felt more secure, knowing he had some effective fire power at last. He had no doubt at all that it would be needed.

There was the sound of running feet outside in the corridor. He snatched up the closest of the controls and whirled to face the door. His heart sank like a cold, leaden stone within him as Janley dashed into the room. 'Don't come any nearer,' he warned her. How could he ever have loved her?

'What do you mean?' she asked. She looked scared, not her usual confident self, and very vulnerable. Despite his knowledge of her betrayal, Valmar felt sorry for her.

'I overheard your conversation with Bragen,' he said bitterly. 'But neither of you can stand up to the Daleks. Your schemes will come to nothing.'

'Not my plan,' she insisted, 'Bragen's.'

'It's the same thing.'

Janley shook her head. 'Not any more.'

He laughed scornfully. 'Do you expect me to believe that?'

'I had to go along with him,' she protested. 'He was going to kill me too, if he thought I was against him. I didn't know you were here.' She put all the conviction she could into her voice. 'I came here to do what you've just done: show Bragen the power of the Daleks. He has no real idea how strong they are. He's got to be stopped.'

Valmar wanted to believe her, but he had been betrayed once. Whatever she said, she *had* been willing to betray them all and let Bragen assume power. The only thing that seemed to have swayed her was the prospect of massacring the rebels. *If* she was telling the truth this time. Still, even if she were going up against Bragen simply out of self-preservation, she could be a useful ally.

As he pondered, one of the Daleks spoke to him. 'You will lead us to the middle of your party of human beings?'

It must mean the rebel leaders, Valmar realized. 'Yes,' he agreed. While he didn't exactly trust the Daleks either, they were powerless as long as he held the firing controls.

'Then we will fight for you,' the Dalek stated.

Janley nodded, urgently. 'Believe me, Val, we have to do it. It's the only way to save all of our lives.'

Still hesitating, Valmar asked her: 'Did you know that the Daleks are duplicating themselves?'

'Yes,' Janley replied. That much had been obvious from Lesterson's rantings. And it did explain their need for electricity and parts.

'But we are your friends,' the Dalek argued.

'We will serve you,' the second one added.

'Take us to the centre of your group,' the third one finished.

Valmar wavered. 'Can we trust them?' he asked Janley.

'We must,' she insisted. 'Bragen's given his guards the order to wipe us all out. We *must* use the Daleks to fight them. Come on!'

Reluctantly, still convinced he was making a mistake, Valmar nodded. He handed her one of the Daleks' firing controls and took the other two himself. 'All right,' he sighed. 'Let's go.'

For good or ill, he had committed them to this line of action.

Without warning, the Doctor dashed past Quinn and into the rest room. His eyes darted about the cramped quarters, coming to rest finally on the picture window. 'Does this window open?' he asked his companions.

Ben glanced at it. 'Dunno.'

'Well, it'd better, or we're done for,' the Doctor answered, feverishly trying to work the latch. Quinn pushed him aside and snapped the lock back.

'What do you mean?' Polly asked. The Doctor seemed in a state of virtual panic.

'The Daleks are on the loose,' he replied, throwing up the window. 'The corridors are full of them. We've got to get back to Lesterson's lab immediately. Outside is our only chance! Come along!'

Polly didn't need a second invitation; she shot through the glass and out on to the bare rocks beyond. Ben and Quinn followed her out, while the Doctor bounced up and down impatiently, his eyes darting back and forth between the window and the door.

There was a burst of machine-gun fire in the corridor outside, and Kebble threw himself inside the room. His mouth opened in shock, and then there came the rattle of a Dalek gun firing. Kebble screamed as he died, falling face-down on the floor.

The Doctor hopped through the window and ran for his life after the other three.

Kebble's body was pushed aside by the Dalek that had killed him. Entering the room, its eye-stick swung about, scanning for other life. It came to focus on the open window and the recent heat-traces.

Now that the final round was being played out, Bragen allowed himself to feel a sense of triumph. He stared out at the surface of Vulcan, *his* world. Even now, the guards would be slaughtering the remnant of the rebels and imposing his order on the entire colony. Deciding it was time for another reassuring word with his subjects, he returned to his desk and tapped the broadcast button on his comm unit.

'A group of rebels is attempting to take over the colony,' his voice rang out through the corridors and rooms. 'It is the duty of all loyal citizens to help the guards resist them. Stay in your rooms. Order will be restored. Listen for my bulletins.'

Four Daleks glided into the terminal of the moving sidewalk. There were few people left here. Two rebels were dead on the floor, and several guards were ushering workers into cover.

The Daleks spread out and opened fire. Screaming in spasms of agony, guards and workers alike fell in the blaze of Dalek guns.

'Exterminate all humans!'

Thane and the three rebels left with her fell back towards the rocket room. There they had planned this insane fiasco. It seemed to be an appropriate place to end it. The medic was under no illusion that any of them would survive. The guards had them trapped and possessed riot shields and better weapons.

Her second kicked open the door behind them, and she ducked in with him. There was a judder of shots, and the other man collapsed, his body riddled with holes. Thane loosed off a burst, which splattered against the shields ineffectually.

'We're dead,' her companion said. All anger and fear had drained from his voice hours ago. Only resignation was left.

'Maybe.' Thane refused to surrender her hopes. Then she saw a new reason for them: two Daleks had entered the corridor behind the guards. Were these Valmar's pets?

The guards glanced back, but didn't seem to be worried. It was their final mistake.

Both Daleks opened fire, saturating the three guards with lethal blasts. The men collapsed, their screams cut off by death.

'They're helping us!' Thane's companion shouted happily. He leaped to his feet, waving his thanks.

The Daleks' next burst cut him down, his face caught half-way between elation and terror.

'Exterminate all humans!' the Daleks grated, closing in on Thane. She fired off a burst from her gun, shocked. Her body was acting on instinct, her mind a total blank. The bullets whined off in all directions, not even denting the Dalek metal. She threw herself backwards as the Daleks fired.

She was dead before her body hit the ground.

Bragen heard the sounds of rifle-fire and screams. He smiled happily to himself. The rebels were doomed. Soon, soon . . .

One of his squad leaders dashed into the room, terror on

his face. 'The rebels!' he cried. 'They're using the Daleks to kill our people!'

Stunned, Bragen reacted with anger. 'Well, fight them, then! Don't come whining to me! What do you think your guns are for?'

'Guns don't work against the Daleks,' the man replied. 'They're annihilating us!'

Furiously, Bragen gave the man a violent shove. The guard stumbled back into the doorway. 'Get back out there and fight them!' Bragen ordered. He held up his pistol. 'Or, by heavens, I'll shoot you down like a dog!'

The guard eyed Bragen's pistol, clearly weighing up his chances of dying outside against the certainty of death right here. Finally, he turned and ran into the corridor outside.

Janley and Valmar walked behind two of the Daleks, protected by their armour, as they worked their way down a corridor towards Bragen's office. The rebels had set up a barrier there, which the guards were storming. One rebel died in the hail of bullets as they approached.

Pointing at the guards, Janley ordered the Dalek: 'There!'

It fired, and the two guards rushing the barricade collapsed in the lethal rays. Then the Dalek twisted to bring its weapon to bear on two of the rebels.

'No!' Janley ordered. 'They're on our side.' She hit the cut-off button.

It had no effect. The Dalek gun fired, mowing down the startled rebels.

Valmar was shocked. 'You were supposed to cut the gun off!' He was obviously thinking that she had betrayed him after all.

'I did!' she insisted, showing him the control.

'It killed our own men,' Valmar said. 'Must be a flaw in the programming. We'll have to dismantle this one, that's all.'

The Dalek pulled away from Janley, and spun to face them. Its gun-stick rose.

'Look at it!' Janley screamed.

The two Daleks that Valmar was leading jerked forward,

whipping the control boxes from his hands. Then they turned as well.

The box had never worked, Valmar realized. The Daleks had been deceiving them all along.

'Exterminate all humans!'

Before they could open fire, the Daleks were attacked from the rear. The remainder of the guards in the corridor leaped the barricades, machine guns blazing. The three Daleks spun around to fire on the more dangerous foes.

Grabbing Valmar, who was in a state of shock, Janley dragged him to the temporary safety of a side corridor. 'Come on!' she yelled.

Quinn stopped beside a window. 'This is the closest to Lesterson's laboratory,' he announced.

Ben tried it. 'It's locked on the inside,' he complained.

Quinn smashed the butt of his machine gun against it. 'Not now, it isn't,' he replied, smiling slightly. He used the butt to clear away the glass as Ben reached in to unlatch the window and open it. Quinn went through first. As the others clambered into the room, he dodged past the bed and into the outer room. Nobody was home. He opened the outer door just enough to enable him to scan the corridor. A hastily built barricade had been shoved aside. A smouldering corpse lay atop it. There were no signs of life at all.

'All clear,' he reported, as the Doctor and his companions joined him.

'Right,' the Doctor said. 'Now, let's head for the lab. Stay together, everyone.'

'No,' Quinn said. 'Look, I'm no good here.' He held up the gun. 'And this is useless against the Daleks. I'm going after Bragen. If I can make him see that this in-fighting is only helping the Daleks, maybe we have a chance.'

The Doctor sighed. 'I wouldn't like to bet on your chances of getting Bragen to see reason,' he replied. 'But I understand that you have to try. Good luck.'

'He'll see either reason or the business end of a bullet,' Quinn promised. With a nod, he set off over the barrier.

'A brave man,' the Doctor murmured. 'Right, let's go.' He

led Ben and Polly quickly down the stretch of corridor to the laboratory doors. There were bullet holes in the walls, and scorch marks all over the floor, but the room was empty of Daleks.

To their utter astonishment, Lesterson's head popped up behind a stack of crates. He looked very calm, and he beckoned them over to join him.

As they did so, Polly stared at him. 'It's madness to hide in here.'

'Do you fancy your chances in the corridors?' Ben asked. 'The guards are bound to have orders to kill us, and the Daleks are just murdering everyone!'

'Ssh!' Lesterson insisted. He pointed towards the capsule, which was barely visible through a narrow crack in the stack of supplies.

A Dalek emerged from the portal and glided out of the laboratory door.

'They're still turning out new Daleks,' Lesterson explained. His voice had an unnatural calmness to it. 'You must be absolutely quiet. They know everything that's going on. They even know what you're thinking.'

The Doctor gnawed on his knuckles as he stared at the scientist. Ben and Polly exchanged worried looks. It was quite clear that Lesterson had finally cracked under the strain.

Ben turned his gaze on the cables that snaked across the floor. He gestured at them. 'Where are they drawing their power from?' he asked.

'Oh, I tried to turn the power off,' Lesterson replied dreamily, 'but they were miles ahead of me. Marvellous creatures.' He smiled at the three of them. 'You have to admire them, don't you?'

'Well, I don't!' Ben retorted. 'We've got to stop them.'

Lesterson shook his head. 'It's far too late for that.' He spoke like a person who had undergone a religious conversion and had finally seen the light. 'They're the new species, you see, taking over from Homo sapiens. Mankind's had its day.' He smiled again, happily. 'We're finished.' Then he held up a finger to his lips for silence.

Another Dalek came out of the capsule. The previous one

236

returned to the laboratory. 'The static circuit is nearly completed,' this one reported.

'Then we can soon abandon the power source we are currently using,' the Dalek in the capsule stated.

There was a fresh burst of gunfire some distance away. It was followed by several screams.

'All humans are now being exterminated,' the first Dalek stated. It returned to the capsule, and both of them disappeared inside again.

'Doctor,' Ben whispered in horror. 'Did you hear them? They're almost ready to use their own power now.'

'The cables they've laid all over the colony,' the Doctor agreed. 'It will allow them to set up a static charge throughout.' He chewed on his lower lip. 'The trick I used on them before won't work now.'

'Don't worry,' Lesterson told him, smiling happily. 'It's far too late. We're all finished. All we can do is to marvel at the creatures taking our place.' He beamed at them all.

Janley led Valmar towards the laboratory. Maybe there was still time to stop the Daleks. They were still drawing their power from the colony's generators, so she and Valmar together might be able to cobble up something to stop that drain. 'Come on,' she called over her shoulder to Valmar.

'No.' He stopped. 'That way's too dangerous.'

'Come on,' she insisted.

Valmar stood uncertainly. He jumped as Quinn suddenly appeared from a side corridor. Quinn grabbed hold of Valmar's arm. 'Let her go,' he said.

'She's out in the open,' Valmar argued. 'Don't be a fool!' he called to Janley.

She turned to face him.

Behind her, a Dalek moved into killing position. Hearing it, she twisted to face it. 'No!' she cried. 'I helped you!'

It didn't even bother to reply. Its gun-stick aimed and fired.

In her final split-second of life, Janley realized how futile her quest had been. She had wanted power so badly, and had been willing to work with Lesterson, Valmar, Bragen or anyone else who was willing to help her. But none of them had true power. Only the Daleks did. And they were willing to help no one.

She screamed, a mixture of agony and lost hopes. Her body fell to the ground, smouldering slightly.

Janley's death scream had been clearly audible in the laboratory. Polly shuddered, realizing that it might be her own throat crying out next as the Daleks continued their killing spree. They would not rest as long as any human remained alive on Vulcan.

Ben placed a comforting arm about her. 'Steady on, Pol,' he said.

'Can't we do anything?' she demanded. 'They're murdering everybody, one by one.' She glowered at Lesterson. 'It's all your fault!' she accused. 'You did this. Why did you ever give them power in the first place?'

The Doctor shook his head slightly. 'I think he knows that he's to blame, Polly,' he said softly. 'That's why he's retreated into madness. He simply cannot face the guilt.'

'I could control it,' Lesterson said to her, as if trying to justify his actions. 'The Daleks were only allowed what I would give them. But Janley got one of her men, Valmar I think.' He nodded decisively. 'Yes, that's the one. He rigged up a secret cable. It's carrying power directly from the colony supply.'

That caught the Doctor's attention. 'Another cable?' He grabbed Lesterson's arms and shook him roughly. 'Where? Where is it, Lesterson?'

'You'd have to ask Valmar,' the scientist replied. 'He's the only one who could answer that. Or the Daleks, of course. They know everything. Yes, you know, you should ask the Daleks.'

Ben shook his head. 'We'll have to find Valmar, then,' he said to the Doctor.

'If he's still alive,' Polly said. 'The Daleks are murdering everyone. Everyone!'

The Doctor came to a quick decision. 'You stay here with him and Polly,' he told Ben. 'I'll see what I can do.' He popped his head out for a quick look at the capsule. As there was no sign of Dalek activity, he hopped to his feet and dashed out of the door.

The corridor was still empty. He scuttled down it, heading for the source of the scream they had heard. If there was anyone left alive, that was their most likely location. As he ran around the corner, he almost stumbled over Quinn and Valmar.

As soon as the Dalek had killed Janley, it had set off after fresh victims. Valmar had run out of hiding and cradled Janley's dead head in his lap. He stroked her hair gently.

'You've got to leave her,' Quinn urged, looking about for further Daleks.

'You don't understand,' Valmar said softly. 'She wasn't as bad as you think. Really she wasn't.'

The Doctor moved over to join them. At the end of the corridor a guard suddenly ran into view. Before any of them could react, he arched in a death spasm, a soul-wrenching scream tearing from his mouth.

'Get down, both of you!' the Doctor said urgently, falling to the floor himself. He pulled his jacket up over his head.

Around the corner came a Dalek. It moved past the dead guard and towards the clutter of bodies further down. For a moment it paused and scanned the group of four fallen figures. Their body heat seemed to be high. Then it caught sight of the tell tale marking of death on the female human. They had been killed very recently, which explained their heat-retention.

It moved away and down the next side corridor.

The Doctor sat up, letting out a sigh of relief. 'Valmar,' he whispered urgently. 'Where is the Daleks' power supply?'

There was no response from the technician. He was staring mutely at Janley's face, which was still beautiful even in death. Quinn grabbed his shoulders and shook him hard.

'We've got to stop them, Valmar. She's dead. We all will be if we don't stop the Daleks. You can't do anything for her, but you can still help the rest of us.'

With an effort, Valmar managed to wrench himself out of the bleakness of spirit in which he had been wallowing. 'The . . . the main cable's inside the capsule,' he told the

Doctor, his voice dead and drained of all emotion. 'But there's nothing you can do.'

'There must be some way to cut the power off,' Quinn urged.

The Doctor looked at him in astonishment. 'What makes you think I want to do that?' Before Quinn could question that outrageous query, the Doctor added, 'We must have more time. A diversion!'

'What?' Quinn was hopelessly baffled.

'You were off to see Bragen, weren't you? Well, he must have more guards. We must use them to keep the Daleks occupied. You've got to get to Bragen – now.'

Quinn nodded. 'I'll do what I can.' He patted Valmar encouragingly on the shoulder and then set off as fast as he could.

'Right,' the Doctor said, hauling Valmar to his feet. 'We've got work to do. Come on!' If they only had the time to do it.

27

The Law of the Daleks is in Force

Throughout the corridors, there were dead bodies everywhere. Some were rebels, slain by Bragen's guards. Some were guards, shot in the fighting. The vast majority of the corpses, though, had been gunned down by the Daleks. As Quinn moved, he constantly had to hide from parties of two, three and even four of the murderous machines. There seemed to be hundreds of them, all over the colony. The sounds of fighting and resistance were growing fainter. Few humans still held out in the Hub.

Even if the Doctor could pull a miracle out of thin air, how many would be left after all this?

Bragen raged about his office, fuming. What had happened to his men? Where were the nice, orderly reports that he demanded? How was he supposed to run a colony if his men wouldn't keep him updated? He stopped at his desk and snapped on the comm unit.

'Section One,' he yelled, 'where is your report? Are you there, Section One?' As before, there was no reply. What the devil were they doing? 'Section Two!' he screamed. 'Why don't you answer me? Three?' There was nothing but static. 'I am the Governor!' he howled. 'Why won't you answer me?'

His face twisted with frustration, Bragen slammed his fists down on the unit. What was going on? Why wouldn't his men reply?

Was it possible that the squad leader was right? Could the Daleks conceivably be working with the rebels? Well, it didn't matter if they were. He knew how to deal with that. He tapped on the controls for a general broadcast. Then he composed his thoughts and voice. It wouldn't do to sound worried.

'This is Governor Bragen speaking. This is to the Daleks. Daleks, listen to me!' Despite his intentions, his voice rose to almost a whine. 'I am the Governor! You must work for *me*. Do not trust the rebels. I will give you whatever you want. Immobilize your guns. *This is the Governor speaking!*'

In the laboratory, Ben stared incredulously at the speaker in the wall. 'He's off his chump,' he announced. 'Trying to bargain with the Daleks!'

'There is no need,' Lesterson agreed. 'They will take over anyway.' He stared in awe at the capsule. 'There are more of them on their way.'

Ben didn't care for the thought. He glanced around and saw a cabinet, close to the capsule, but pushed to one side. 'What's in there?'

'Nothing,' Lesterson replied. 'It's quite empty.'

'Good.' Ben pulled Polly to her feet. 'In there, quick.' He shoved her inside and jumped in after her, pulling the door almost closed. Through the slight gap they saw several Daleks emerge from the capsule and then move out into the corridor.

Bragen fumed as he sat at his desk. The Daleks had not replied to his demands either. Was his control falling apart about him? Why wouldn't anyone tell him what was going on? How could he govern in a state like this?

'Do you hear me, Daleks?' he yelled into the comm unit again. His voice came back, tinny and panicked. 'You will obey my orders!'

There was a movement in the doorway. For a second, Bragen thought it was his squad leader, coming finally to report. But behind the muzzle of the guard's gun stood a grim-faced Quinn.

'It's no use, Bragen,' he said. 'The Daleks have finally shown their true colours. They've stopped obeying *all* orders.'

Rising to his feet, Bragen half-reached for his pistol, which lay on the desk. A quick motion from Quinn with the barrel of the gun stopped that. 'Guards!' Bragen screamed.

242

'It's no use, Bragen,' Quinn told him bitterly. 'They're all dead. The Daleks have slaughtered them all.' He crossed to the desk. 'But you must still have your guard units in the interior. How long will it take them to get here?'

'It depends,' Bragen hedged.

'Order them in here!' Quinn waved the gun at him. 'Now.'

'But the Daleks will hear me and intercept them!' Bragen protested.

'Exactly,' Quinn agreed. 'That will draw the Daleks away from here. It should give the Doctor time to deal with them.'

Those guards were Bragen's last men; without them, he would be finished. 'I refuse to allow my guards to be sacrificed.'

'Haven't you been listening?' Quinn demanded. 'The Daleks are killing everybody! Those guards are as good as dead already. If you bring them in to fight the Daleks, at least they won't die pointlessly. As you will do in five seconds . . .'

Angrily, Bragen hit the key on the comm unit. 'All guards! This is Bragen speaking. All units must report to the Hub immediately. Be prepared to face rebel Daleks.' He cut the signal and glared at Quinn. 'There. Satisfied?' His face twisted into a sneer.

Quinn held his weapon firmly on Bragen. 'I only hope it works.'

Returning to Lesterson's laboratory, the Doctor paused to check that there were no Daleks inside. Then he slid in carefully, Valmar sticking close to him. There was no sign of Ben or Polly. The Doctor called out softly to them.

The cupboard door opened quietly and Ben and Polly emerged, looking shaken.

'Did you hear that announcement?' Valmar asked them. 'Let's hope that the Daleks have all gone to take on the guards.'

'A lot of them just came out of the capsule,' Polly replied. 'They went down the outer corridor a moment or two ago.'

'Good,' the Doctor said, rubbing his hands together. 'Then I'm going inside.' Before anyone could stop him, he shot through the capsule opening.

243

Ben started to move after the Doctor, but as he did so, the scruffy little man reappeared. He was carrying one of the junction boxes Valmar had fitted earlier into the craft. Long cables trailed after him.

'Is this it?' he asked Valmar.

'That's one of them,' the technician agreed.

'Right.' The Doctor set it on the workbench. 'Ben, get me one of the short cables over there. Polly, keep watch by the door. Valmar, keep your eye on the capsule.' Pulling a screwdriver and wrench set from the scattered tools on the bench, the Doctor began to take the junction box apart. The others hurried to do as he asked. As Ben handed him the short cable he'd requested, the Doctor stared at the mass of wiring within the box. It looked more complicated than he had expected. Nervously, he wrenched free one of the wires. Then he took Ben's cable. He looked uncertainly at his companion, then back at the box. Taking one end of the cable, he held it out gingerly, then plunged it into the place he'd torn the wire from. He had his eyes screwed shut. Carefully, he opened one of them and stared suspiciously at his makeshift connection.

Ben could stand it no more. 'Do you know what you're doing?' he asked.

The Doctor looked offended. 'Of course I do!'

'Really?' Ben asked sceptically. As the Doctor wired in the cable to the box, he added: 'Why don't you just pull all of their plugs out and cut off the power?'

'Because,' the Doctor said, miffed, 'I prefer to do things my way.'

Before Ben could think of a suitable retort, Polly called a warning from the doorway, then ran bck to join them. Valmar, a worried expression on his face, pointed to the capsule, then moved to be with them. The four of them ducked behind the workbench as one Dalek came through the lab doors and another emerged to meet it from the capsule. The Doctor's eyes were rivetted on the edge of the bench. He could just see the end of the small cable.

'Static power is being stored,' the Dalek from the capsule announced. 'We can now dismantle the humans' electrical system.'

244

'The Law of the Daleks is in force,' the second Dalek replied. 'All humans are being exterminated.'

The first Dalek moved from the capsule. Its eye-stick followed the lines of Lesterson's original cable. Then it locked on the box that sat on the workbench. 'Our cables have been moved!'

The four refugees behind the bench held their breaths. They could hear the Daleks moving towards the bench, and inevitable discovery.

Suddenly, Lesterson jumped to his feet on the far side of the lab. 'And I could tell you who moved it,' he said, cheerily.

The Daleks spun around to face him. 'What are you doing in here?' the first one demanded.

'I came to help you,' Lesterson replied. 'I know that you are the superior beings.'

As the Daleks regarded Lesterson, the Doctor pushed the other end of the cable home in the junction box. Then he grabbed the loose end of the wire he had disconnected. Ben looked at him expectantly, but the Doctor shook his head: *stay where you are!* Then, carefully, making no sounds, the Doctor began to inch his way towards the generator, trailing the wire to the junction box beside him.

'Why do you want to help us?' the Dalek demanded of Lesterson.

The scientist smiled insanely. 'I am your servant,' he announced, in a stiff impression of their own voices.

'We do not need servants,' the Dalek replied. It raised its gun.

Lesterson stared at the Dalek in confusion. 'Surely you wouldn't kill *me*?' he said. 'I gave you life!'

'Yes,' the Dalek agreed. 'You gave us life. We give you death.' Its gun spat. ·

The deadly jolt of power shook Lesterson. As it cut off, he dropped lifelessly to the floor. The Daleks turned from him and moved towards the workbench again.

Polly and Ben were directly in their view now. The guns inched upwards.

Frantically, the Doctor rammed home the wire he held into

245

the generator linkages. He gave the unit a quick smile that was suddenly wiped away when nothing happened. Had he miscalculated? In a frenzy, he jumped up at the panel. The power was turned off. Of course! Lesterson had said he'd shut it down, without effect.

The Daleks whirled around to gun down the Doctor. Feverishly, he twisted the power modulator to full setting.

There was a whine as the generator came to full power.

In the centre of the room, the two Daleks suddenly began to spin in unison. Their lights strobed, and smoke began to emerge from every crack in their casings. Both issued mechanical screeches that increased in intensity. Then, in a flash of light and thunder, the domes of both Daleks exploded.

Quinn and Bragen whirled around as a Dalek moved into the office.

Its gun was aimed. 'Exterminate all humans!' it said.

Quinn was staring at his own death.

In a whine of mechanical agony, the Dalek suddenly went into some kind of frenzy that ended with billowing smoke and an explosion as its top half erupted in flames.

'What happened to it?' Bragen asked, astonished.

'I don't know.'

'It appears that your friend the Doctor was successful after all,' Bragen said.

The guards were retreating down the corridors away from the Hub. An endless stream of Daleks was converging on the small area. In a few moments, they would all be dead.

Then the Daleks began to spin on the spot, in some kind of wild dervish dance. Smoke and fire spat from their casings, and then they all blew apart.

The bewildered guards stared at the masses of blazing metal.

Quinn stared at the burning Dalek, elation flooding into him. The Doctor had done it! The Daleks were all being destroyed! Despite the sickening stench emerging from the body of the machine, he felt a huge wave of relief.

Then Bragen hit him from behind. Quinn fell to the floor,

the machine gun clattering from his fingers. Bragen scooped it up and stood over his fallen foe. There was a fanatical gleam in Bragen's eyes.

'Now I shall restore law and order on this planet.'

Disgusted with his stupidity, and with Bragen's megalomania, Quinn shook his head. 'Not "your" law, Bragen. That's finished for good.'

'You'll obey me,' Bragen insisted, swinging the gun to cover Quinn. 'Or you will die.'

'Your day is over,' Quinn replied. 'No one will obey you now.' After all he had been through, Quinn had no fear of what was to come.

Bragen's face twisted in fury. 'I am still the Governor!' he snarled, and tightened his finger on the trigger.

A shot rang out, but Quinn felt nothing. Then the gun rattled as it hit the floor in front of him. Quinn looked up. Bragen, his face a mask of pain, held a hand clutched over his right shoulder. Blood was spurting from a gaping wound there, flowing over fingers and uniform in a bright flood.

Valmar, still panting from his efforts to reach the office, stumbled into the room. In his hand he held one of the dead guard's pistols. It was trained on Quinn.

'Valmar,' Bragen began. His voice had lost some of the imperiousness now, as he struggled with pain. 'You must do what I say and – '

'Enough!' Everything that had happened here in the past few days was Bragen's fault, Valmar knew. The rebellion, the oppression, the murders, even the powering of the Daleks had been because Bragen had wanted a weapon. And Janley's death had been directly due to Bragen. Without remorse, Valmar fired again.

Bragen choked on his own blood and staggered forwards. Then his heart gave a final spasm. Valmar's third bullet went through his brain, killing him instantly.

'Thank you,' Quinn said, climbing to his feet. He looked down at Bragen's body. 'It was a near thing.'

'He deserved it,' Valmar said, without pity. Then he threw the pistol down in the pool of blood. 'Enough of guns. We have so much to do.'

247

Quinn nodded and offered his hand. 'We must rebuild – together.' Valmar accepted the grip. 'What is the extent of the damage?'

'I don't know,' Valmar replied. 'I don't even know if it's possible to repair. So much devastation . . .'

'Then we'd better check, hadn't we?'

As Quinn entered Lesterson's smoke-filled laboratory, Valmar was beside him. Both carried pads as they were assessing the damage. People were starting to emerge now that the fighting was over and the Daleks smouldering ruins. Quinn knew he'd have to get on to the comm units and broadcast a plea for unity soon, but he wanted to be able to give out some concrete information on their status when he did so.

Polly and Ben looked up from where they crouched beside the Doctor's still form.

Quinn's heart almost failed him. 'Is he all right?'

'He's okay,' Ben replied, grinning. 'He just took a jolt of power and knocked himself out.'

As they spoke, the Doctor's eyes flickered open. His initial terrified expression calmed into a big, lop-sided grin as he realized that they were all still alive.

Quinn elbowed past the smoking Dalek casing. 'It was a miracle,' he told the Doctor. 'How did you do it?'

The Doctor hated explanations. 'What happened?' he asked, feigning ignorance. That often worked. Clambering to his feet with Ben's help, he stared as if in shock at the wreckage of the Daleks. Smoke was billowing out of the mouth of the capsule, too. He put a finger to his mouth, like a guilty school-boy. 'Oh dear, what did I do?'

Ben clapped him on the back, grinning wildly. 'You destroyed the Daleks, that's what you did.'

Polly added: 'Don't be so modest!'

With a satisfied smile on his face, the Doctor looked around him. 'Did I do all this?'

'You know you did,' Polly accused him.

Valmar laughed. 'You used the power from the colony's generators and amplified it, then fed it back into their static

248

power lines. It sent massive surges through the Daleks and blew them apart.'

'Did I indeed?' The Doctor looked smugly pleased with himself.

Valmar's tone grew a little less congratulatory. 'You may have stopped the Daleks, Doctor, but do you have any idea of the damage you've done to the colony?'

The Doctor blinked hard and his face fell. 'Oh.' He glanced back at the smouldering wreckage of the power generator. 'Bit of a blow back, was there?' he asked, apologetically.

'A *blow back*?' Valmar couldn't believe it. 'Our power supply has been *destroyed*! It'll be months before we can get things back to normal!'

Quinn gave the technician a dig in the ribs. 'Valmar . . .' He shook his head.

'Oh dear,' the Doctor murmured uncomfortably. He fidgeted under Valmar's glare. 'This *is* unfortunate.'

'He did save all our lives,' Quinn pointed out.

Valmar gestured at the devastated room. 'But did it have to be this way?'

'Did a lot of damage, did I?' the Doctor asked guiltily. Valmar threw up his hands, giving up. The Doctor nudged Ben and Polly. 'Come on,' he whispered. 'I think we'd better get out of here before they send us the bill!'

Epilogue

The surface of Vulcan was unchanged. One day, the Doctor knew, the humans would remake the world. The bleakness would vanish under a canopy of green. The colony would become just the first of many cities. The humans would thrive.

Of course, the next few months would be a bit rough on them. Still, the results should be worth a bit of adversity. Pulling out his recorder, he started to pipe a cherry jib. With his hat back on his head, he felt quite a new man once again.

Ben followed behind, still locked in an argument with Polly he'd begun when they had slipped out of the colony. 'I mean, I didn't exactly expect brass bands to be playing, but I would have thought at least a thank-you would have been in order.'

'Ben,' Polly answered, 'I suspect they're only thinking of all the victims, both of the Daleks and of Bragen. They're in mourning, not a mood for celebration.'

'I know,' Ben agreed, 'but the Doctor saved the whole colony from being completely wiped out!'

The Doctor took his lips from the mouthpiece for a moment. 'Ah! Then you do accept that I'm the Doctor, then?' He didn't look back, so they couldn't make out his expression.

'Yes,' Polly said firmly, and then glared at Ben as if daring him to contradict her.

'You've got to be,' Ben said, with a laugh. 'After all, you've got his way of solving problems, haven't you?'

'It's a knack,' the Doctor admitted, modestly.

'More like a blast,' Ben said. 'And you're just as hard to pin down, too. Still, you did try and warn everyone back there about what was going to happen. But would they listen?'

'Well, I don't know,' Polly put in, defending Quinn again. 'Sometimes he wasn't very convincing. Doctor?' He gave her an innocent look. 'You did know what you were doing all along, didn't you?'

He simply raised his eyebrows and tootled a couple of notes. Then he flashed her a big grin and a wink. He led them through the rocks, careful to avoid the mercury pools The familiar shape of the TARDIS loomed suddenly as they rounded a corner.

Beside it stood one of the shattered Daleks. The Doctor gave a start of surprise.

Ben slapped the broken casing. 'It's all right,' he laughed. 'It's perfectly dead.'

The Doctor fished the TARDIS key from his pocket. 'Don't be too sure,' he cautioned Ben. 'They were dead before.' He sighed. 'Daleks are like cockroaches: just when you think you've got rid of them all, they pop back up and you're infested again.'

Ben refused to let the Doctor's gloom infect him. 'On which happy note,' he said, 'it's time to go. And try and make it somewhere cheery next, okay?'

They entered the TARDIS. 'Somewhere with a beach and sun,' Polly begged.

'England,' Ben suggested.

'You can't have it both ways,' the Doctor said. 'Make up your minds.' Not that I could get you there, he added to himself.

There was a soft breeze blowing across the barren ground of Vulcan. It stirred the dust, but little more. With a raucous rattle of noises, the TARDIS shimmered and then faded from the surface, its interrupted journey continuing once more.

All was still, except for the vague flurries of dust.

The shattered Dalek stood alone in the rocky ruins. A soft bubble sighed on the surface of the mercury pool close by.

The twisted eye-stick of the Dalek shivered, perhaps from the breeze.

Then it inched upwards, as if seeking the warmth and light of Vulcan's immense sun.

Author's Note

Though I have now written several dozen novels, few of them ever give me as much pleasure as novelizing a *Doctor Who* script. And though it is my name on the cover as the 'author' of this book, I'm never the only person who produces the end result. In the case of *The Power of the Daleks*, more than most, there have been a number of people involved, without whom this book would have been vastly different.

First of all, there is Terry Nation. He not only created the Daleks back in the beginning, but he's also been very supportive and indulgent in letting me work with them.

Next, of course, is David Whitaker. The original story editor and one of the creative forces behind *Doctor Who*, he also penned the original scripts from which this book was adapted. David has long been one of my favourite *Doctor Who* writers, and I am immensely happy to have been given the chance to turn his excellent scripts into (I hope!) an excellent book! His own novel – the first of this series – *Doctor Who and the Daleks*, influenced my own style more than a little.

Thanks are most certainly due to actress June Barry. *The Power of the Daleks* was commissioned by producer Innes Lloyd and story editor Gerry Davis when they knew that William Hartnell was leaving the show, but before Patrick Troughton was cast in the role. As a result, David's scripts were written without his knowing who would be playing the role, or the direction this actor would take. When Patrick Troughton was cast, the scripts were rewritten to reflect his new character. However, David Whitaker was not able to perform the revisions as he had moved on to a new assignment in Australia. As a result, one-time story editor Dennis Spooner was given the task of reworking the scripts. The end result as filmed was an amalgamation of many people's work, then, from David's basis.

I met Dennis Spooner in 1981 and he told me about having rewritten the scripts, and that David's originals had contained a lot of material which they had been forced to prune out in order to make room for the character touches for the new Doctor. I was intrigued by the thought that these might still exist somewhere in their original form. Not only did they survive, but June Barry bravely salvaged them from her attic and kindly made them available so that I could use them for this novel. She was married to David during his time as story editor on *Doctor Who* and had retained his work. Thanks to her generosity, I have been able to restore a lot of the passages from his scripts that had been edited out for the television version. While most readers of the book probably won't know which passages these are, most of the show's fans will. I hope they will be as grateful to June as I am.

Since the filmed version of *The Power of the Daleks* is one of the stories no longer in the BBC's vaults, I couldn't watch it to get the visual feel for this story. However, I was able to get a great deal of visual help from a photonovel of the story. This was produced by Gary Leigh as a non-profit venture approved by all parties involved. It is an excellent production and I do recommend it to all readers.

My thanks also go to Jeremy and Paula Bentham, who read and offered helpful comments on the opening few chapters of this novel.

A heart-felt thank-you must go to the people behind the scenes: to my agent on this and other Dalek books, Roger Hancock, and to my editors Peter Darvill-Evans and Riona MacNamara. All three helped make this book a pleasure to write. Finally, as always, thanks to my wife, Nan, who has had to put up with my writing and talking about Daleks for weeks on end and still remain cheerful!